# SUMMER BRIDES

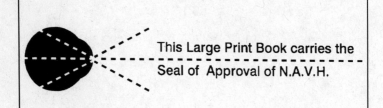

This Large Print Book carries the
Seal of Approval of N.A.V.H.

# SUMMER BRIDES

## A YEAR OF WEDDINGS
## NOVELLA COLLECTION

# MARYBETH WHALEN,
# BETH WISEMAN, AND
# DEBRA CLOPTON

**THORNDIKE PRESS**

*A part of Gale, Cengage Learning*

GALE
CENGAGE Learning

Farmington Hills, Mich • San Francisco • New York • Waterville, Maine
Meriden, Conn • Mason, Ohio • Chicago

GALE
CENGAGE Learning·

**LIBRARY OF CONGRESS CATALOGING-IN-PUBLICATION DATA**

Summer brides : a year of weddings novella collection / by MaryBeth Whalen, Beth Wiseman, and Debra Clopton. — Large print edition.
    pages cm. — (Thorndike Press large print Christian fiction)
    ISBN 978-1-4104-8136-8 (hardcover) — ISBN 1-4104-8136-0 (hardcover)
    1. Christian fiction, American. 2. Weddings—Fiction. 3. Large type books. I. Whalen, Marybeth. June bride. II. Wiseman, Beth, 1962– July bride. III. Clopton, Debra. August bride.
PS648.C43S86 2015b
813'p.01083823—dc23                                    2015016562

Published in 2015 by arrangement with The Zondervan Corporation LLC, a subsidiary of HarperCollins Christian Publishing, Inc.

Printed in Mexico
1 2 3 4 5 6 7 19 18 17 16 15

# CONTENTS

# A June Bride

MARYBETH WHALEN

*For The Bridegroom. You are all we need.*

*February 14, 2009*
She stands on the veranda overlooking a beautiful outdoor complex featuring infinity pools, cushy lounge chairs, waterfalls cascading into unnaturally blue water, and swim-up refreshment areas. The place has been cleared of onlookers and lit with an abundance of tiki torches, the smoke dancing in the air above them. Beyond the pool area, the ocean crashes in and recedes. She draws a breath and holds it for a moment, steadying herself, centering her thoughts on this moment, and not others. All around her the crew works steadily and stealthily. "Pretend we're not here," they say. And yet each time someone arranges a stray hair or puffs her nose with powder, their presence is undeniable. She hears one of the crew make a remark and another crew member laugh. She can't help but suspect they are joking about what is about to happen, taking bets over who she

will choose.

She has wondered the same thing herself.

In a moment the group of men will come in dressed in tuxes, each one more handsome than the last. They will face her with looks of expectation, their skin shining with bronze toner that has been applied to them like it has been applied to her. Their teeth will appear even whiter against the dark night. Their hope will be evident for all — especially the millions of viewers — to see. They want to be picked. By her. This fact is still unreal. And that is when the thought she has been banishing creeps in.

In remembering the girl she used to be, she remembers the boy that girl went with. She sees his face, sans bronze toner, void of bleached teeth. She thinks of his lopsided grin, his cocky demeanor that has nothing to do with cameras and demographics and ratings. His was born of an inner knowing, a confidence. And when she was with him, that confidence rubbed off on her. Her heart clenches at the thought of him watching this. Would he? Did she want him to?

"We're about to bring the guys in and go live, Wynne. You ready?" the producer, Donna, asks, her voice soft and even.

She nods and watches as the men file in, looking exactly as she suspected. She grips the oversized gold key they gave her, the one she is supposed to hand to the guy she has chosen. She sees him come in, third from the last, and tries not to let anything register on her face that might give it away to the viewers. She grips the key harder, the ridges pressing into her flesh. It is, as they've touted on national television for weeks, the key to her heart. And yet, as she surveys the group of men — men she's learned to surf with and climbed mountains with, walked hand in hand with and, yes, even kissed over the last few whirlwind weeks — she doesn't see the one face she wants most to see. The lopsided grin is missing, his teeth crooked and off-white from a serious sweet tea habit. She wants that smile to be the smile she sees at this moment.

She still wants to give the key to her heart to the one person who no longer wants it at all. She scans the faces once more, but the one she longs to see isn't there.

# PART 1

*3 Months Later*

"Ladies and gentlemen, welcome to a very special edition of *Charlotte Live*! We have got such a treat in store for you. An exclusive! You are not going to believe who we have live and in person in our studio today! Some local girls who've achieved national fame!" Karen Dodd, the bubbly, down-home southern host of *Charlotte Live*, arranged her face in what Wynne guessed was supposed to be a look of surprise. Wynne thought it came out more like a look of gastric distress. She tamped down the urge to laugh and tried to remember she was about to have the cameras turned on her.

She was grateful she didn't have Karen Dodd's job, with cameras on her every day at precisely 11:30, just before the noon news. She'd had her fill of cameras for the rest of her life. Unfortunately, the cameras

15

weren't quite through with her yet. She just had The Wedding to get through and then they would go away, their rabid attention aimed at some other poor, unsuspecting innocent who foolishly believed all of this would be "fun." She twisted the diamond around on her left hand, thinking of Andy, counting down the days until she said "I do." After the cameras went away, she could focus on married life, catch her breath as she set up housekeeping with this man she had chosen.

Finished with her opening monologue, Karen turned her attention to the woman sitting beside Wynne. Wynne had met her briefly that morning in the green room, such as it was. (The room was actually a bland beige with two folding chairs and a pot of coffee that looked and smelled like it had been made first thing that morning and left to char for hours.) Stuck in the tiny room with Meredith, it had taken Wynne all of two seconds to surmise that the two of them had little in common beyond their hometown and reality TV show success.

Now Meredith Welsh seemed to hum with a barely suppressed compulsion to leap into action. Her eyes danced, her face beamed as she soaked up Karen's long introduction of her and all her accomplishments. Photos

flashed of Meredith in all her many forms
— wife, mom, activist, athlete, adrenaline
junkie and, most recently, reality TV star.
As the camera turned on her, Meredith
leaned into it, her smile widening as Karen
introduced her as the current winner of the
popular reality TV show, *Marathon Mom.* On
the show, uber-moms completed
superhuman tasks in order to be crowned
the Marathon Mom.

Meredith had used, Wynne assumed, the
same bleaching procedure on her teeth as
those guys who courted her. Wynne wanted
to shield her eyes from the brightness.
Instead she tucked her hands under her
knees as Karen turned her attention to her
and launched into her intro. She felt the
familiar redness creep across her cheeks as
they played the tired old audition video that
had become a viral hit and earned her a spot
on *The Rejection Connection,* a dating show
that paired recently dumped women with a
host of eligible bachelors. Wynne's video
had featured her honest, heartfelt tale of
her recent breakup with her high school
sweetheart and fiancé. She'd been a little
too vulnerable, a little too open in that
video, using the camera her best friend
Picky aimed at her as a sort of confessional.
In a spectacularly weak moment, she'd let

Picky enter it to be considered. No one had been more surprised than she when the video struck a chord with women everywhere, their own tears mingling with her cyber ones. Her most embarrassing moment was captured forever, then celebrated as she not only got picked for the show, but then went on to have, as the promos for the show had said, "A second chance at love."

In truth, no matter what it had earned her, Wynne still wished she could find that video and burn every form of it, eradicating it. It never got easy to see her heartbreak splashed across the screen, never became passé to see herself spilling her guts and wiping her nose. Because the truth was, in spite of the fame and perks and "second chance at love," that hurting girl now sobbing openly on the screen was still her.

When the video ended and the live audience expressed their "awws" and "ohs" and one "you go girl, you showed him" that made everyone laugh, Karen turned to face Meredith and Wynne. She spent a few minutes gushing over their fair city's unusual fortune at having not one but two reality TV stars in their midst, then began the typical barrage of questions. Each time she hurled one at Wynne, it felt like being hit with a small pebble. Not enough to do

18

damage, but enough to sting. She'd grown tired of having pebbles hurled at her by the greedy, curious public. She tried to focus as Meredith happily returned Karen's volleys. How was it that this woman seemed so genuinely happy to be grilled by people who didn't know her and would forget about her by the next ratings sweep? Wynne had a few more weeks to go before this circus folded up its tent and went away. Maybe she could learn a thing or two from Meredith.

Karen turned to Wynne, her face appearing open and genuine, but this close Wynne could see that her eyes didn't match. In her eyes, Wynne saw something that resembled jealousy. It was easy to see how this local talk show host might mistake Wynne's sudden fame and fortune as bigger and more significant than hers. She wanted to tell the whole truth, right then and there. Set this woman — and the audience — straight. Tell the world that, yes, it had been fun and kind of surreal at first, but the more popular she became, the less fun it all was. She thought about her contract, her family, her best friend Picky, and Andy. But she kept silent, forcing her face to match Karen's. She knew that her eyes did too.

"Everyone's just ecstatic that you've chosen Sunset Beach, North Carolina as your wedding location." Karen paused to let the crowd send up an obligatory cheer in response to their home state's mention. "Having your wedding in the best state in the US!" she added with a smile for the camera as another cheer erupted. Wynne had read in her bio that Karen was actually from a small town in Tennessee, so she doubted that Karen truly felt that way. But she wasn't about to point that out.

"What made you choose Sunset Beach?" Karen asked.

She didn't say that she and Callum had talked about getting married there, right on the beach. She didn't say that they'd hiked to Bird Island and left promises to each other in the legendary mailbox there one romantic, memorable afternoon back when she believed fairy tales could happen to real people. She didn't say that, as the producers of the show grilled her on places she found romantic, the first place that popped into her head had been Sunset Beach. And that it was ultimately the producers who'd run with the plans, even going so far as to secure her wedding date for her, sending out a press release with their intentions before she'd even given her OK. She didn't say that she still felt like a traitor to Callum and to the memory of what they'd once had, as ridiculous as that sounded.

She'd confided that truth to Picky — and gotten an earful in response. "He dated you all through high school and college and then he dumped you when it was time to get married! How in the world can you possibly feel like *you* betrayed *him*?"

Instead, she gave her practiced, beatific smile and said to Karen and the viewers, "It's my favorite place in all the world. I grew up vacationing there every year and . . . it's where my heart lives." How many times had she given that same exact response, delivered that practiced line with that exact same look to go with it? Surely someone had to be catching on by now. Callum. If he was at all aware, he would notice. She pushed the image of his face out of her mind and substituted Andy's. Sweet, caring, attentive Andy. Andy, who loved her.

"So the big day is coming right up!" Karen powered on with the interview. "You're going to be a June bride." She turned to the camera, looked right in it to address the viewers at home. "Doesn't that just make you swoon? It's so perfect!" The in-studio audience clapped their approval. "And I hear it's going to be televised?"

"Yes, since Andy and I are one of the first *Rejection Connection* couples to make it to the altar, the producers wanted to celebrate with us and give our fans the chance to, also." Another tired, practiced line. Beside her she could actually feel Meredith's energy shimmering in the air — she was buying this. She was as excited as the crowd. Wynne guessed that, if she asked, Meredith would agree to be her matron of honor right then and there.

She already had a maid of honor. Picky had designated herself for that role moments after the final episode aired, the one where Andy gave her the ring she now wore on her left hand. Picky was after her to make sure a key contingent of the guys that didn't make the cut from her season had VIP invites to the nuptials. Picky was still incredulous that Wynne hadn't picked Devin. "I don't care if he didn't have much of a personality. You could've just looked at him the rest of your life!" She scanned the audience and wished Picky were there. Picky, who could always make her laugh. Picky, who had known her forever and loved her no matter what. Picky, who had gotten her into this mess with her "Take a chance! It'll be fun!" refrain as the video camera rolled.

Instead, it was Meredith who reached over and grabbed her hand, flashing her ring in front of the camera as the audience made approving sounds. "Take a look at that rock!" she exclaimed as everyone laughed.

Wynne looked down at her hand. She had suggested to Andy that he re-propose when they were alone, so it could be more heartfelt, away from cameras and crew and viewers. She'd hardly heard the words he said the first time, she was so consumed with how she appeared and how she could keep this turn of events quiet until the show aired . . . and whether or not she should say yes. Andy had agreed that a private proposal was a good idea, and yet, in the whirlwind of wedding preparations, the moment had just never materialized. Wynne wondered sometimes if another proposal happened, would she say yes again?

Now she said to the camera and Karen, "It really is lovely, isn't it?"

As she spoke her eyes landed on one lonely-looking woman in the audience nodding heartily. She knew without even having to ask that woman had her on a pedestal, wanted this fairy tale she seemed to be living. Would it shock the woman to know that the closer they got to the wedding, the more doubts filled her mind? She swallowed, pasted on her most winning smile, and told the world she was so excited for the wedding, urging viewers to tune into the special episode of wedding highlights, honeymoon footage, and "exclusive interviews." She had, at least, talked the producers out of airing the wedding live.

Karen rushed to wrap up the show and give her signature wave that looked like a cross between a high five and the old *Dating Game* smooch. (Picky had once pointed out that *The Rejection Connection* and the *Dating Game* had many similarities, then had pulled up YouTube videos to prove her point.) The lights and cameras faded as the audience filed out. An assistant rushed over to direct Meredith and Wynne back to the green room to collect their things. Wynne checked her watch as they filed silently down a corridor. She had a bit of time before her meeting with the minister. The one thing about the wedding that was solely hers: her own minister — the man who had directed her in the children's choir and lowered her into the water for baptism — was officiating the wedding. She was actually looking forward to their meeting today to talk about the ceremony. But first, she needed some lunch.

She gathered her purse and the book she had brought to read, a collection of advice for brides her mother had given her. She hadn't cracked the cover yet, never seeming to need added advice since everyone associated with the show, and more than a few viewers, offered it unsolicited every other minute. Sometimes she couldn't even open her Facebook page because she didn't want to hear any more about The Wedding. Why didn't she and Andy just elope and let the talking heads analyze it on morning television?

"You don't need that book," Meredith spoke up, startling her.

Wynne tucked the book into her purse and looked over at her as she pulled the purse strap over her shoulder. "I don't?" she asked.

Away from the lights Meredith looked less electrified and much more normal. If Wynne was seeing right, she even looked a little tired. She knew the woman had four kids, a militant fitness regimen, and a side public relations business, not to mention a husband and a home to run. Add a stint on a reality TV show that required some tough weekly challenges and Wynne would've been toast. Wynne hadn't watched the show all that much — who had the time? — but the episode she had seen involved cooking a complete gourmet meal for the families at a Ronald McDonald House and then doing all the families' laundry, only to come home and do it all over again (albeit on a smaller scale) for her own family. Wynne had wanted to cry for her as she'd sunk down in front of the pile of kids' laundry to fold it while everyone else in her house slept, darkness outside her windows. One of the reasons Meredith had won, according to what Karen had just said, was her sunny personality no matter what challenge had come her way. And yet, standing in that beige green room, Meredith didn't look very sunny.

"I'm starving. Got time for lunch?" The cloud rolled away for a moment and the sun emerged again on Meredith's face. "I can give you all the marriage advice you need."

"Um, sure? I was going to get lunch anyway so that'd be . . . nice." Wynne had planned to go through a drive through, and sit in her car and eat while reading her book before heading to the meeting with her pastor. "I have a meeting with my pastor today so I can't go for long though," she added.

"Your pastor?" Meredith asked.

"Yeah, my church likes for couples to go through a series of pre-wedding counseling sessions before you say 'I do.' "

"I've never heard of that," Meredith said. Then she mumbled something to herself.

The two fell into step as they headed toward the parking lot, arriving at the row where they'd both been instructed to park when they arrived hours ago. "Okay, I know a little hole-in-the-wall place near here where we can go. No one will make a fuss and, I don't know about you, but that sounds great to me."

Wynne couldn't help but grin. "Absolutely. I'm ready to be anonymous."

"Okay, follow me and I'll get us there. Then you can get to your . . . meeting."

Wynne gave a little wave and climbed into her car. As she waited for Meredith to get into her car and pull out, she dashed off a quick text to Andy: "Interview over, thank goodness. Now off to have lunch with Meredith Welsh from *Marathon Mom.*"

Andy's return text waited for her when she pulled into the restaurant parking lot. True to Meredith's word, the place looked like a dive, a low-slung nondescript white brick building with no signage to speak of and a gravel parking lot. She parked and read his return text. "Wow! Didn't see that coming. Is she as much of a tiger lady as she seems on TV?"

Wynne grinned and shot back a text. "She's as much of a tiger lady as I am sweet and demure." The network had really played up Wynne's sweet, vulnerable side, the Southern Belle done wrong who needed rescuing. But Andy had seen that, beneath her sweetness, lurked what she liked to think was a tough interior, a resolve and tenacity that the cameras hadn't captured. Andy, it seemed, was the one guy among the ones competing for her attention who had not only seen that side of her but tapped into it, believing in her and encouraging her whenever they spent time together. It was, she remembered fondly, what had made her choose him.

Andy quickly responded. "Touché. There are some things you just can't know about people unless you spend time with them. See you at our meeting!"

She texted back with a smiley emoticon. She was looking forward to their meeting, anxious to hear Andy's answers to the questions Reverend Stanton would pose. She seemed to learn more about this man she was marrying each time they met with the pastor. She guessed that was the point, but sometimes she felt as if they were being graded on their compatibility. She worried that Reverend Stanton was turning in some sort of score to her parents on the sly. She shook her head and got out of the car as Meredith approached with her confident stride. She was being silly, her insecurities about the hastiness of their nuptials coming through. She knew what her friends and family thought, and she wanted so badly to prove them wrong.

Over the weekend her mother had gone so far as to pull her aside in the kitchen as Andy stood outside with her dad at the grill. "You don't have to go through with this, honey," her mother had said. "I don't care what those TV people say. This isn't their lives, their future." Had her mother seen something in Andy that concerned her? Even now Wynne wondered if she should've asked her mom that very question instead of what she did do, which was shrug off her mom's statement and carry a platter of meat outside to her father and Andy. She'd given Andy a hug for no reason and he'd kissed her on the cheek. "You OK?" he'd asked, and she'd told herself that his insight in that moment was only proof that he was the one for her.

"I'm great," she'd responded. But she'd stayed out at the grill with her dad and Andy instead of returning to the kitchen to help her mother.

Meredith secured them seats in the back and, true to her word, the few diners in the place barely even looked up as they made their way to their seats and accepted the greasy plastic menus from the waitress. Meredith leaned over and whispered conspiratorially, "I don't know about you, but I'm having the biggest, greasiest cheeseburger I can get my hands on." She giggled and added, "With bacon."

Wynne groaned in response. "You don't have to fit into a wedding dress in a few weeks." She put her hand across her flat middle section as if willing it to stay that way.

Meredith waved her hand in the air. "You look great. One cheeseburger isn't going to change that."

But when the waitress returned, Wynne ordered the healthiest thing she could find on the menu, a grilled chicken wrap with a side salad. And a water.

Meredith ordered a frosty root beer and fries to go with her bacon cheeseburger and, after the waitress disappeared, she confessed, "This is my tradition after any publicity thing I do. I reward myself with something I absolutely shouldn't have."

"Really? You always seem so cool and collected in every interview I've ever seen," Wynne replied, not bothering to hide the astonishment in her voice.

"Yeah, because I know once I get through

it, I get this!" The two laughed, and Wynne found herself relaxing in Meredith's presence, warmed by the camaraderie she felt. This woman understood her unique set of circumstances better than anyone. "Of course, this afternoon I'll be in the gym burning off every calorie I ingest." Wynne groaned in response. The burden to be fabulous — to look fabulous — was part and parcel of the gig. Though she'd always tried to stay fit and trim when she and Callum dated, she'd never had to push herself to the degree she did now.

"So tell me all about the wedding," Meredith said. She took a big sip of her root beer and fixed Wynne with her piercing amber eyes. Wynne wanted to be the one to ask her questions. The first one being, how did she do it all? And so well?

"Well, it's going to be at Sunset Beach," Wynne began, feeling the pang she always felt as she said it, that momentary flash of guilt and regret that she was getting married to Andy at the place she had intended to marry Callum. But her big mouth had landed her in this place and there was no changing it now. The show had already dispatched a whole crew of people to attend to a myriad of preliminary details before she and Andy arrived for the main event.

From what she'd picked up on, they were leaving no stone unturned and the tiny island was overrun with Hollywood's finest. She couldn't decide if the citizens were going to hug her or kick her for making the place famous.

She continued, telling Meredith all about the "nautical" theme she'd selected after a surprisingly fast meeting with the stylist the show had hired. She found herself gushing as she described the bold navy and white stripes on the cake, the signs and ribbons adorning the aisles. She described the rope knots that would serve as place card holders at each table and the lime green accents the stylist was scattering around for pops of color. She even told Meredith about the anchor symbolism that they would be weaving into the ceremony. She almost spilled the beans about the gorgeous gown she'd chosen, but she'd been sworn to secrecy until the wedding. She could see the seersucker dress, a complete departure from what she'd envisioned, and yet, the breezy fabric blended perfectly with the beach backdrop. She'd never thought a wedding dress could be comfortable, that she would feel like herself as she walked down the aisle to meet her groom.

"We're getting married on the beach, then

they've got this gorgeous house for the reception close to Bird Island — that's this undeveloped stretch of coastline that is just breathtaking — so we'll have these amazing views as we dance the night away." She sighed. "It's going to be perfect." She may have planned to marry Callum at Sunset Beach, but she would've never had this kind of wedding if she'd married him. Not that she'd cared about that stuff back then, but now that she had it, she intended to enjoy it to the fullest.

Her phone buzzed from within her purse. "Do you mind if I check my phone real quick? I just need to make sure Andy hasn't hit a snag with making our meeting today. He's been so busy with this new job on top of everything else." Andy had willingly moved to her hometown so she could be near her family and friends, the church she loved, and the life she knew. He'd found a job in short order and had mostly settled into life there.

Though his mother still made comments about him moving so far from his home. "Seems the diplomatic thing to do would've been to pick a place halfway between the two cities," she'd mused the last time Wynne had seen her. She had never said so, but Wynne suspected his mom thought this whole thing was preposterous and had gone too far. She suspected that because her mom thought the exact same thing and reminded her whenever she could work it into conversation.

"Sure, sure. I'm sure I've got a few texts to respond to, also," she grinned and busied herself with her cell phone while Wynne retrieved hers from her purse. It turned out she was glad Meredith wasn't watching her, because she might've picked up on the shock on Wynne's face when she saw who the text was really from.

She'd thought she'd deleted his contact info from her phone in the wee hours of a particularly strung out, sleepless night. Nevertheless, there was his name on her screen, her phone remembering what she'd tried so hard to forget. Heart racing, she opened the message, her eyes taking in his first words to her in over a year: "Saw your interview just now. You look good, but you don't look happy. And Sunset Beach, really? We need to talk."

She swallowed hard and threw the phone back into her purse, as if she could throw the message away too. "Bad news?" Meredith asked.

"Oh no. Just wedding stuff. You know, so many details to keep up with." It wasn't a total lie. This was a new detail she'd have to keep up with — her ex sniffing around when she was weeks away from saying "I do," and on television no less. Her heart continued to pound so hard she wondered if Meredith couldn't hear it. She reached for her water glass and downed the rest of it, then crunched on her ice.

"I remember so well," Meredith said. "All I can say is, better you than me, girl."

Wynne was about to ask Meredith about her wedding, maybe learn a bit about Meredith's husband and kids when the waitress came over and presented them with the check. Meredith made a show of picking up the tab. "My treat," she insisted. "A little wedding present." She winked and busied herself with tabulating the tip and signing the check.

"So I guess now you've got your meeting to get to?" Meredith asked when she was finished.

"Yeah, good thing my church isn't too far away."

"My husband and I just got married by a justice of the peace. I couldn't imagine jumping through all those religious hoops too," she said.

"Oh, I really like meeting with our pastor." She caught herself. "I mean, my pastor.

Well, I mean I guess he'll be Andy's pastor after we're married." She laughed and waved her hand in the air. "Oh, what does it matter? I'm learning about marriage and that's a good thing. I want to be prepared."

Meredith rose from the table and hoisted her large leather bag onto her shoulder. "Honey, nothing can prepare you for marriage." She gave a small bitter laugh, then rested her hand on Wynne's shoulder and gave her a look Wynne could only describe as sympathetic. "But I wish you all the best." Then she gave her that megawatt smile she'd flashed on camera. "I'll let you get to it, then."

"Thanks for lunch, Meredith. I enjoyed meeting you. Maybe we could . . . do it again sometime? After the wedding?" Meredith might be a good friend to have — she was the type of person you couldn't help but like.

Meredith whipped out her cell phone. "Give me your number. I'll call you." Wynne obediently spilled the number, then got out her phone and logged Meredith's in as well. Thankfully there were no new texts from Callum. But the thought of his message set her heart racing again.

"Let me know if you need anything," Meredith said. "I'm good with most any emergency." She gave a little wave. "How do you think I won *Marathon Mom*?" She winked and breezed out of the restaurant, leaving Wynne holding her phone, resisting the urge to read Callum's message one more time.

"I don't know what's keeping Andy," Wynne said, the tone of her voice apologetic as Pastor Stanton tented his fingers and fixed her with his gaze.

"It's fine, Wynne," he said. "Gives us a moment to catch up. He'll be here."

She glanced behind her, as if Andy could be sneaking in the door, then looked back at the reverend. "I just talked to him before lunch and he said he was coming."

"Like I said, he'll be here. Don't worry so much." He laughed and shook his finger playfully at her. She blushed and looked down at her lap. It had been a full day and she was starting to feel exhausted. She still had several wedding things she had to do. Her mother had wanted her to drop by the house and look at some seashell necklaces she'd found that would make "uh-dorable" bridesmaids' gifts. Wynne wondered what her mother would say if she begged off, went home, and crawled in bed instead. Probably not, "You go girl."

Oh well, maybe her mom would have something good for dinner. Andy had a tux fitting scheduled, so without intervention, she was looking at cold cereal for dinner. She hoped Andy didn't harbor fantasies of her morphing into some great cook after the wedding. Maybe that was something to bring up with the pastor. She glanced down at her purse where her cell phone sat silently. No text from Andy explaining his lateness. No more texts from Callum.

She looked up at Reverend Stanton. "Should we just get started?" She knew he picked up the uncertainty in her voice.

"I guess we could," he said, giving her a reassuring smile. "Anything you'd like to talk about while we've got some time alone?"

She shrugged. "Not really. I'm just ready to get the show on the road."

"No reservations or concerns? I know your mom was expressing —"

She put her hand up. "My mom is the one who worries too much. Marrying Andy is the best decision I could make. I have no doubts whatsoever." She was glad she wasn't hooked up to one of those lie detector machines. She would fail miserably. If she didn't have concerns before she got the text from Callum, she most certainly did now. But that wasn't something to discuss with your minister, was it?

"Well, that's good to hear. Some people who haven't known each other long when they plan to marry can have moments of doubt or uncertainty." She started to argue, but he held up his hand. "I just want you to know that if you have those moments, it's normal." He chuckled. "It's even normal for couples who've been together forever."

Together. Forever. That was what people used to say about her and Callum. They had been together since they were teenagers, and everyone thought — including her — they'd be together for the rest of their lives. Maybe she'd stopped believing in "together forever" when Callum ended their relationship. Maybe the best thing to believe in was "together right now."

But she wasn't about to say that to her pastor. He might refuse to do the ceremony, require her to attend some sort of remedial class on love. The secretary — a friend of her mother's — poked her head into the room. "Can you take a call?" She glanced over at Wynne apologetically. "It's urgent." She stage whispered, "Bill Lauer. Emergency surgery."

Wynne stood. She held up her own phone. "You take the call, and I'll go try to catch up with Andy."

The pastor nodded and reached for his phone as she, gratefully, fled the room. She didn't want to make any more small talk. She wanted to find Andy and get on with the plans for this wedding. She sank into a chair with a sigh. She'd so looked forward to this meeting, relished the thought of making plans for their ceremony. She and Andy wanted to write their own vows. She'd been excited for Andy to meet — and make a good impression on — her pastor. She'd wanted him to reassure her family that Andy was a good guy, someone who could be trusted with her future.

She pressed the button to automatically dial Andy's number and listened as it rang a few times before rolling over to voice mail. She was trying not to worry or get upset, but she couldn't help but wonder if he'd been in an accident. Or headed for the hills. What if he'd somehow found out about Callum's text and decided he wasn't up for the drama? She was being paranoid. There was no way that Andy could know about that. Her guilty conscience was getting the best of her. And yet, what did she have to feel guilty about? She hadn't texted Callum and she hadn't responded to him.

Yet. The word snuck into her mind before

she could banish it. Callum was under her skin. And that was what she felt guilty about. She would be lying if she said she didn't want to see him again. Just one more time before she took the plunge. She would only see him to gain closure once and for all, to finally get the answers to the questions that had haunted her since their last, terrible phone call. That wasn't so bad, was it? Anyone would want that from someone they'd once planned to marry, someone they'd once loved.

She opened the text from Callum once more, her fingers hovering over the "send" button on her cell phone. One press of that button and she was setting something in motion, something that would be hard to stop if she did, something that could run away with her and change everything in her carefully made plans. Her family thought this whirlwind of agreeing to go on the show and then agreeing to marry Andy was the craziest thing she'd ever done. And yet, responding to Callum felt even crazier.

With a deep breath, she let her finger land on the button and, before she could belabor it anymore, she began tapping out a response. She kept it brief and breezy and squeezed her eyes shut as she hit send.

When the phone rang later that night, she froze, her stomach leaping into her chest as it had every time a new text arrived with its shattered glass alert or the phone rang with the silly song Picky had put on as a joke. "Going to the chapel and we're gonna get married," the Dixie Cups sang as she checked the screen to see who was calling. Her heart slowed as she saw — surprisingly — Meredith's name there.

Callum had not texted her back. And Andy was safe, sound, and accounted for after calling to apologize profusely for missing the meeting with Reverend Stanton. His new boss had called him in just as he was about to leave work and, being a new hire, he'd not felt he could say anything, nor could he call or text while his boss droned on and on. She'd been more than happy to extend forgiveness, seeing as how she was in need of some forgiveness of her own. She wanted to tell Andy about Callum's text, but when the moment came in their conversation that she could have, she said nothing.

She answered Meredith's call with a cautious hello. It was odd to hear from her, and so soon after their impromptu lunch. Wynne thought about the moments during their lunch when the bright, together-looking Meredith appeared dim and weary and wondered if maybe Meredith needed a friend.

"Hi, Meredith! What's up?" she answered.

"Oh well, not much. Just calling to see how your appointment went today." She gave a little laugh. "Was it as fun as you thought? Or more like the root canal I expected?"

"Well actually, my pastor had an emergency so we had to reschedule." This was not a lie. After the phone call from an anxious Bill Lauer's wife, Reverend Stanton had apologized and rushed out to the hospital. Though they hadn't rescheduled yet, she trusted that somehow they would. Never mind that the days were getting fuller and the time to leave for the actual ceremony was fast approaching. Never mind that the pastor had already worked them into this slot, squeezed in between her constant publicity and wedding preparation demands and Andy's new work schedule. Never mind that she still hadn't found that perfect moment to dig deeper into what Andy thought about faith and church and God. She'd always assumed they'd talk about it at some point, but as the whirlwind of their hasty engagement picked up speed, there had always been something more pressing to discuss. And the truth was, at this point she was a little afraid of hearing what she didn't want to hear. It was surprisingly easy to let life just carry you along, never rocking the boat simply because you didn't want your boat to be rocked. Whenever Andy steered the conversation away from church or God, she let him, ignoring the niggling warning she felt deep inside.

"Well, I guess you dodged the bullet for another day." Though she meant it entirely different, Meredith's words eerily echoed her own thoughts. "It'll all work out. You'll see," Meredith said. Her voice sounded different, Wynne noticed. The hard edge was gone. Instead, she sounded like she was floating on a raft in a peaceful lagoon, nearly lulled to sleep.

"So what are you up to tonight?" Wynne asked. She still couldn't figure out why Meredith had called.

"You know, just hanging out. Gary and the kids are out so I'm getting a much-needed mommy break."

"Oh, that sounds nice." Wynne had no idea what wives and mothers went through

— not yet — but she imagined it was a lot. And, from what she had learned about Meredith, her plate was even more full than the average mother's. "So you're having an evening to yourself? I bet you don't get those often. It must be so intense being a wife *and* mom. I'll know soon enough, I guess!" She gave a little laugh, but Meredith didn't laugh with her.

"Mmmm," Meredith said instead, gulping a drink and swallowing noisily into the phone before continuing. "I just wanted to follow up after our lunch and tell you I meant what I said about helping you out. I keep thinking about the way your face looked as you described all the stuff you have to get accomplished in just a few weeks. It sounded overwhelming." Meredith paused, then added, "And if there's one thing I know, it's how to multitask."

On the clip they'd showed from *Marathon Mom* this morning at the talk show, Meredith had been juggling — literally. They'd brought in a professional juggler who taught the moms how to juggle. Then they'd competed for different feats: longest time juggling without dropping anything, most items juggled, who could juggle the heaviest or most dangerous objects, etc. In the clip Meredith had tossed several rings with ease, catching additional ones as the instructor threw them at her and continuing to juggle with dexterity and determination. Even the other, usually snarky, contestants had stopped to watch the smooth way that she moved, the serious yet open look on her face.

"That," Karen the host had said that morning, "was when I knew you would win." The whole audience had clapped their approval.

"So I've heard," Wynne said now, and laughed.

"Well?" Meredith asked. "Is there anything you can think of that I could do? I could come by as soon as tomorrow morning. Now that the show is over and the publicity is dying down, I'm kind of a woman without a country." There was a beat. "So to speak."

For just a moment she wondered what her life would be like once all of the hoopla around her and Andy died down. Could they do normal life? Would they be happy together when there were no cameras following them around anymore? Would they have anything to talk about if they weren't talking about the show or the wedding? She made a mental note to bring up these concerns the next time they met with the pastor.

*You worry too much.* The refrain came back to her. Maybe these things just worked themselves out.

She promised to think over what Meredith could do before Meredith arrived at her place the next morning. "I'll bring breakfast!" she crooned just before they hung up. Wynne closed her eyes and pulled the covers to her chin. She felt her brain rev into motion, thinking, thinking, thinking as she was prone to do whenever she got still for a moment. She thought of those necklaces her mom said she should order for her bridesmaids, the final dress fitting, the caterer's checklist that needed to be proofed, the still shots the photographer wanted of her and Andy to be used for the show. She thought of her promise to spend some time with Picky before she left for Sunset Beach, just the two of them, one last time before she was an old married lady, as Picky had joked. She thought of the meeting she'd said she'd have with the representative from the cruise line who was "sponsoring" their cruise after the wedding. She still hadn't made that happen. Could Meredith take over any of those things, or did it all require her specific attention? If she could delegate even some of the details, she'd feel a great sense of relief. She rolled over and squeezed her eyes together tightly like she did when she was little, a pitiful effort to induce sleep.

On the nightstand her phone buzzed in the silent room. Her eyes popped open, but she didn't even have to squint at the screen to know who it was. It was 11:11, their old tradition. No matter what, they always talked at 11:11 in the a.m. and p.m. Good morning and goodnight. She couldn't deny the little thrill she felt that he had remembered. She thought he'd forgotten all about the special things they once shared. She reached for the phone, ignoring the guilt that pinged inside her as she said hello. This wasn't betraying Andy, she told herself. This was tying up loose ends, giving him the explanation he'd asked for about choosing Sunset Beach as the location for her wedding. She owed him that, and one quick phone conversation wasn't going to change the wedding she'd committed to, the life she'd planned with Andy.

Meredith showed up the next morning with coffeecake muffins and a piping hot thermos of coffee. Bleary-eyed, Wynne reached for a muffin, for once not thinking of what it would do to her figure. Instead, she savored the crunch of the pecans, the satisfying sweetness of the cinnamon sugar on her tongue. She followed the bite of muffin with a gulp of black coffee. Bitter to chase the sweet, just like she liked it.

"Thanks so much for coming over this morning. I couldn't stop thinking about your offer to help last night, and there's really no time to waste," she said to her new friend between bites.

"I'm glad to do it. I'm so bored in that house without Gary and the kids."

She stopped chewing and gave Meredith a quizzical look. "Oh, when you said they were out, I thought you just meant last night. They're . . . gone?"

Meredith grinned and rolled her eyes. "On a visit. To my husband's parents' house. His dad took a fall last week, and Gary wanted to take the kids up there and check on everything, get his dad's mind off what happened. The grandkids always seem to cheer him up."

Wynne thought of Andy's mother's disapproval over their hasty marriage and hoped she'd get over it in time to be a good grandmother to their hypothetical children. Andy would make an excellent father. She just knew it. She took another swallow of her coffee and tried not to think about all that had happened after she said hello at

11:11 last night, focusing instead on her guest and plans for the wedding.

"Do you think you'll still have time to help once they get back from their trip?" she asked, hope edging her voice. Now that she'd thought of all Meredith could help her do, she hated to lose her.

"Oh, absolutely," she said, nodding in that intent way of hers. "I just spoke to Gary on the phone this morning, and he's saying that since the kids' school is already out, he might just stay awhile. They live on this great farm and have this huge garden. It's a kids' paradise."

"Are you sure you don't want to join them?" she asked.

"No," Meredith said. "I'll feel better staying here to help you. They don't need me up there." She took a long drink of her coffee and a bite of her muffin. "So, I'm at your disposal! Anything you need!"

Wynne shrugged, thinking through her day. She'd promised her mom that since she hadn't stopped by the night before, she would stop by today. "I have to go look at these necklaces my mom thinks would be good for bridesmaid's gifts this morning and —"

"I'll go with you!" Meredith said, springing to her feet.

Wynne felt funny about taking this stranger to her parents' house, but she didn't have the heart to say no. There was something about the look on her face, a longing Wynne couldn't quite pinpoint. She thought about Meredith's attempts to forge a friendship, to her admission that she was, for now, totally alone while her family was gone. Ironic that, despite the fame, Meredith was lonely. She knew that Meredith was counting on her understanding this. And she did.

She returned Meredith's smile and obeyed her order to go and get dressed. "I'll just tidy up out here!" Meredith hollered as she walked away.

Thirty minutes later they were in Wynne's car, headed to her parents' house. Meredith babbled as they drove the short distance. She talked and talked, Wynne noticed, but didn't really say anything. Wynne alternated between trying to follow Meredith's ramblings and recalling the night before, the secret she was now keeping from everyone.

She pulled into her parents' drive, grateful she had Meredith with her to serve as a distraction. Without Meredith her mom would focus solely on her. And she might be able to tell something was going on.

There was no way she was ready to spill her guts. And to her mother, least of all. The last time they'd talked about it, her mom had said she hadn't waited long enough for Callum to "come around," and that it was the show that had come between them.

"He got cold feet," her mother had said. "Plenty of men do."

If Wynne was honest, she had to admit those words still haunted her. And after last night, they were resounding inside her, echoing in time to the beat of her heart. What if her mom was right and what if this whole thing was one giant mistake?

She ushered Meredith into the house, calling out for her mom, intent on keeping her voice bright. She was, she realized with a smile, imitating Meredith. Her mom rounded the corner and found Wynne in the kitchen, Meredith on her heels. "Mom, this is Meredith," she said.

Her mom's reaction was priceless. She'd followed *Marathon Mom* almost as closely as she'd followed *The Rejection Connection* and seen the interview on TV the day before. "I know exactly who you are!" She ignored Meredith's outstretched hand and went in for a hug. "It is so nice to meet you!" She let go of Meredith and shoved Wynne playfully. "You didn't tell me you were bringing a celebrity over!" Her hands fluttered to her hair and down the front of a stained T-shirt commemorating some long-ago church event. "I look a sight!"

Meredith chuckled and waved her complaints away. "You look lovely, Mrs. Hardy." She glanced from mother to daughter. "Just like your daughter!"

Her mother, Wynne could tell, was charmed. "Meredith's helping me with some wedding stuff," she informed her. "I came by to see the necklace, but I don't have much time."

Her mother looked over at Meredith, "This one and all her rushing around." She shook her head. "Maybe with your help she can slow down a little. You're so efficient; I'm sure you'll be a huge help." The admiration for "Marathon Mom" Meredith was evident in her mother's voice. She led them into the next room and rummaged around to produce a bag. "Now, I've kept the receipt, so be honest because I can take it back." She pulled out a simple gold shell with a pearl centered inside it. Her heart began to race as she stared — not at the necklace, but at her mom's face, which remained vacuous. Did her mom really not remember?

She felt Meredith's hand on her arm.

53

"Wynne? You look like you've seen a ghost."

She made herself laugh, hoping her smile erased what Meredith had seen. "That necklace just . . ." She couldn't tell the truth, couldn't put into words how that necklace made her feel inside, her stomach rolling as she watched it swing from her mother's hand. Instead, she lied. "It just looks like something I had as a teenager."

Her mother started to protest, still not getting it. But Meredith interrupted. "You know, I wasn't going to say anything, but I had the exact same thought. That maybe it looks a little . . . young." She winked at Wynne and then began to exclaim over the cutest ideas for bridesmaids' gifts she'd seen just the night before on Pinterest.

Wynne silently thanked God for Meredith's presence and listened as she detoured her mom right around that sticky situation without her even feeling the change in direction. She could see how Meredith had won *Marathon Mom*. Meredith, she was learning, was good at winning. Wynne watched as the necklace was packed away and the receipt was found and, by the time they left for their next errand, her mother was online discovering the glories of Pinterest and exclaiming aloud to no one in particular.

"She'll be busy for hours now," Meredith

54

said as they closed the door. "And we'll go find you bridesmaids' gifts you feel good about." She gave Wynne a smile that made her believe she would. Just having Meredith around made her feel like it would all get done. That her wedding would happen just the way she wanted. It *would* be perfect.

Wynne and Meredith headed back to Wynne's apartment, both visibly exhausted yet still upbeat. Meredith cranked up the radio as she rubbed her feet, wiggling in her seat to the music and making Wynne laugh. "I'm starving," she said dramatically, her voice loud to compete with the music.

"Me too," Wynne agreed. They'd skipped lunch, making do with a quick stop for lattes.

"I guess you have plans with Andy tonight?" Meredith asked. Wynne could hear the note of hope in her voice.

"We haven't really made plans, actually. I've been so busy and he's working so much so he can take time off for the wedding and honeymoon. He'd probably be fine if I made some other plans. Did you want to order pizza?"

Meredith gave her an "are you crazy?" look. "That's kid food! I'm thinking we go somewhere we can sit and be waited on.

Doesn't that sound nice?"

Wynne nodded and hit the turn signal so she could head toward a nearby strip of new restaurants. Meredith let out a whoop and went back to dancing in her seat. "This has been so great," she said, and rolled down the window to let her hand surf the currents of air as they whooshed by the car. Wynne felt free and happy and almost distracted enough to stop thinking about Callum. But just as they were getting seated in the restaurant, her cell phone went off. She didn't even have to look at it to know who had sent her a text. It would be Callum, seeing if she would keep her promise to see him later. She looked at Meredith and realized that she had, without knowing it, given her the perfect cover story for Andy. He would believe that she was with Meredith all evening. And she hadn't even had to think about it. She quickly responded to the text, letting Callum know she'd be true to her word and would see him later.

When Meredith asked if that was Andy, she smiled and said yes. Meredith, she suspected, had her little secrets. What did it hurt if Wynne had hers? She needed to see Callum one last time, and there was no harm in that. One last time, one final good-bye for the sake of closure. Then she would marry Andy and never look back.

# PART 2

It turned out the evening ran later than she'd expected because Meredith had too much to drink at dinner, lingering at the table as if she didn't want to go home. Yet no matter how many times Wynne tried to get Meredith to talk about herself on a more personal level, she'd always managed to steer the conversation back to the show, the wedding, the publicity. Wynne suspected things weren't well in Meredith's world, and she wished that her new friend would let her in. But so far Meredith was keeping her at arm's length.

She pulled up outside Meredith's house and noticed how quiet the house was, utterly void of the little signs of family life most homes had. There were no cast-off little shoes, no abandoned bikes, no stray balls or gardening tools lying in the yard. Everything was neat and orderly and very, very still. There were no lights on inside, no warm glow emanating from within. She knew that Meredith's husband had taken the kids to his parents, but watching her lurch up the sidewalk and fumble to get her key in the lock, Wynne thought that the house didn't just look empty. It looked abandoned. Still, Meredith opened the door, flipped on a light, and turned to give that brilliant smile and a little wave before slipping inside and closing the door.

Wynne sat in the drive for a second longer, thinking of all the right things she could do at that moment, things that would guarantee a happy ending to her fairy tale story. She was playing faster and looser than she ever had. She shifted the car into reverse and eased to the end of the drive. One direction would take her home and the other direction would take her to Callum's. There was what she should do and what she wanted to do. There was what was expected and what was a surprise, even to her.

She thought of Callum's voice on the phone as they talked for hours, missing sleep as they caught up on each other's lives. *He's just an old friend,* she'd told herself over and over as the minutes turned to hours and the clock by her bed revealed times she didn't normally see. When he'd asked to see her once more before the wedding, she had said no. But eventually he'd worn her down, just like he always had. She might always regret it if she didn't take the chance now while she had it, she reasoned. Before the wedding it was still sort of OK. But after the wedding she would be a married woman and there was no justifying that. The truth was, she did want to see him. She wished she didn't, but she did.

She hesitated for just a moment before she drove the wrong way. Or maybe it was the right one. It depended, she supposed, on how you looked at it. And how it all turned out.

Callum was standing on his front porch when she pulled up, which meant that she didn't have a moment to take a few deep breaths to gather her courage, to tell herself again that this wasn't wrong, what she was doing. She turned the key in the ignition and tossed it into her purse, blocking thoughts of that huge key she'd given Andy. Callum waved from under the porch light, beckoning her as if this was nothing. And perhaps to him, it was. He wasn't the one engaged to someone else, planning a wedding that would be broadcast to millions of people in a short time. He couldn't ruin everything with this little visit.

She got out of the car and walked slowly toward him, grateful it was dark outside, using the space between them to take those deep breaths. She wondered how she should greet him. A hug? A handshake? The stiff, distant, arms-crossed greeting he deserved? And yet, as she climbed the stairs of his porch, he met her there at the top step, leaving her no time to think as he took her into his arms and hugged her, the feeling so familiar and comforting that for a moment she forgot everything that was on her mind. For a moment it was just like old times — her and Callum embracing, the smell of his skin enveloping her senses. She inhaled, relishing the onslaught of feelings without dissecting them. She had waited for this moment since that last awful conversation between them. She deserved this moment. Didn't she?

She stepped away and the spell was broken. She squinted up at him, silhouetted in the bright porch light. She couldn't see his face. "Do you want to come inside?" he asked.

Her heart pounded as she thought of setting foot inside his house, the little house she'd helped him find, assuming she would one day live there too. They'd held hands as they walked through with the Realtor, that other diamond new and sparkling on her left hand. She wondered where it was now. Probably still in the box she'd overnighted to him the day after their big breakup. She'd fully expected him to show up in a few days with that ring in his hand, begging her to wear it again and apologizing for his foolishness. But days turned to weeks, then months, and there was no word from him. Eventually she'd given up, let Picky talk her into that ridiculous video and . . . here they were. Now she wore another man's diamond, and Callum was still living in the house she'd once thought of as theirs.

"Wynne?" he asked.

"Sorry," she laughed at herself. "I'm —"

"Thinking too much," he chided with a grin. He opened the door. "Come on," he said and held the door open for her. She stood still for a moment, her glance straying to her car sitting in the driveway, the engine emitting little clicks as it cooled. She could get in and drive away, go straight to Andy and tell him everything. She could stop this madness now.

"It's okay, Wynne. It's just a visit with an old friend," he said, the tenderness in his voice soothing her nerves and coaxing away her reservations. Even now, he knew her, and she couldn't help but be comforted by that. He gestured to the open doorway.

She ducked her head and walked through.

He had taken a seat on the couch, so she had purposely chosen the big overstuffed chair opposite it. She wasn't about to sit beside him. As she stiffly lowered herself and refused his offer of a drink, she ignored the memories that assaulted her. They had bought this sofa and chair, bickering over the fabric choice, debating the merits of bold color versus neutral patterns. They'd talked about durability in a house with toddlers someday. Or had it just been she who had talked and he who listened? She couldn't remember that part. He'd seemed to be invested and interested. But maybe that had only been what she wanted to believe.

"Thanks for coming tonight. I know it was kind of a risk for you." He smiled and gave her a bashful look. "I guess you didn't tell him?"

She shook her head and looked away. "I tried but . . . I didn't know how to explain what I was doing."

He shrugged and sipped his tea, the ice cubes knocking against the glass. "Maybe you'll feel better about telling him after the fact, once you know everything turned out

OK and you have nothing to feel guilty about." He smiled again and set his glass down on the coffee table, characteristically ignoring the stack of coasters she'd bought to protect the wood. The set was from Sunset Beach and featured pictures of the old bridge. She wanted to laugh that he'd actually kept those coasters from one of their trips, yet he still managed to avoid them. She chose not to let those coasters make her feel any more guilty over her wedding location than she already did.

"I just thought it would be good to see each other one more time before, you know. You're . . ."

Was she right, or was he unable to say Andy's name or the word "married"? She bit back a little vengeful smile. It served him right. "I guess we both need some closure," she said, then added quickly, "I mean, more than a phone conversation can bring."

"I really just wanted to ask you why you chose Sunset Beach of all places. I was thinking maybe I'd vent a little about that and then, you know, get on with my life." He didn't look exactly angry, she thought, but perhaps a little indignant.

She started to argue about his right to vent about any of this, but he stopped her. "I know, I know. I have no right to have those feelings, and you're free to do what you want but I . . ." He reached over and grabbed one of the coasters, turned it around in his hand before putting it back down on the table. "I was just really, really surprised when I saw you on that show, and I couldn't understand why you'd do that."

She opened her mouth to answer, her heart torn between explaining how it all transpired and denying him an opinion in the matter, but he shook his head. "But now that you're here, Wynne, I realize it doesn't matter. It was just good to hear your voice, to hear about your life and . . . I realized how much I'd missed that. And then I just . . . needed to see you. I . . . actually didn't expect that." He met her eyes. He reached for his tea glass and took a long swallow, his Adam's apple bobbing up and down in his throat as he did. He set the glass back down on the coaster this time and looked back at her. He blinked with heavy lids, and she wondered how much sleep he'd gotten since the day the show aired. "I guess I thought we'd always have time."

"Time for what?" she asked, her voice scratchy and thick. She hoped he would say what she wanted to hear him say. Yet what would hearing it change?

There was a long stretch of silence as he

chose his answer. He was, she knew, weighing his words, deciding how vulnerable he
should be. That was the trouble with knowing someone as long or as well as she knew
Callum — she could still read him whether
she wanted to or not.

"Time to come back. To us," he finally
said.

Her heart began to pound and she swallowed again, her throat burning as her eyes
began to well up. "You made it clear you
didn't want that."

His voice was strained, emotion bubbling
just below the surface. "In hindsight maybe
it wasn't the smartest thing I ever did, but I
thought we should see what else was out
there. That we'd spent our whole lives
together and we owed it to ourselves to
make sure we were right for each other
before we did what you're about to do."

"You mean marriage? You can't even say
the word, Callum."

"I mean committing to another person.
For life. Before you and I stood in front of
everyone we knew and made promises to
God." She studied her hands to avoid the
way his eyes implored her to understand. "I
took that very seriously. Do you?"

She thought about Andy's proposal, how
it had somehow caught her off guard even

as the cameras whirred and the air around them got very, very still. She hadn't really intended to get engaged, and yet the "yes" had come out of her mouth. Everything that had come after had been on the tide of that one, split-second decision. She twisted the ring on her finger. It was bigger and flashier than the one Callum had given her, and she'd seen him notice. "You have no idea how seriously I take all this," she said.

He leaned back on the couch and stared her down. She ignored how handsome he looked in those worn-out jeans, which she knew he'd had since high school, his feet bare and already tanned even though it was barely summer. "Well, good," he said, an ironic edge slicing into his voice. "I'm certainly glad to hear it. I guess my concerns that this *marriage* of yours is just to spite me are completely wrong."

She sputtered as she tried to think of the way to respond. She finally settled on, "You have some nerve, saying that to me."

He nodded and smirked. "Guess I do." He inhaled a deep breath that sounded more like a resigned sigh. He looked up at her, his eyes changing from bitter to almost sad. "But am I wrong?"

She stood up, clasped her hands in front of her as she searched for the right words.

"I'm going to leave now. I think it was a mistake to come." She started walking for the door, expecting to hear his feet following. But when she put her hand on the door and turned around, he was in the exact same spot, his head down.

"Bye," she said, more as a dare than a parting. *I'm leaving, in case you didn't notice.* Why did she want him to chase her? Even now? She jiggled the door knob in her hand, remembering that the key never fit quite right in the lock. She wondered idly if he'd ever gotten a new key fitted. The sound of his voice jarred her back to the present.

"What did you say?" Her voice was hesitant and uncertain, revealing, she was sure, just how much she'd wanted him to say something before she was gone. This was about closure. Isn't that what she'd been telling herself? One final exchange between them. All the things they needed to say before they couldn't say them ever again. This would be, after all, the last time they ever saw each other. In another week she'd be at Sunset Beach with the producers, preparing her big wedding. Another week after that and she'd be married.

"I'm sorry," he repeated. "For being unsure and putting you through what I put you through. If I —" He stopped, and she felt herself reaching, straining for those words he didn't say, the ones she could see he was keeping inside.

"If you what?" she prompted.

He gave her the same smile he gave her when her grandfather died and he sat by her side at the funeral. The same smile he gave her when she didn't get the score on the SAT she needed to get into Chapel Hill. The same smile he gave her when she got mono and had to miss the junior prom. Little more than a firm line with the ends of his mouth turned up, it was a smile that said, "I don't know what to say, but I'm here for you no matter what." But he wasn't there for her anymore, and his familiar, sympathetic smile only made her more aware of that than ever. "Nothing," he said. "Go and live your life. Be happy. I want that for you, even if you don't believe me."

"I believe you," she managed. He was telling her good-bye and she had no choice but to hear him. To hear him and, this time, accept it with grace and dignity. She forced herself to smile back without begging him to reveal whatever he was withholding. It wouldn't make any difference. She had made a promise, forged a life with someone else, moved on, just like all her friends and family had urged her to do.

She bit the inside of her jaw to stave off the tears that were threatening. "I want you to be happy too." She restrained herself from hugging him good-bye, even though every fiber of her being wanted to cross that room and wrap her arms around him. There was a time when a hug from Callum could change the whole trajectory of her day. Instead, she gave him a little wave, not unlike the one Meredith had offered her earlier that evening, and exited his house for the last time.

She got back into her car and gripped the steering wheel, wondering why moving on didn't feel nearly as good as people made it sound. For a moment she watched the porch to see if he would come outside and stop her from driving away. But the porch stayed empty, and after a few minutes, the light flicked off. She drove away, telling herself she was driving toward her future, that the best was yet to come. She forced herself to think of the ocean and the wedding plans, the little touches they'd planned for the big day. She had so much to look forward to — all this looking back was ridiculous behavior. She was going to be a June bride and have her perfect wedding in the place she'd always dreamed of. That was enough. She pressed harder on the accelerator. It was enough.

# PART 3

"You sure you're OK?" Andy asked, squeezing her shoulder as he looked down at her with concern in his eyes. "You're not acting like yourself."

Wynne nodded and smiled harder.

"If you ask me, you're letting them stress you out too much," he said, pointing at Donna and Paul, the producers of the show. "This is your wedding." He chuckled, then amended himself. "*Our* wedding." He pulled her closer. "Not theirs." He rolled his eyes and lowered his voice for privacy, not that Meredith was paying any attention. She was enjoying the attention from the producers too much to pay them any mind. "Or hers for that matter. I still don't understand why you let her come to this meeting with us. All of a sudden she's like your shadow."

Wynne sighed and took a few steps away, just to ensure that Meredith didn't overhear anything. "I can't explain it. She just seems sad. And this stuff makes her happy."

Andy gestured to Meredith, now demonstrating the Macarena as the producers all laughed. "Yeah. She looks just positively broken up right about now."

"Meredith is actually helping. She's great at wedding planning, and she loves all this fame stuff. I would rather avoid it so she's taking the heat for me." She wrapped her arms around his waist and kissed his cheek. "Which leaves me free to stand here and talk to you."

He smiled and bent down to kiss her. "Well, I'm not arguing with that," he said. "So you ready to hit the road tomorrow?" He put his arm around her. "This time next week we'll be married. Can you believe it?"

*It's all I can think about.* Guilt crawled up her spine. She needed to tell Andy the truth about seeing Callum. But each time she thought about what to say, her mouth clamped shut and the right words escaped her. She'd promised herself she would confess before they got married. It wasn't right to start their marriage off with a lie hanging between them. She just hoped Andy understood.

As Andy went over to talk to Paul, Wynne stood and thought about the only conversation they'd ever had about Callum. A conversation that had, actually, taken place during their date on the show. Though the footage of them talking had been edited down to about two sentences, it was that conversation that had made Andy stick out in her mind, his kind smile and warm eyes raising him above all the other guys in her eyes. Sure, the other guys had made comments about how Callum had been stupid to let her go, but it was Andy who really got how she felt, who let her talk about what had happened and actually listened.

In the end Andy had taken her hand and kissed it gently. He'd said, "I know you're hurting, but it's not going to always feel this way." Then he'd winked and thanked her for a nice night, leaving her to ponder just what it was about Andy that made him so good, that made her feel like she could trust him and tell him anything. "You have to be friends," her mother had always told her. "The passion fades. It just does. But the friendship — if you're lucky — will always be there."

Andy had been her friend. But did that mean she loved him? Enough to become his wife? Oh, that confounding Callum, walking back into her life at the precise wrong time, butting into her thoughts with his lopsided grin and his ability to take one look

74

at her and know exactly what she was thinking. She thought back to his off-base theory that she was only marrying Andy to get back at him. Sure, it might appear that way. She and Andy were still getting to know each other. She and Andy didn't have one-tenth of the history she and Callum had. But that didn't mean they weren't meant for each other.

It was Andy's diamond on her finger. Andy to whom she'd given the key to her heart in front of a nation of viewers. That had to count for something. And it wasn't like Callum had offered, even after they'd seen each other again. He'd hinted that he didn't like her marriage to Andy. But he'd never said, "Marry me instead."

Was that what she was waiting for? Would it change things if he had? These were her thoughts, hundreds of little popcorn kernels popping inside her head — when what she wanted was to think of the wedding only. She needed to focus.

Meredith came over and bumped shoulders with her, knocking her off balance and laughing as she did. "Hey, you are not going to believe what Donna just asked me!" she said.

"What?" Wynne smiled and hoped that Donna just asked her if she wanted to star in some other reality show. It was clear that Meredith was having a hard time letting go of the limelight while Wynne couldn't shed it fast enough.

"She wants me to come to your wedding! She said it'll be great for ratings. And —" Meredith squeezed Wynne's upper arm a wee bit too hard as Wynne winced. "Oh, sorry." She rubbed her arm and gave her an apologetic smile. "And, she said she wanted me to make a toast to you and she will make sure it gets into the final show!" She held her hand up for a high five, grinning as broadly as Wynne had ever seen. Wynne obliged by reaching up to slap her up-stretched palm, feigning the same kind of excitement Meredith had. But all she could think of was what Andy had said when he saw Meredith at the meeting: "I'm just grateful she's not going to be at the wedding."

Meredith, oblivious, said, "I'm going to go tell Andy!"

"Yay!" Wynne mustered as Meredith speed-walked over to poor Andy, who was unsuspecting in more ways than one. Oh well, he'd get over it. It seemed they all had things to get over.

Wynne stepped out onto the screened-in

porch of her room at the Sunset Inn, a lovely place where they were all staying. Producers, crew, and "cast," for lack of a better word, had filled the inn. Her family and friends had rented rooms at nearby condos and a resort on the mainland. Picky and her family had rented a gorgeous home on the ocean for the whole week. Somehow Meredith had scrambled around and found somewhere to stay at the last minute. Wynne was silently grateful it wasn't in the inn where she was staying. She hadn't anticipated Meredith actually tagging along at the wedding and, she hated to admit, her new friend was starting to be a little too much. She knew that Meredith's popularity was sagging and couldn't help but suspect that her sudden, intense interest in Wynne and the wedding was an attempt to reclaim the camera's attention.

She took a seat on the porch swing and kicked her feet to set it in motion. She felt guilty for judging poor Meredith that way. The woman clearly had an empty life and was trying to fill it with fame. And yet, she could never get her to talk about what was really going on in her life. It seemed that the only thing that made Meredith truly happy was the fame she'd found on *Marathon Mom,* and yet *Marathon Mom* was behind her. She thought about the many times she'd seen Meredith drink too much, that empty house where she'd dropped her off. Funny how her initial impression of her had been so different. On TV she had seemed so together, so fulfilled.

And now she was excited about getting back on TV again. But what could she really gain from hanging around her wedding and toasting their marriage in front of the cameras? It didn't make sense. Wynne put her feet down and stopped the swing. But it wasn't the only thing around her that didn't make sense. She thought about their meeting with the pastor, the one she'd finally secured in the nick of time. She and Andy had met with him just before leaving Charlotte to drive to Sunset Beach. In that moment, looking out across the water as she sat alone, she found herself thinking through what had happened and what it meant.

Pastor Stanton had talked to them about marriage, about commitment and family, and sharing a life with someone else, and all that came with it. Did they understand the seriousness of what they were about to do? Had they talked through all the things they needed to address? She had her moment to finally address the faith issue. She'd turned to Andy, looked back at the pastor as he nodded his encouragement.

"Andy, you know my faith is very important to me and I . . ." She searched for the right words. "I just wondered if you, um, feel the same way? I mean, when we're married will you go to church and raise our kids in church?"

Andy had faltered. It hadn't been long — a fraction of a second — but in that moment she'd seen his hesitation. He had recovered nicely, said all the right things after that. He just wanted what she wanted. He would be committed to her faith. But he'd called it that: her faith. Not his.

She thought back to the one time faith had come up on the show. They'd filmed an episode at her church and each guy had talked about his faith — or lack of — on their "date" to a church service. The episode had been a very good way to weed out the guys who were wrong for her. But it had also been a whirlwind of quick conversations and — always — the cameras and lights and people hovering around. She'd loved what Andy said about his family's religious traditions and church attendance and had believed he counted himself when he talked about his family. And yet, that assumption might've been totally wrong on her part. She thought of all her mom's warnings, how she just didn't know Andy well enough. This kind of thing, she suspected, was exactly what her mom had meant.

She'd looked back at Pastor Stanton, seen the concern on his face. He, too, had recovered nicely, giving her a smile as he said, "Well, I'm glad you two were able to talk about that issue. I know it was weighing on Wynne's mind and I think you've started a nice dialogue."

Sitting on the porch, she wondered what the pastor had really been thinking at that moment. She'd heard that the show was giving him a nice donation for the church's building campaign in exchange for his participation in the ceremony and any interviews. She hated to think that would motivate him to go along with all of this even if he thought they were making a mistake by getting married. And yet, he'd kept quiet at the moment he could've said something. But what would he have said? And how would she have reacted?

She took a deep breath. Maybe she was the one making a big deal out of it. Maybe he'd seen other couples begin just this same way — and it had turned out fine. She smiled and shook her head. Picky had warned her that true reality — not the TV show version — would catch up with her sooner or later and she shouldn't second-guess herself when it did. She was bound to have concerns as the moment to say "I do" approached. Plenty of brides got nervous about getting married without their wedding being on national television to a man they'd known less than a year.

She pulled her knees up to her chin and wrapped her hands around her feet as the swing moved in the breeze, trying to decide if, even in the heat of a June afternoon, her feet felt cold.

Picky called right in the middle of a meeting with the wedding planner . . . and Meredith. Meredith had found some lovely anchor earrings for the bridesmaids, and the wedding planner had suggested she find a quote about friends being anchors that she could read to them before handing out the gifts. It would be great on film, everyone agreed — so emotional. Meredith had gotten teary-eyed just talking about it, and Wynne couldn't help but wonder just whose wedding this was. Meredith came on like a hurricane. There was no stopping her. She knew Picky had seen the publicity the producers had leaked, little insider glimpses of Meredith right in the middle of things that piqued the public's attention. What was the winner of *Marathon Mom* doing helping *The Rejection Connection* bride? People wanted to know.

Picky probably most of all. After the meeting she retrieved her phone from inside her purse and dialed her best friend's number. She prepared herself for admonishment from Picky for being so hard to get ahold of. She expected Picky to say something about her choosing Meredith over her or getting caught up in her fame and forgetting the little people. But Picky said none of that. She just sounded genuinely excited. "This time tomorrow we will be together!" Picky nearly sang when Wynne answered the phone.

"Yeah," Wynne said. "Then the real fun begins."

"You said it," Picky agreed. "So, are you nervous yet? Has it hit you this is really happening? And more important that you have *moi* to thank for it?"

She chuckled. "Something like that."

"So what are you doing right now? Getting ready for a big night out on the town with your new bestie?"

There it was. "She's not my new bestie. She's actually kind of annoying if you want to know the truth. I'm still wondering how she ended up here, I actually never —"

Picky, laughing, interrupted her. "Kidding, Wynne. I was totally kidding with you. I know you couldn't replace me!"

Wynne thought of the friendship that she and Picky had shared since the first day of Sunday school in the sixth grade. They had shared the gamut of emotions and experiences in the years that followed. That kind of lasting friendship wasn't replaced in a few weeks of wedding hype. She was being overly sensitive and worrying too much. But what else was new?

She steered the conversation back to something safe. "I'm going back to my hotel room and planning to call it a night. My bed is super comfortable and it's calling my name."

"So there's nothing going on beyond that over there? I'm disappointed. I was hoping for some hopping nightlife when I get there."

"Oh, a group is going out. I just opted not to join them."

"Is Andy going?"

"He said he might. A bunch of them are."

"Wynnie, Wynnie, Wynnie. Haven't I taught you anything? You're actually sitting alone in a hotel room while your fiancé goes out?" She tsked through the phone lines.

"You go put on a cute outfit and make him happy he's marrying you in a few days."

Wynne smiled. "He's happy he's marrying me. I'm not worried about it. We're getting ready to spend a lifetime together. He won't miss one night. Plus, I'd like to have just five minutes to myself before the intensity of this blessed event cranks into overdrive. If I don't go sit at a bar with these people one evening, it won't be the worst thing."

Picky's sigh was loud and dramatic. "Suit yourself. But when I get there we are going to do everything there is. We're going to make the most of this experience."

Picky could hardly wait to get there and join the fun she was convinced they were having. And Wynne knew she had her eye out for Devin's arrival too. "Deal," she agreed.

As if on cue, Picky added, "And you're going to find a way to introduce me to Devin. And convince him to fall helplessly, hopelessly in love with me."

"Deal, again," she said with a smile.

Picky was quiet. Then, "You OK?"

"Yeah," she exhaled. "Busy. Overwhelmed. Tired."

"That's all?"

She paused, wondering what Picky was digging for. Because she was definitely dig-

84

ging, in her Picky way. "Sure. I'm about to get married. Why wouldn't I be OK?"

Picky sighed. "I saw Callum at church. He asked me to have lunch. He told me about . . . you two."

Wynne's heart rate accelerated. At this point, she had no intention of admitting the truth about Callum to Picky. She would have to tell Andy, but Picky? No way did she need to hear that lecture. "I don't know why he would talk to you about that."

"Because he's confused. He feels things with you guys are . . . unfinished. And he knows it's too late." She paused to wait for Wynne's response. When Wynne didn't offer one, she continued. "And I think he blames me. In a way. I'm the one who made that video. So he wanted to talk to someone who sort of . . . knows the situation. It was kind of sad, actually."

"Let me get this straight," Wynne said. "You're defending Callum?"

"Noooo. Not defending him. Just sharing what he said. I thought you should know."

"Okay, well now I know." She turned the lock on her hotel room door, went straight to her bed and sank down, fighting off the urge to climb under the covers and stay there.

"What are you going to do?"

"I'm going to marry Andy. And move forward with my life just like you — and everyone else — have told me to do."

"And you're fine with where things are with Callum? Because he's not."

Her voice sounded like a robot when she responded. "It's like you said. It's too late."

They were both quiet. "Just know I'm here if you want to talk. I had no idea this was even going on and I —"

"It's fine, Picky," Wynne cut her off. "If it wasn't, I would've told you. Yes, I saw Callum and I probably shouldn't have. But I felt I owed it to both of us — if nothing else just to bring closure for us both before I entered this new chapter of my life."

Picky was quiet again. Wynne knew she was debating saying more, pushing harder. In the end she made some excuse about needing to go finish packing. "Just tell me one thing first, though," she said. "Tell me you got closure. And that you're totally done with Callum."

"I am," she said, thankful that Picky couldn't make her pinky promise like she used to when they were kids. They hung up after stating how excited they both were to see each other and to celebrate the much-anticipated nuptials. It was good to distract Picky from the Callum subject, good to hang up on a positive note. She put her phone down and stared at it for a moment, feeling bad for lying to Picky, but uncertain what the truth was anymore.

She picked up the remote control and idly flipped through the channels, seeking something to take her mind off Picky's voice saying Callum's name, the way her blood whooshed through her veins, hot and fast, when the subject came up. She needed a good crime show to immerse herself in, something that had nothing to do with romance. But as she flashed through the channels, she saw her own face, and then Andy's, and then Meredith's on the screen. She sighed and stopped surfing long enough to see what this gossip show was saying about them.

She saw Meredith giving a quote to a reporter, her permagrin turned to full wattage. "I'm just so thrilled to be a part of this celebration," she gushed. Beside her Andy stood there, and she reached out and gave him a little squeeze. "This guy's going to make the best husband." He grinned at Meredith like they were good buddies — like he actually liked her. Looking at him on the screen, Wynne realized she felt like she was watching a total stranger, like he was just some guy on TV, not the man she was marrying in three days. Her blood coursed through her veins again, heating up her face and making her stomach hurt. What was this feeling? Was it just nerves or was there more to it? She clicked the TV off and stared at the blank, dark screen, thinking of Picky's admonitions that she should be spending every available minute with Andy. It seemed that, in the last few weeks, they'd been spending very little time together, always with the promise that they'd have plenty of time together after the wedding. But maybe all the distance and distractions had created a wedge between them. Maybe that was why she was struggling with doubts — she just hadn't spent enough time with her fiancé.

After all, something had made her pick him. Something had made her say yes to his proposal. She looked at the clock. She would go down and surprise them, tell Andy they should go for a walk alone on the beach in the dark afterward. They could hold hands, kiss, talk, spend some much-needed time alone. Maybe they would broach the subject of the talk they had with the minister. Maybe she'd be brave enough to tell Andy the truth about Callum. Maybe he would put her mind at ease and dispel some of these doubts she was having. She had been so stupid, getting caught up in all these wedding preparations and not focusing on the marriage that was to come.

She hopped up and checked her face in the bathroom mirror, slicking on some lip gloss and running a brush through her hair. The public had found her "Unassumingly pretty." "Natural." And "Wholesome." She paused for a moment and, as always, wished they'd described her as "alluring" or "sexy." She laughed and shook her head, her reflection moving in the mirror as she did. She would never be those things and had done her best to come to terms with it. Satisfied that she was presentable, she turned off the bathroom light, grabbed her keys and headed to find her fiancé.

She stood stone still, watching the scene play out in front of her as if she was watching a bad reality show — the kind she would never have agreed to be in. The kind of show that featured bleeped out words, bar brawls, and desperate women throwing themselves at feckless, weak men. Because that was exactly what seemed to be playing out between Meredith and Andy as they sat across from each other, alone, in a dark corner table at the bar. Had anyone from the crew ever been there with them? It didn't appear so. They looked quite cozy, leaning in, and oblivious to the rest of the world. She watched as Meredith threw back her head and laughed, her hand resting easily on Andy's forearm, that radar gaze focused solely on him.

Wynne's heart raced as she debated what to do. Pretend she hadn't seen them and get out before they saw her? Or stride across the restaurant in full-on combat mode? Too bad for the producers that there were no cameras here tonight. They would've bilked this for higher ratings if they had the chance. If she stood there much longer, she felt sure she might see something more. If she left now, there wouldn't be anything she couldn't get over. She watched as Meredith handed Andy her drink so he could taste it, the act somehow intimate and foreboding. She needed to get out of there quick.

How did she get here? The question had been popping into her mind with more and more frequency lately. Even more than when she was actually making the show week in and week out. Then it had just seemed like some nice fantasy, a little departure from the mundane reality of life. Never again would a cute, girl-next-door like her have guys trying to console her in droves. Never again would she be the object of so much affection. So what if most of them were actors just trying to make their mark? She had found the one authentic guy in the bunch. Or had she? She watched as Andy leaned forward and said something that made Meredith laugh again.

She took a step back, then stood frozen as Meredith looked over and saw her there. She said something to Andy, who jumped up and started moving toward her. Wynne turned and walked out, grateful she was near the door and had a head start. She heard first Andy, then Meredith, call her name.

She moved faster and faster, breaking into an outright run to escape them. It helped that they had both apparently had a lot to drink. It helped that she was sharper and more focused. It helped that neither one of them had any business getting behind the wheel of a car to chase her. Had she not come to find them, she would've never known about this. First their on-air interview she'd had no idea had even happened and now the chumminess in the bar. The questions of what else she didn't know began to crowd her rationale.

Suddenly Meredith's voice rose over the ones in her head, shocking her enough to make her pause in her flight. She turned just as Meredith caught up to her. Andy held back, and Wynne refused to look him in the eye. "This isn't whatever you think it is. Please don't run away." Meredith's eyes under the streetlight in the parking lot were pleading. And tired.

"I need to just go," Wynne said. "Clear my head. I shouldn't have come here. I was . . . I thought I'd surprise you, and I guess I did."

"Just please don't make this a big deal. Andy and I don't want anything to ruin this wedding. It's a big chance for all of us."

Wynne's heart picked up speed again. Chance? For all of us? "I'm not sure how my wedding is your chance, Meredith." She straightened her back, prepared to square off with this woman who had come barreling into her life and whose presence was still confusing to Wynne. She wasn't sure why she was there and why she had allowed it. Her glance flickered over to Andy. And how he'd suddenly gone from "could barely stand her" to giggling over drinks in a dark corner.

"I'm trying to make my mark. Just like you," Meredith responded. Behind them Andy shuffled his feet as if he was thinking about fleeing the scene.

"Meredith, this isn't a publicity campaign.

This is my wedding." She realized what she'd said and amended her words, her gaze falling on Andy. "*Our* wedding. This is real life, not some TV show."

Meredith's laugh was more of an unlady-like snort. "You actually thought this was real? That is just precious." She reached out to pat Wynne's shoulder sympathetically, but Wynne moved away before she could. Unfazed, Meredith continued. "We're actors. In a television show. We're all just playing a part." She narrowed her eyes at Wynne. "It's all part of the game."

"What game, Meredith?" Wynne spat out. "What you call a game, I call my life." She looked around them, at the empty street and the massive new bridge crossing the dark horizon. She lowered her voice. "This is my marriage. My future. What about you? Your future? Don't you want something more for your kids? Your marriage? Don't you get tired of all this . . . this . . . fakeness? Don't you want some —" She gave an ironic laugh as she realized what she was about to say. "Don't you want some reality?"

Meredith's face changed. The smile Wynne had grown accustomed to seeing seemed to break as she watched. "Reality?" she scoffed. "Why would I want anything to do with reality?" She gestured to the scenery around them. "Look where I am. This is my reality!" She gave Wynne a knowing smirk. "Reality is what you make of it. If one version doesn't match up, you go make yourself another. You of all people should know that." She crossed her arms as if the conversation was over.

"Um, I'm just going to go settle up," Wynne heard Andy say. Out of the corner of her eye, she saw him back away, grateful for an escape.

"But your kids. Your husband," Wynne said as she watched Andy reenter the bar. "I mean, they've been at his parents' house for awhile. Don't you even want to go be with them?"

"My husband took the kids and left." Meredith stared straight ahead, and for a moment, neither of them spoke. "He got tired of my 'need for constant attention.' " She held her fingers in the air to make quotation marks. "He said it was either the show or him."

Wynne started to say something about choosing fame over family but Meredith held up her hand and continued. "What kind of person would make me choose between them and something that makes me happy? How selfish is that?" She shook her head as if she was still trying to figure it out. "I told him if he would even ask that of me, he clearly didn't understand or love me. And you know what he said to that?" Wynne started to say she didn't know but Meredith plowed on without noticing. "He said, 'Well then, maybe I don't.' The next day, he suddenly needed to go to his parents and he took the kids with him." She shrugged. "But did I sit around crying over it, lamenting my lot in life and dissecting the situation like some people?" She angled her eyebrow in Wynne's direction. "No! I met you and decided that maybe I could help you and get my mind off the situation at the same time." She held up her hands. "I made a new reality." She gave Wynne a look that told her she believed that settled it.

But Wynne didn't see it that way. "But what if you called him? Maybe he's waiting to hear —"

Meredith held her hand up, her jaw trembling as she did. Her voice shook as she spoke, and yet she still said the words Wynne hated to hear. "I don't want to call him. Don't you see? I'm done. I've got other things to do, other things to focus on. And if he and the kids are happy, then so be it. In the meantime, they're tossing around ideas for some shows I could be involved in." She gave Wynne a smile, her jaw gone rigid. "I'm still in the game." She reached out and tugged on her hand, a plea. "That's what Andy and I have been talking about. He understands. I hoped you would too."

"But what I saw in there. That wasn't just understanding."

Meredith laughed. "Poor Wynne. I wish life was as simple as you want it to be."

Wynne saw Andy's dark shadow approaching. "I can't handle this. I need some time to think." She turned and walked quickly over to her car. Let Meredith explain to Andy what had happened. She'd talk to him in the morning when, hopefully, things looked brighter. Although she couldn't see how. Was he just in it for the fame too? Had she totally misread him? Was he actually into Meredith or had she tried to seduce him? By the look on his face before he'd noticed Wynne, he wasn't exactly pained. Maybe she was reading too much into it but one thing was clear: she didn't know everything there was to know. And her perfect wedding was becoming increasingly less perfect.

Her mind was a jumble of thoughts as she drove over the bridge back to Sunset, her car rolling past the hotel parking lot as if it had a mind of its own. She drove straight into the parking lot in front of the pier. She

parked the car and made her way up to the
mostly deserted pier, pushing aside the
memories of Callum that being there
brought back. At that time of night there
were only a few hardcore fishermen
hunkered over the rails and some random
teens moving in pairs, the dark water churning beneath the planks where they stood.
She moved swiftly past them as the thoughts
churned. Her feet only stopped because she
reached the end of the pier. Out there,
overlooking the vast expanse of ocean in
front of her, she gripped the pier railing and
took a few deep breaths to steady herself.

She stood for a moment, staring out to
sea as she thought about what to do.
Desperate, she began to pray. Prayer was
another thing she'd let slip as she'd raced
through these recent days, frantic to ac-
complish all that needed doing. She'd kept
secrets and hid her doubts, even, at times,
from herself. She'd struggled with the stress
and doubts and confusion without
remembering that she could give it all to
God and trust Him with the outcome. She
looked up at the blank night sky above her.
The moon was the only thing above her,
that one true thing glimmering there like a
beacon.

"Help me," she said silently, her chin

pointed to the moon. "Show me. I'm so lost. Please don't let me be so far off course that You can't get me where I need to be. I've made a mess of things and I need You to make it right again. Because I can't."

She whispered the word "Amen" aloud and then stood in silence as the ocean wind blew wildly. She ran her hands through her hair, as if she could comb through the tangle of thoughts in her mind as she untangled the strands that the wind had whipped into knots.

"You never did have a ponytail holder when you needed one," she heard a voice say.

The voice was familiar — so familiar she thought she was hearing things. She looked in the direction it had come from, her eyes landing on the face that went with it, seeing but not believing. And then, just as naturally as if no time had passed and the last year had not happened, she walked forward, into his waiting arms, the top of her head fitting just underneath his chin like always. She could feel his heart pounding through his thin T-shirt and she imagined he could feel hers as well.

She looked up into Callum's face, reveling in the comfort and familiarity of it even as her conflicted feelings mounted. "I can't believe you're here," she said.

"I told myself not to come, that I was messing with your future. That I didn't have a right — and I don't. I know that. But —" He sighed deeply and stepped away in order to look into her eyes. "I had to come tell you the one thing I didn't say to you. The real reason I contacted you after I saw you on that talk show."

She blinked up at him, the moon shining over his shoulder, the sky void of stars. She knew what he was going to say and she wanted, but didn't want, to hear it. She'd felt it pulsing underneath all the things they'd said to each other since that first text. It was that thing he kept himself from saying that night at his house. The thing she would never push him to say because it didn't matter anymore, did it?

"I came to tell you that I still love you, Wynne. And that I made a horrible mistake when I broke up with you. I wanted you to know that before it was too late. Just in case it would make some difference." She started to speak, but he held up his hand. "Not that I expect it to. I know you're in the middle of this big production and how selfish it is for me to come here, now of all times. But I kept picturing you here." He smiled nostalgically, his teeth shining against his tan skin in the blue light of the moon. "I actually pictured you right here. It's why I came out here tonight, to think about what I was going to say and to pray. And then I looked up and there you were. It felt . . ."

"Too perfect?" she finished for him. She could imagine how he felt when he looked up and there she was. They'd both come here to pray. She wondered if this was like the joke she heard about the man who prayed for rescue at sea but refused the plane and boat that came by to save him, holding out for God Himself to come to his aid. Hadn't she prayed for the answer? But that had been mere minutes ago. Surely this was a coincidence. Instead of finding an answer in Callum's eyes, she only found more questions.

Callum motioned her over to a nearby bench, there at the end of the pier, away from people. He knew privacy was at a premium for her. "Why did you come out here tonight?" he asked.

She shook her head, unable — or unwilling — to explain her flight to this place, fueled by anguish and confusion and even shame. She'd wound up in a situation she didn't know if she could get out of, wasn't sure if she should want out of, didn't know how to get out of. There were so many people involved, so much money and time spent, so much investment. She looked out to the sea, partly wishing she could somehow slip onto those waves and wake up on another continent.

"Just thinking things over," was all she said to Callum.

He cocked his head and raised his eyebrows at her. "Nice try. You act like I haven't known you your whole life." He planted his palms on the bench on either side of him and looked at her hard. "Let me guess. You're not sure if you should go through with this."

"Let's just say I'm not sure about anything," she said.

"Then you shouldn't do it. If you're not sure."

She narrowed her eyes at him.

He held his hands up, the picture of an innocent man. "Look, try to see me here as a friend. I know that seems weird but . . ." His voice trailed off as he dropped his hands back to his side. She noticed his hands were clenched into fists. Once, when they were freshmen in high school, he'd nearly punched a guy who was a bit too aggressive in his pursuit of her one night after a football game. That was the moment she'd realized he was interested in her as more than a friend. Funny how that intense situation led to something that became the best thing in her life.

*Could it happen again?* She felt the words echo through her. But an answer from the rational, sensible part of her — in a voice that sounded a lot like Picky's — quickly shot back an answer: *Don't be ridiculous.* The voice, she knew, was right. She had obligations, commitments, duties. She had people counting on her. This moment she found herself in — here, with Callum on the pier at Sunset Beach moments after learning she didn't know her fiancé as well as she wanted to — wasn't one that would last. It would be gone with the rising sun, gone just like the moon that hung bright and shining above them, its light tinting everything blue.

"If you need someone to rescue you, I'm applying for the job. Even if I just bail you out of this situation and we figure out the other stuff later." He gestured in the direction of the parking lot. "My white horse is parked right out there." His laugh was forced and they both knew it.

Though part of her wanted to take him up on the offer, the other part held fast to the vision she'd had for this wedding, for somehow making this work. Surely this situation was salvageable. To go with her feelings and impulses would only make things worse.

"I can't do this, Callum. Please don't ask me to. You said your piece. But now I just need to go back to my hotel room. And you should go home." She stood up. "Thank you so much for coming here." She gave him a sad smile. "If you'd done this months ago things, might be much different now. But it's too late. I'm getting married." She left him there and fled before he could stop her. She ran right past a woman on the stairs, her elbow grazing the woman's shoulder as she mumbled an "excuse me." Their eyes met but she was moving too fast to register that the woman looked vaguely, fleetingly, familiar.

Later, as she lay in bed she would remember the woman and try in vain to place her face in the sea of faces she'd come in contact with in the last months. Try as she might to think of something else — the woman, Meredith and Andy — her mind kept returning to Callum, and to the way he looked as she said it was too late. Just before she fell asleep she noticed the time and, calculating backwards, realized that they'd been standing on the pier talking at precisely 11:11.

The knock on the door sent her bolt upright in bed. She glanced over at the bedside clock, her mind shrieking an alert that her alarm clock — had she been thinking clearly enough to set it last night — should've barked out an alert over an hour before. Her photo shoot! Her parents! Picky! She shook her head at herself as she ran for the door. She tugged it open to find Donna on the other side, her look of displeasure morphing into a look of shock at the sight of her. "Sorry! I overslept! I —" She started to make an excuse but what could she say to explain the events of last night, especially to the producer of the wedding she was now confused about?

Was she confused enough to not go through with it? There were just so many ramifications if she did. Maybe a quickie divorce after the show aired — one with minimal fuss kept out of the press. That almost sounded easier. She shook her head. She was actually considering a divorce and she wasn't even married yet. Things were way off course.

Donna marched into her room, her eyes scanning the mess with barely masked disapproval. She flopped onto the small loveseat in the room with a sigh. "The photo shoot is canceled," she said. "We've got a bigger mess to fix here." She crossed her arms and fixed Wynne with a stare that made her squirm.

How much should she admit to? Had someone seen her with Callum last night and told on her? Her mind flickered over the woman she'd run past, trying to place her again. She had the sense that she had missed something important.

"Meredith called me last night after you left the bar," Donna said.

She couldn't let on how relieved she was that *that* was what Donna knew about. Wynne nodded and gave Donna her best "woman scorned" look.

Donna leaned forward, balancing her elbows on her knees. She looked past Wynne, suddenly interested in the view of the marsh outside the window. "We need to do damage control here. I mean, you and Andy have a lot to look forward to and it really was nothing. Meredith's willing to leave today if need be. She and I had a nice long talk and — well — I think she understands where things stand. There's nothing going on between those two but if it makes you feel more comfortable, she's fine with leaving, even if it means she can't be part of the show." She looked at Wynne. "You have to know that."

Donna waited for her to say something, but when she didn't, she continued pleading her case. "Meredith's going through a hard time — she told me she was honest with you about her husband. We're negotiating with her about a show about being an uber single mom. We think it could bring about some big ratings. 'Course, she'll have to get custody of the kids, and right now her husband has them, but . . ." Donna stopped short. "Sorry," she shook her head and looked rueful. "I'm always thinking about work. Professional hazard. Everything is fodder." She sighed and held up her hands, which made Wynne think of Callum the night before, saying he would just be her friend. But she had plenty of friends.

"All I'm saying is, please don't let this little thing derail you. I know when emotions get involved it can be real easy to start thinking things. Like how this is a mistake and you don't know each other well and you're moving too fast." She studied Wynne for a second and gave her a little smile. "Am I close?"

Wynne tilted her head from side to side and returned the smile. "Yeah."

"I can imagine," Donna said. She stood up. "Well, you're off the hook for the photo shoot. It would be too awkward for you and Andy to have to pose as the happy couple so soon after, but I've asked Andy to come by so you two can talk." She looked down at the phone she carried in her hand constantly, its presence as much a part of her as her limbs, her attention distracted by whatever she saw there. Wynne thought about how odd it was that she was having this conversation with her producer and not her fiancé. Why wasn't Andy here to defend himself in person? Why did Donna have to ask him to come? And why wasn't she angry at Andy? Probably because she felt hypocritical after her encounter with Callum last night.

"Your family arrives today?" Donna looked up from her phone and changed the subject. Crisis averted, for now.

"Yes, and my best friend. But not till late afternoon."

"Well, let me know if you need any help getting them settled in. I'd say you've got just enough time to see Andy and then attend to them." She looked Wynne up and down. "But I'd advise a shower and some makeup before you see anyone." She gave her a sarcastic wink and left Wynne to do as she was told. She just wished someone would tell her what to do with her heart.

Even though she'd known to expect it, she was still unprepared when she heard the knock on the door. Showered and dressed at least, she pulled the door open to reveal Andy on the other side. He gave her a tight smile and she waved him in as she fumbled for the right opening line. "Donna told me to come over here," he said, pausing in the doorway, his physical presence taking up too much space. She stepped away, her back coming to rest against the wall.

"Yeah, she told me to expect you."

He moved farther into the room. "Well yeah, but that was before she saw this. We were supposed to have an entirely different conversation but now . . ." He handed her a printout from a local news station's website. She saw a photo of Callum and her from high school, lifted straight from their yearbook. "Rejection Connection?" the headline read. She scanned the black and white print, the words nothing more than a jumbled alphabet swimming before her eyes. She got the gist of it. The woman she'd seen on the stairs was a reporter and she'd snagged Callum after Wynne fled. Though he'd apparently been as brief as he could be, his southern manners won out and he'd answered a few questions. Wynne assumed it was because he was unused to being in the spotlight, but Callum had been forthcoming and honest with this woman, who'd probably come across as sympathetic in the moment. Wynne didn't feel angry at him, only sorry he'd been ambushed. And now his picture was in the paper and his story was being shared with the world. She wanted to call him and say she was sorry. She wanted to tell him she knew how that felt all too well. She blinked at Andy, remembering he was her priority now.

She sat down on the bed, laying the paper beside her. Andy perched on the edge of the loveseat in the same spot Donna had occupied just an hour earlier. Donna had probably called while she was in the shower, panicking over the news, sending Andy when she couldn't get Wynne. She reached for her cell phone on the nightstand and saw the missed calls from both Paul and Donna. She held up a finger as she listened to two different voice mails. She hung up and looked at Andy. "They've called a press conference in," she looked at the clock, "oh geez, an hour." She looked down at what she was wearing and quickly surmised she would have to change before she went to the hotel lobby where they were holding the press conference.

Andy appeared not to hear her. "You've been seeing him?" Wynne noticed he almost sounded relieved. Maybe this made them even after last night. Whatever that meant.

"I saw him once, before we came here. Just to say good-bye before we . . ." She shrugged. "It was stupid and I was confused and I had these unresolved feelings and . . ."

"Seeing him only made you more confused."

She met his eyes. "I guess." A long silent moment passed. "I'm sorry," she continued. "I didn't think it was a big deal — at least that's what I told myself — until he showed up last night after I left you and Meredith. I literally ran into him on the pier and I guess some reporter saw us and pounced on him. He's not used to any of this and he . . . fell for it. I haven't talked to him or anything, I'm just guessing," she hurried to add.

"So what do you want to do now?" Andy asked. He ran his hand along the arm of the loveseat as he stared at the pattern in the fabric.

There was silence in the room as she thought of what to say in response. The question seemed to swell, taking up more and more space in the room the longer she was silent. She willed her mouth to say something in response, but the right words wouldn't come. "I have to go to the press conference in a few minutes," she said. "Come with me and we'll say everything's fine. Then this afternoon we can talk through all of this. We can save this."

He glanced over at her and looked away again, this time in the direction of the marsh view from her screened-in porch. A heron was picking his way through the reeds, high-stepping in search of food. "But things aren't fine," he said. "You're in love with someone else."

"I'm not, I —"

In one fluid movement Andy moved beside her on the bed, rested his hand on her leg as he looked at her with intensity. "I won't be your consolation prize, Wynne. That's not fair to either one of us. I know we both care for each other, but I think it's time to admit we've both been having our doubts about all of this. And if this guy Callum really does still want to work things out, maybe you need to consider that."

"But the wedding," she said. "And the show."

Andy gave her a sad smile. "It can all be canceled. I'm sure they can think of something to do instead." He shook his head. "Whatever happens, they'll figure out a way to monopolize on the drama of our breakup. And you and I will go our separate ways."

"I'm not sure that's what I want, though," she argued, still struggling to do what she'd believed was the right thing. She thought of Andy and Meredith last night and seeing Callum and Donna's pep talk and Picky's advice and what a mess it all was when all she'd wanted was to be the perfect June bride, to have a beautiful life. She'd hoped it would be with Andy.

He held his hand up to stop her arguing, the sad smile fading into a straight line across his face as he spoke. "I think it's best, Wynne. And I think it's best if I don't come with you to the press conference. It'll make it easier for you to tell the truth without me sitting beside you."

He looked at her until she met his eyes. "Maybe your happy ending isn't going to look the way you thought. But it'll still be happy." He smiled. "We'll both be happy. You don't have to worry about that." He removed his hand and stepped toward the door. Then he stepped back, and with the same kind eyes and gentleness that had made her pick him above all the other guys, he gave her a kiss on the cheek and then headed toward the door. And then he was gone.

The hotel lobby and breakfast area had been turned into the site of a makeshift press conference, the crew scurrying around her as they prepared to go live. She sat at the long table the hotel staff had dug out for them, a microphone in front of her, imposing and condemning. *Are you going to tell the truth?* it seemed to be asking her.

Donna and the rest of the producers had made it clear she had to straighten out the mess created by that reporter. She scanned the room and, catching the eye of one of the network reporters, gave a polite smile and looked away. It seemed every major news outlet and entertainment network or show had squeezed one of their delegates into this room. Andy's absence felt like a gaping hole beside her. She looked around to see if Donna was there, or someone who didn't seem out for blood. But she found no friendly faces, no one who was on her side. Her parents and Picky wouldn't arrive for a few hours. By the time they got there, this would all be over. She couldn't wait.

"Be with me," she prayed silently. "I've never needed You more."

She was alone, and yet she wasn't. She

took a deep breath as Paul gave instructions to the crowd of reporters. They had promised this would be brief and she would only need to give her statement, take a few questions, and then she could flee to the safety of her room.

She stared down at the words she'd jotted on the yellow legal pad the hotel had lent to her. Her prepared statement. And yet, as she practiced the words in her head, they sounded hollow and false, even to her. She was about to lie to everyone in this room. She bit her lip and took another deep breath. How could she deny the feelings she still had for Callum? She thought back to the night she'd given Andy the key to her heart. It was Callum's face she'd wanted to see as the men filed in to await her choice. She hadn't told anyone that — had even convinced herself that it didn't matter. And yet, he'd come here. He'd said he loved her and wanted another chance. This was the one thing she'd hoped for and yet she'd made a promise to someone else, someone she did care about, even if things weren't perfect with him.

She realized that everyone was waiting for her to speak. And so, for lack of anything better to do, she began to read the words she had scrawled in a rush of fear and adrenaline after Andy walked out. Desperate for order, she'd gone to the easiest answer with the fastest resolution.

"Many of you have seen the interview given by my ex-fiancé, Callum Royce, to a local reporter who found out he had come here to speak with me. And many of you are aware that it was my breakup with Callum that led to my spot on *The Rejection Connection* and to the reason we are all gathered here at Sunset Beach." She looked into the camera, feigning a boldness she didn't feel. "I made the decision last February to say yes to Andy, to commit my life to him and become his wife. And that is what I intend to do in two days." Flashbulbs began to pop like exclamation points. She could already see the entertainment headlines. "Rejection Connection Bride Says Wedding Still On!" "Andy Scores a Wynne!"

Finished with her statement, she put the legal pad down and folded her hands on top of it. Now for the unpredictable part — the questions. The reporter from the stairs stood up, now all too familiar to Wynne. She wore a cat-and-canary grin, enjoying the bit of instant celebrity that the scoop had brought her, the break that Callum's transparency had given her.

It was that transparency that had led to their breakup. He had doubts and he'd been brave enough to voice them. Wynne had freaked out in response to his honesty, accused him of not caring, picked a fight that became a battle that ended in a war. She'd always blamed him but . . . what if? What if she'd been more understanding, more patient, more open? She'd held everything so close, so tight, so controlled, always wanting things to be perfect, to go the way she expected. But, that wasn't faith. If Callum had wanted time, she should've given it to him willingly. Not because she trusted Callum's plans — but because she trusted God's. If she truly believed that He held her future in the palm of His hand, and that He had a good plan for her life, why was she afraid of anything that happened?

She looked at the expectant faces, all waiting for whatever secrets she would divulge. She thought of Callum on the pier the night before. She thought of how she'd landed where she was, doing what people expected, giving the right answers and going through the motions just like she'd done all her life. All in an effort to be perfect, to make things perfect. And yet, in spite of her efforts, they were far from that.

She thought of that beautiful wedding that

was to take place in two days — the attention to every detail, the meticulous plans and countless hours invested. It was, to be sure, going to be her dream wedding. Yet. But. Except. There would still be that missing face. She had almost made it through the questions, answering robotically. She thought of Meredith saying, "You don't actually think any of this is real?" But she had wanted to believe it was. Or it could be.

The final question came from someone from the Entertainment Network, a face she'd seen many times when scrolling through the channels, a woman who had done her fair share of red carpet interviews. And now here she was in this small Carolina beach town, probably wondering just what all the hoopla was about. "Wynne," the woman said, her mouth forming a half smile, half grimace. "Be honest. Are you sure you don't have any feelings for your former fiancé, Callum, is it?"

Wynne barely nodded and looked down.

The woman gave a knowing nod to the colleague next to her. Wynne could already envision the segment that would run about this. They would play *The Rejection Connection* video of her blubbering on about Callum and then they would play this next bit, this answer to her question. And what would that bit be? She opened her mouth to answer but no sound would come out. The room stilled. It seemed everyone in it had inhaled as the question was asked and they were all still holding their breath, Wynne included. She scanned the faces in the room, her heart picking up its pace as she struggled to form words. But nothing sounded right.

She felt her face growing hot, then hotter. The sound of stillness changed to a high-pitched whine that grew in width and intensity, until it was all she could hear. Until the sound inside her head began to sound like the scream she had been holding in since that day at lunch with Meredith when a text flashed on her phone screen and everything she thought she knew about the future shifted. She tried to speak again, but when her mouth opened all that came out was a gasp. She blinked at the pairs of eyes staring a hole through her, saw the expectation on all the faces. But she couldn't say what they expected, not anymore. She cast a glance at Paul and Donna, now hovering in the back of the room, waiting for her to act the part as she'd been doing for the last several months.

Instead of doing "the right thing" and giving the expected answer, she simply turned and fled the room, her feet carrying her down the front stairs of the inn and across the gravel parking lot. She focused on her feet hitting the gravel, keeping her head down so she didn't have to make eye contact with anyone. She just wanted to get away, to not be looked at by another set of eyes. Which was why she never saw the person standing there at the edge of the parking lot, watching the media circus from a safe distance. She ran smack into him and looked up to find the face she'd been wishing to see all along.

# EPILOGUE

*3 Months Later*

From behind the curtain she heard Karen Dodd offer the lead-in. "Well, everyone, I'm thrilled to introduce our next guests. Wynne Hardy is a celebrity after her stint on *The Rejection Connection* and her much-publicized breakup with former fiancé Andy Baker. And we have a treat today because Wynne is here with the guy she ditched him for!" She paused for the audience to clap their approval and titter to each other. "So please welcome Wynne Hardy and her first, and one true love, Callum Royce. Come on out, guys!"

Callum gave her a "What have you gotten me into" look, gripped her hand tightly, and together they walked out onto the little soundstage as they'd been directed to do. Two chairs had been placed for them with another chair nearby for Karen, who was already in her seat, beckoning them over as if they were neighbors just stopping in for a regular chat. Wynne felt herself relax as Callum slid into the seat next to her. She tried never to compare Callum to Andy — because, why? She saw all the signs now, the many moments she'd known Andy wasn't the right man for her, but had refused to see it because she was afraid that if he wasn't, she'd find herself alone.

And what would've been wrong with that, she wondered now. What would've been so wrong with her being alone for a while? What would be wrong with praying for God to send the right man for her when it was His timing to do so, to lean into Him while she waited? In a way, she thought with a smile as Karen grilled poor Callum while the audience of women looked on with delight, that's what she'd been doing these past few months.

Oh sure, she and Callum were seeing each other. But mostly she was taking her time, standing on her own and learning that a full life was possible in a lot of other ways, if only she remembered to see it. She saw it now in her mom's homemade vegetable soup and Picky's "helpful" fashion tips and her new puppy's wet nose as he licked her hello. She saw it in the change of seasons and another sunrise and freshly picked flowers. It wasn't found solely in a gold band on her left hand. Love, in all its forms, was her true anchor.

Karen asked the questions people always asked. What did she think of Meredith's new show that would be premiering soon? She told Karen that she wished Meredith well, but she didn't add that she often prayed that Meredith would work things out with her husband and stop chasing the elusive fame she craved. Next of course was the "Andy question." Again, she answered politely, that she wished him well and that she'd heard he quit his job and moved back to his hometown. She didn't add that she knew his mother must've been elated.

The cameraman indicated they needed to wrap up, and Wynne felt relief wash over her. "So, Wynne, don't shoot me for asking this, but before we go to commercial, I can't resist." Karen turned and gave the audience a conspiratorial grin. "Can we expect a wedding announcement from you two anytime soon?" The audience guffawed over her bold question.

But Wynne had expected it. After all, she got it often enough from her mom and Picky and even people in the grocery store. And she thought about the ring in the box in the junk drawer of Callum's kitchen, the one he'd told her was hers to wear again when she was ready. Perhaps she would be soon.

"Maybe you'll be a June bride next year instead?" Karen pressed, giddy, her face shining.

Wynne gave her a smile that told the camera she knew something they didn't. It would set everyone to wondering and that was the fun part. It was good to wonder. "You never know," she said as the show went to commercial and the camera turned its focus away from her.

# ACKNOWLEDGMENTS

Special thanks to the other authors of A Year of Weddings. I'm honored to be counted among you.

# DISCUSSION QUESTIONS

1. "This story is about 'the rest of the story' — the parts we don't see" in the reality TV world. Do you ever think about what happens after the cameras are turned off, or away, from the reality TV stars?
2. Why do you think that Wynne said "yes" to Andy's proposal?
3. Did Wynne make the right choice in the end?
4. How did you feel about Meredith? Is there a reality TV star she reminded you of?
5. Do you think the author had any reality TV stars in mind when she wrote this story?

# ABOUT THE AUTHOR

**Marybeth Whalen** and her husband Curt have been married for twenty-two years and are the parents of six children, ranging in age from college to elementary school. They live outside Charlotte, NC. Marybeth is the author of five novels. The newest one, *The Bridge Tender,* brings readers back to Sunset Beach, NC and releases June 2014. Marybeth spends most of her time in the grocery store but occasionally escapes long enough to scribble some words. She is always at work on her next novel. You can find her at www.marybethwhalen.com.

# A July Bride

BETH WISEMAN

*To Daddy*

# PROLOGUE

Alyssa Pennington grasped the crescent bouquet of orchids with both hands, careful to hold the flowers slightly below her waist the way the florist had suggested. Her father looped his arm in hers, and when he whispered, "I love you, Daughter," she brushed away a happy tear. She was sure Dad had never looked more handsome in his black tuxedo, crisp white shirt, and the red rose boutonniere Alyssa had pinned to his lapel an hour ago. His dark hair, graying at the temples, was freshly cut, and the familiar aroma of his Old Spice aftershave calmed her jittery excitement. A little.

Until recently, her father had been the number-one man in her life. But he'd happily stepped into second place when Brendan Myers proposed nine months ago. And now, on this July afternoon in La Grange, Texas, she would profess her love for Brendan in front of their families and friends.

The scene was playing out as she'd imagined it for years, exactly as planned. All the attendants were in place, arrayed across the front of the church Alyssa had grown up in. Her friend Sherry stood beaming in the matron-of-honor dress they'd let out — twice — to accommodate her pregnancy. Little Raelyn and Joshua had performed their duties as flower girl and ring bearer perfectly. And there was Brendan in a white tuxedo with tails, his brown hair bronzed a tawny gold from his work at Lenny Wick's ranch. Even at a distance, those deep brown eyes seemed to see inside her soul. Pastor Dean stood beside him, holding his Bible with both hands. Soon Alyssa Pennington would be Mrs. Brendan Myers.

Mrs. St. Claire started the bridal march, and everyone stood. Dad tried to ease them forward, but Alyssa froze, unable to force one foot in front of the other. Unfazed, he reached down, gently pulled one of her hands free, and squeezed it. Three squeezes, and she released the breath she was holding. Still looking forward, she squeezed back three times. They had started doing that in church, this church, when she was a little girl. The tradition had stuck, and they both knew three squeezes meant "I love you."

"It's normal to be nervous," he whispered as he took her arm again and they stepped forward. He kept them at a slow, steady pace down the aisle, each pew decorated with white baby's breath, greenery, and white bows. It was her moment. The moment every young woman dreams about.

She passed Glenda Hightower on her left. Glenda got credit for Alyssa's hair on this special day. She had managed to take Alyssa's unruly dark curls and tame them into a beautiful updo beneath her veil. Alyssa smiled at her friend, then noticed Bob Shanks to her right. Bob had been her first boyfriend when she was in the seventh grade. Now he was happily married to Amy, and Raelyn and Joshua were their four-year-old twins. Alyssa glanced at the people she loved on each side of the aisle — around two hundred — but she couldn't keep her eyes from drifting back to her soon-to-be husband. The most handsome and wonderful man on the planet.

But as she drew close to him, something twisted in her heart, a heaviness she would remember for the rest of her life. Pastor Dean asked, "Who gives this woman to this man?" As planned, her father said, "Her mother and I." But that part was a blur, like jumbled voices echoing in a tunnel of her brain that wasn't tuned in.

All she saw at that moment was the sweat pouring down both sides of Brendan's face and the tears welling in his eyes as he whispered how sorry he was. *For what?*

A long, brittle silence loomed between them like a heavy mist, and Alyssa couldn't breathe.

"I can't do this," he finally said.

And he bolted out of the church.

# ONE

Alyssa lifted her wedding dress onto the counter and handed the hanger to Loretta Klatt, swallowing back the lump in her throat.

"Hon, are you sure 'bout this? You love this dress. You've been eyeing it for years, and it fits you like a dream. Sure you don't want to keep it, just in case?" Loretta draped the dress over one arm and sighed as she glanced up at the wall. Hundreds of photos hung there, all brides that Loretta had dressed and sent down the aisle in the forty years she'd owned the shop. Alyssa had assumed her own bridal photo would be hanging there by now.

"No, thank you." She nodded to make it definite. "It's been two months. I'm not getting married. Not to Brendan anyway. Maybe never." She pulled her eyes from Loretta's and hung her head for a few moments before she looked back up to see Loretta hanging Alyssa's beautiful dress on a rack behind her. She blinked a few times, resolved that there would be no more tears. She took a deep breath and forced a smile. "Thank you, Loretta. For taking the dress back."

Loretta stuffed her hands into the pockets of her jeans, her plain white button-up shirt straining against a full bosom. For someone who made a living dressing people in wedding attire, Loretta was not exactly a walking advertisement for her business. Her long gray hair hung to her waist, and her short cropped bangs were cut high above gray eyebrows.

"I'm just so sorry about what happened. I've seen my share of couples, believe you me, and I really thought you and Brendan were the real thing. If ever a man was crazy about a girl . . ." Loretta shook her head and frowned, bringing together a road map of wrinkles.

Alyssa wasn't sure how much more pity she could swim in. She was drowning in it. Forcing a smile — again — she said, "Evidently not." She gave a quick wave before she walked out of the shop. As the bell on the door clinked against the glass, she was reminded how many times she'd been in and out of Loretta's store for fittings, to choose bridesmaid dresses, or just to chat with Loretta about her wedding.

Her wedding to Brendan Myers. The only man she'd ever loved. But now hated.

Brendan counted out the last of three hundred dollars to Rudy Schmutz.

Rudy shook his head. "I'll take your money, but I can't promise it'll do any good." He stuffed the bills into one back pocket and pulled a can of chewing tobacco from the other. He put a pinch between his cheek and gum. "She ain't gonna get back with you, fella. You humiliated that girl in front of the whole town."

"I'm not giving up. Ever." Brendan looked up at the blue sky above, imagining the banner trailing behind Randy's crop duster and the look of surprise and wonder on Alyssa's face. "Now remember what I said. You gotta fly over Monument Hill at two o'clock next Saturday. That's when they start the reenactment. Alyssa will be there for sure. Her dad makes sure the family goes to that stuff."

Rudy shrugged his broad, bony shoulders. "Whatever you say." He spit out a brown stream, then raised his bushy brown eyebrows. The guy was about fifty, but he looked more like eighty to Brendan. His

face was weathered, he walked with a limp
— supposedly from falling off a bull — and
he was always scowling. But he was the only
guy with a Pawnee crop duster who was
willing to take the job at a price Brendan
could semiafford.

Brendan had gotten back the deposit he'd
put down on a small house for him and
Alyssa, but he'd given it to his parents on
top of the rent he already paid them. At the
time, that had seemed like the right thing to
do, especially since his mother had been
diagnosed with breast cancer. But based on
the amount of booze in the house, he didn't
think the extra money was going toward his
mother's health care. He'd already started
putting money away for another deposit.
Rentals in small towns didn't come along
often, but he wanted to be ready when one
did. He really needed his own place.
Another reason he shouldn't be spending
money on stuff like banners.

Not that that would stop him.

"I have to get back to work before Lenny
gets back from the Lions Club meeting."
His rancher boss was a great guy, but Lenny
expected a full day's work for a fair wage,
and Brendan had always given Lenny a
hundred percent. It wasn't just a matter of
being a good employee. Brendan loved the

work, especially tending to the horses.

Rudy chuckled as he limped back to his truck. "Shoulda just married the girl when you had the chance."

Brendan pushed back the rim of his Stetson, a Christmas gift from Alyssa. "I know that, Rudy. And I aim to get her back before it's too late."

Alyssa found Sherry at the back of the café in the booth where they always sat. Her blond hair was braided into pigtails, which only made her chubby cheeks look even rounder. She waved and then stood awkwardly to greet Alyssa with a hug.

"Are you okay?" Sherry eased herself back against the bench seat and folded her hands across her enlarged belly. "That couldn't have been easy, returning the dress." Sherry still had another few weeks until her due date, but Alyssa's lifelong friend looked like she was about to pop any minute.

"It went pretty much like I expected. Loretta tried to talk me out of it, but she took the dress back in the end. That dream is over. Every wedding gift has been returned, every last wedding detail undone. That was the last item on the list. Time to move on." Alyssa slid into the seat and put her purse beside her. "What about you? You look miserable." She picked up one of the paper menus that was already on the table. Not that she needed it. She always ordered the same thing — a tuna melt with a side of fruit.

Sherry sighed. "All that stuff they say about glowing during pregnancy . . . well, it's not true. The first four months, I threw up. And the last four, I've spent unable to see my toes and with a waddle that would make any penguin proud."

Alyssa grinned. She knew lunch with her former matron of honor would be the perfect thing to do after returning her wedding dress. "Well, you don't have much longer. Another few weeks and we'll be holding Monroe Junior."

"You do realize how much I love my husband, don't you? Why else would I let that man name our firstborn Monroe?" She shook her head. "I'm afraid li'l Monroe Modenstein is going to be teased his entire life."

"I doubt it. He'll probably be a big boy like his daddy. No one will pick on him." Everyone in town loved Sherry's husband. He was six foot seven and a tad heavy, a size that had served him well on the football field all through high school. He was a big old teddy bear, though, and he adored

Sherry, who barely reached five foot tall.

"I'll have a double cheeseburger, fries, and a chocolate shake." Sherry spieled off her order to the waitress. From the time she'd found out she was pregnant, Sherry had taken that as the go-ahead to indulge in all the dietary luxuries she'd never allowed herself before. "Oh, and one of those brownie parfaits."

Alyssa slapped her menu closed. "I'll have the same."

Sherry's eyes widened. "You're not pregnant *too*, are you?" She giggled. Alyssa's best friend knew good and well that Alyssa and Brendan had never done the act.

"It's time for some changes." Alyssa sat taller. "I'll start slow with a new lunch selection."

"So tell me," Sherry said as she shifted her weight in the seat. "What has Brendan done lately to win you back?"

Alyssa slouched into her seat. "Can't we talk about baby clothes or diaper choices . . . or anything besides Brendan?"

Sherry quickly covered her mouth, then burped. "Good grief. I've got more gas than a flatulent linebacker."

Alyssa laughed. "Or we can talk about your gastric issues."

"Ugh. Not a good topic. So are you going

to tell me or not? You know I live to hear about Brendan's shenanigans."

Sometimes Alyssa wished she could leave La Grange, even if it was just for a while. She feared she would always be the girl who got dumped at the altar, and Brendan was only keeping the embarrassing story alive by trying to woo her back. "He's making a fool of himself," she finally said. "My dad went and talked to him last week and told him to quit sending things to the house."

Sherry smiled. "I think it's romantic, all those flowers he keeps sending."

"Last week he sent me a kitten with a note that said, 'You make my heart purr.' Can you imagine?"

Sherry laughed out loud. "He's so goofy."

Alyssa sighed. It was one of the things she'd loved about Brendan. "Well, he needs to stop, and that's what Dad went to tell him. To leave me alone." She paused. "What kills me is that he doesn't have the money to spend on things like that. Especially now that his mom is sick."

"Aw, poor guy. He's made it clear how much he regrets what he did. Can't you find it in your heart to forgive him and give it another shot?"

Alyssa shook her head. "I've forgiven him already. But I just can't trust him." She drew in a big gulp of air, then let it out slowly. "I just want to get on with my life, and he's making that impossible."

"Well, I think you're making a mistake. Monroe said that all the boys were ribbing him at the bachelor party, joking about the end of the good life and all that." She lifted one eyebrow. "Not my Monroe, of course, but the others. And you know how those boys get when they're together sometimes. Brendan was probably already nervous to be stepping up to the plate, but I'm sure those guys were partly responsible for running him off the field. And then there's Brendan's family situation."

Alyssa was well aware of Brendan's dysfunctional family. The whole town was. She and Sherry were quiet as the waitress set their food down. Then Alyssa said, "None of that is reason enough for leaving the woman you love at the altar. I don't care how bad the guys were trash talking about marriage. And I know how afraid Brendan was of turning out like his parents. We'd talked about that."

"I just think you're hurting yourself by not giving him another chance." Sherry took a giant bite of her burger and hadn't quite finished chewing when she added, "He's never gonna give up."

"Well, he's going to have to."

Alyssa was finally able to veer the conversation in another direction, and Sherry spent the latter part of their lunch talking about her upcoming labor and delivery. "Monroe knows I have a high tolerance for pain. I don't expect I'll be needing all those drugs they offer up."

"Maybe have them on standby. You know, just in case." Alyssa dabbed at her mouth with the napkin as she recalled Sherry's trip to the dentist last year. Alyssa had taken her to get a tooth extracted, and she wasn't so sure about Sherry's high tolerance for pain.

Alyssa let the last of the brownie parfait settle against her palate, savoring it, before they split the bill.

When they got outside, Alyssa hugged her friend. "I knew you would cheer me up, Sherry. Thanks for meeting me for lunch."

Sherry chuckled. "That's what I do, you know. I *eat*. All the time." She gave a quick wave and started walking toward the bank where she worked. Alyssa took off in the other direction, and she was almost to her car when someone called out her name. She turned around, brought a hand to her forehead to shield her eyes from the sun, and peered at the gorgeous man approaching her from down the block.

"Hey, Dalton," she said. "If you're looking for my brother, he's with Dad at the fairgrounds."

Dalton sauntered up to her. Her brother's friend was possibly the best-looking man she'd ever laid eyes on, and Alyssa had spent her first seventeen years on earth adoring him from afar. Until Brendan. Even now, the man could make her pulse quicken. He'd always been way out of her league, though. In high school he'd dated every cheerleader until he'd finally latched on to Pamela Herring. Gorgeous Pamela Herring. They'd even kept dating when Pam went away to school in Houston.

But gorgeous Pamela, apparently, had dumped Dalton sometime in the spring — and by text message. Alyssa remembered thinking that was really cold. And who would dump Dalton Landreth in the first place?

"I wasn't looking for Alex." Dalton smiled. "But I'm glad I ran into you. I was going to call you."

"Oh?"

"I was wondering if you'd like to go out with me next Saturday."

"Uh, I . . . uh . . ." Despite everything with Brendan, it felt like a betrayal to even consider a date with another man.

149

"Just dinner." Dalton took a step closer. "We can see how it goes. I know we're both coming out of something, but . . ." He shrugged. "I'd really like to take you out."

Alyssa wanted to say yes. And that was confusing. Shouldn't she still be mourning the demise of her relationship with Brendan? But then she remembered. "Oh, I can't. The whole family promised my dad we'd go to Monument Hill next Saturday for Texas Heroes Day. You know, they're having the battle reenactment, and I think the county judge will be there, and the high school band, and . . ." She paused. "It goes on all weekend, but I think we're leaving the house around one on Saturday. It usually runs into the early evening. Anyway, I can't miss it."

"Well, maybe we could go there together and get dinner afterward."

*Hmm.* Here they were, both single for the first time since junior high. She thought for a few moments. *Why not?*

"Yes. I'd like that," she said. Maybe Dalton Landreth was exactly what she needed to put Brendan out of her mind. Maybe even for good.

# TWO

Dalton walked along the sidewalk of the town square toward the bank. Twice he'd turned back to sneak another look at Alyssa before she got into her car. Finally, a real date with her. So many times he'd had dinner with Alex, Alyssa, and their parents, and in the past few years it had been torture to watch Alyssa leave to go meet Brendan Myers later in the evening.

Everyone had been devastated the day Brendan left Alyssa at the altar. Everyone but Dalton. And he planned to give it everything he had to win her over.

He glanced at his watch and realized he only had ten minutes before the bank closed. He picked up his pace and hurried into the building, glad to see that Sherry was working today. He placed his paycheck and deposit slip on the counter and wondered if Sherry knew about the dab of ketchup on her chin. He smiled as he touched his own chin. "You've got, uh . . ."

She quickly swiped at the ketchup with her hand. "Well, that's what I get for inhaling my food." She logged Dalton's deposit and handed him the receipt. "I don't usually take a lunch on Saturdays since we close at one, but this small person inside of me was hungry." She pointed to her tummy and smiled. "So I grabbed a quick bite with Alyssa."

"How's she doing?" Dalton knew Sherry was Alyssa's best friend. "Do you think she's over Brendan yet?"

Sherry was quiet as she finished the transaction, then said, "She'll never be over Brendan. I don't care what she says." She shook her head as she handed him a receipt. "And Brendan is certainly going to extremes to try to win her back."

Dalton had already heard about Brendan's tactics to win Alyssa back. He was a good guy, but he'd had his chance. "Well, I'm going to hope you're wrong about her never being over the guy, because I'm taking her to Monument Hill next Saturday and then to dinner afterwards."

Sherry's eyes widened. "Really? She didn't mention that at lunch."

"I just asked. And she said yes."

"Huh. I didn't know you had an interest

in Alyssa."

Dalton smiled. "I've always had an interest in Alyssa. The timing just hasn't ever been right."

Sherry grunted. "I'm not sure the timing is good right now either." She smiled. "Sorry to tell you that, Dalton, but I don't want you to get your hopes up where Alyssa is concerned."

"It's just one date. No big deal." He tried to sound casual, even though his hopes were definitely up. It was unforgivable what Brendan had done to Alyssa, and Dalton wanted to help her get over it. He grinned at Sherry. "Aren't you due like any day now?"

Sherry scrunched her face into a scowl. "Dalton Landreth, I know I'm huge, but that is not something a lady wants to hear. I have a few more weeks."

"I — I didn't mean anything by it. I think you look very pretty. Glowing." Everyone loved Sherry, and Dalton didn't think there was a happier couple than her and Monroe.

She rolled her eyes and huffed. "If I hear that word one more time — glowing — I might puke. And Lord knows I've done enough of that throughout this pregnancy." She put her hands on the counter and leaned forward — as much as she could with her rounded belly. "Pregnant women don't glow. We vomit and waddle. And in case Monroe hasn't mentioned it, we get a wee bit mean at times too."

"Now, Sherry. I can't imagine you being mean."

"Oh, don't give me that. You've known me all my life." She waved a hand. "Now go. Prosper. Have a great weekend — or whatever. I need to start getting this place shut down so I can go home and go to bed." She rolled her eyes again. "That's also what pregnant women do. When we're not eating, we sleep."

Dalton chuckled before he left the bank, a little bounce in his step. He couldn't wait until next Saturday. He glanced behind him as he walked out the main entrance and saw Sherry on the phone. Dalton figured she was calling Alyssa to get the scoop. By next Saturday everyone in town would know Dalton was taking Alyssa out.

Alyssa put the rolls on the table, then sat down when her mother did. Her brother Alex said the blessing, then her father started talking about the reenactment the following Saturday.

"I heard that two of the local radio stations will be covering it — and Fox News might even be there." Dad scooped a generous helping of greens onto his plate. Mom shook her head. "I still don't understand the allure of these reenactments. All you grown men getting dressed up and pretending to shoot each other." She grinned. "Returning to your childhoods perhaps? Like playing cowboys and Indians?"

"There won't be any Indians, Corrine. It's a tribute to the men who died during the Dawson Massacre and the Mier Expedition in 1842." Dad turned to Alyssa. "You're coming, right?"

Alyssa nodded as she swallowed a bite of roast. "And I have a date."

All eyes shot in her direction.

"With who?" Alex halted his fork midway to his mouth.

"Dalton Landreth."

Her mother actually clapped her hands together. "Oh, that's wonderful."

Alyssa's father gave a nod of approval also, but Alex just stared at her. "I don't think that's a good idea. For either one of you."

"Well, it's not your choice to make," Alyssa told her brother. "And he's your friend. Why isn't it a good idea?"

"Uh, well, I don't think it takes a brain surgeon to figure that out. You're suffering from a broken heart over Brendan, and I don't think Dalton's over Pam yet." He pointed his fork at Alyssa. "Someone's gonna get hurt."

"Alex, it's just one date. I think everyone should be glad that I'm trying to move on. It doesn't mean that Dalton and I will be anything more than friends."

"Yeah, whatever." Alex shook his head as he stabbed at a piece of meat.

"Yeah, whatever," Alyssa mumbled under her breath.

"That's enough. You're both too old for that kind of bickering." Mom smiled at Alyssa. "Family supports family, no matter what. And if you want to go out with Dalton, do it."

Dad pushed back his chair. "Apparently that talk I had with Brendan last week didn't do a lick of good — more flowers arrived for you this morning." He pointed to the living room. "I put them with the others. Looks like a funeral parlor in there."

The mention of Brendan's name still brought a lump to Alyssa's throat. "Maybe he'll give up once he hears I'm going out with Dalton."

Sherry had called her the minute Dalton left the bank this morning, singing Dalton's praises as if Alyssa didn't already know how great he was. She wondered if Brendan would be at Monument Hill next Saturday. Maybe it would do him good to see her out with someone else.

Especially someone like Dalton.

Brendan ate his dinner on a paper plate on the front porch. He could still hear the yelling inside, but over the years he'd learned to tune it out. One drunk in the house would be bad enough, but when both of them were drinking, it just wasn't safe to be around them. Both Brendan's older brothers had taken off at seventeen, and one of them hadn't made a very good go of it. Last he heard, Danny was doing time in a Houston jail. Craig was married and living in Eagle Lake, less than an hour's drive away. But he'd pretty much washed his hands of Mom and Dad. Brendan didn't blame him.

He jumped when the screen door opened but was relieved when his mother emerged. His father could be nasty when he drank.

"Why're you sitting out here?" Mom sagged into the other rocking chair on the front porch of their old house.

Brendan shrugged.

"Your dad had a bad day at work today, so he's in a mood." Mom kicked the rocker into action.

"You shouldn't be drinking. That's what the doctor said."

"Cancer doesn't grow 'cause you drink a couple of beers. Don't make a big thing out of it. I just need a little help to deal with your father." She leaned her head back against the high-back rocker and closed her eyes. She had bags beneath her eyes, and she was really pale. And Brendan knew good and well that she'd had more than two beers.

"Mom, it's not about making the cancer grow. It's about keeping you healthy enough to fight this stuff."

"Hmm." She rocked a little more. "I'll think about it."

"I hope so." He finished the last bite of his chicken and set his plate on the small table in between the rocking chairs. "You should go to bed now, Mom. You look tired."

She stopped the rocker but didn't get up. "You having any luck winning Alyssa back?"

"No." Brendan figured Alyssa's parents were glad their daughter wasn't marrying into this family — though they'd always been really good to Brendan, assuring him that he was no reflection of his parents, that he'd be able to carve his own path in this world. Brendan couldn't think of a better family to marry into. And he knew he'd never love another woman the way he loved Alyssa. But he'd blown it.

"Maybe it's just as well you didn't marry that girl. We're from different sides of the tracks, so to speak. And her people always seemed a bit uppity if you ask me. They aren't like us."

*Thank goodness!* "They're not uppity, and it didn't matter to them which side of the tracks anyone was on." He paused, thinking this conversation was pointless. "I love Alyssa. And I would've worked hard to take care of her. It would've worked out."

"We'll never know now, will we?"

Brendan bit back an angry response. The Lord was surely testing him these days. Mom and Dad usually managed to keep it together on Sunday mornings, and ironically they'd made sure that Brendan and his brothers went to church regularly. But the things that went on behind closed doors at his house would shock most people in La Grange. Folks around here just thought they knew everything about the Myers family. Even Alyssa didn't know the half of it. His parents were basically living the same way both sets of grandparents had lived. It was a pattern Brendan was determined to break.

"Love ain't always enough," his mother finally whispered. She sighed, opened her eyes, and pushed herself up from the chair. She gazed down at Brendan, and Brendan knew what was coming. First his parents would fight, then the crying would start. Mom covered her face with her hands as her shoulders shook. "I'm sorry we ain't been better parents."

Brendan slowly got up, put his arm around his mother, and edged her toward the door. "I know, Mom. Let's get you to bed."

They tiptoed across the living room where Brendan's father was snoring on the couch, and they both jumped when he sat up. But after eyeing them both and scowling, he finally lay back down. Neither Brendan nor his mother moved until his father started to snore again.

# THREE

Alyssa snapped a few pictures of her father in his battle attire while her mother gathered gallon jugs of sweet tea, her contribution to the event.

"Alex, put these in the back of the truck, will you? Then we need to get on the road." Mom turned to Alyssa. "Is Dalton picking you up?"

Alyssa took one more picture, then nodded. "He should be here any minute." Mom smiled her approval. She loved Brendan and had been like a second mother to him. But if another suitor was on the horizon, Mom was glad it was Dalton.

Alyssa wasn't sure about her father, though. Dad had formed a strong bond with Brendan when Brendan worked for him at the feed mill, before he and Alyssa had even started dating. Dad had admired him for his hard work and dedication to the business, and he'd been crushed when Brendan walked out — not to mention angry at him for hurting his daughter.

Dad had sold the mill a few years back, about the time Mom retired from teaching elementary school. Both her parents were enjoying their early retirement, though Dad spent a fair amount of time as the auctioneer for cattle sales and various fundraisers.

"I'm taking my own truck." Alex hefted a box filled with four gallon jugs and headed for the door.

Mom nodded, then turned to Alyssa. "Have fun today. I'm glad you're giving Dalton a chance. He's a great guy."

Alyssa smiled, but she was tempted to voice her mother's unspoken words: *a great guy with a great family.* Alyssa's parents had never complained about paying for the entire wedding. But Alyssa was sure Brendan's background still bothered Mom a little.

It was ten minutes after they all left when Dalton drove up in his red Silverado. He'd only had the truck a few months, a birthday gift from his parents for his twenty-first birthday. Dalton had grown up completely different from Brendan, but both men were hard workers. Dalton went to the community college half days but also put in long hours at the lumberyard in town. And he'd been fortunate to find a small farmhouse to rent about six miles out of town.

"Sorry, I'm late," he said as he walked up to the front porch. "You ready?"

"Yep." Alyssa had taken special care on her hair today and had it pinned up in a clip with tiny ringlets dangling on each side. She had on a new pink blouse and her best jeans. Brendan never took her anywhere without telling her how beautiful she looked. But Dalton just opened the door of the truck so she could get in without saying anything. It was a first date, though, and it would be silly for her to expect Dalton to treat her the way Brendan had the past two years.

The parking lot at Monument Hill was almost full, and Dalton had to drive around until he found a spot on the far side of the lot.

They walked toward the festivities in the open area near the monument that gave the historic site its name. Alyssa was sure that God couldn't have blessed them with a prettier day. There wasn't a cloud in the sky, the high temperature for the day was seventy, and a gentle breeze swirled through the live oak trees. Like a postcard, she thought as she glanced around. She wasn't much of a history buff, but the site was one of her favorite places to visit. On most days it was quiet, with only a few tourists, and there were beautiful walking trails along the Colorado River atop the sandstone bluff. One of the trails led to the remains of the historic Kreische Brewery. Heinrich Kreische's house was still on the property as well.

She could see her father in the distance chatting with other like-minded reenactors, and several of the townsfolk had set up booths relevant to the 1840s. Some had artifacts on display, and others were selling jams, jellies, homemade noodles, and cookbooks. Alyssa recognized the aromas wafting through the air, and she was sure that somewhere on the grounds you could find sausage on a stick, funnel cakes, turkey legs, and cotton candy. She saw many people she knew as she scanned the crowd, but there was only one person she was looking for. She hoped Brendan was here, and she hoped it stung like a hornet for him to see her with Dalton.

"Well, don't you two make a handsome couple." Sherry waddled up to Alyssa and Dalton. "Love your shirt, Alyssa. Pink has always been your best color." Then she turned to Dalton and eyed him up and down. "And that navy blue shirt of yours and tight jeans almost make you worthy of

Alyssa's company."

"Really, Sherry? Did you really just say that?" After all these years, Alyssa was surprised that Sherry could still shock her.

Dalton chuckled as he pushed back the rim of his cowboy hat. "I know that I'll have to earn your approval, Ms. Sherry." He winked at Sherry, then glanced at Alyssa, his magnetic blue eyes locking with hers. "And I will," he added.

Alyssa pulled her eyes from his, feeling a blush creep into her cheeks. Dalton turned back to Sherry and asked her where Monroe was. As her friends fell into a conversation about food, Alyssa studied Dalton for a few moments. He was much taller than Brendan and, unlike Brendan, had perfectly white, straight teeth. Brendan's not-quite-perfect teeth had always lent him a boyish look. It was something Alyssa had always loved — Brendan's smile.

Alyssa's date had a beautifully proportioned body with broad shoulders, and he carried himself with a confidence Alyssa assumed came with such good looks. Dalton's hair was dark, his complexion olive, and with that black Resistol hat he could have been a cowboy model for a truck commercial. Alyssa had wanted to get Brendan a hat like that for Christmas last year. But her budget had only allowed for a Stetson, not the four hundred dollar number Dalton was sporting. Brendan had loved her gift, though. Alyssa could still recall the look on his face when he opened the box with the Stetson.

"Are you even hearing what I'm saying?" Sherry leaned in close, and Alyssa realized that she'd zoned out of the conversation with thoughts of Brendan.

"Sorry. What?" Alyssa felt her face reddening again and she looked over at Dalton, who was looking down at his boots. Gorgeous Tony Lama ostrich boots that cost a fortune. Alyssa remembered her brother drooling over them when Dalton was at their house for dinner a few months ago.

Sherry shook her head. "Never mind. I see Monroe heading my way with my funnel cake. And I'm going to meet him halfway, then dive into that thing with a vengeance." She pointed at Alyssa and Dalton and winked again. "You kids have fun." She turned and headed toward her husband.

Dalton smiled as he scratched his cheek. They both watched Sherry picking up the pace as she got closer to Monroe. "Do you think she knows that once the baby comes, she's not going to look like the same Sherry as before she got pregnant?"

Alyssa laughed. "I know. I keep thinking the same thing. She's always been so tiny, but she's really ballooned during her pregnancy. She's not going to like all that leftover baby fat."

Dalton's eyes were still on Sherry and Monroe. "I don't think Monroe would care. Those two have something really special."

Alyssa watched Monroe hold the funnel cake while Sherry took a bite. "I couldn't agree more. And I think they will be great parents too." Her eyes involuntarily began searching the area again.

"He's over there." Dalton pointed to his left. Sure enough, there stood Brendan talking with a group of other men. And once again, Alyssa felt herself blushing.

"I wasn't looking for Brendan." She shrugged. "If that's what you were thinking."

"Yeah, you were." Dalton turned to face her. "And that's okay, Alyssa. It really is." He shifted his weight, but kept his eyes on hers. "Listen, I know you're not over Brendan. And I'm willing to play this however you want to."

Alyssa opened her mouth to tell him he was wrong, that she was over Brendan, but she bit her lip, not wanting to be guilty of another lie.

Dalton gently latched onto her shoulders. "I like you, Alyssa. I want to get to know you better. I know two months isn't long enough for you to be over Brendan — believe me, I know. All I'm asking for is a shot." He spoke to her softly and added a smile. "But for today, you tell me how you want to handle our being together, and I'll go along with whatever you want."

"I — I'm not out with you just to make Brendan jealous." It was true, but if her being with Dalton hurt Brendan to the core, then so be it. No sooner had she had the thought than her chest tightened, and another round of mixed emotions swallowed her up. *I don't ever want to hurt Brendan. Even though he destroyed me.*

"I know that's not the only reason you're out with me." Dalton dropped his hands to his sides, then hooked his thumbs in his back pockets. "But I'm thinking you might still want to get in a few digs with Brendan." He reached for her hand, and started walking in the direction of the circle of men where Brendan stood.

"No, let's don't go over there." Alyssa dug her feet into the grassy area, rooting them beneath her.

"That's fine." Dalton still had hold of her

hand, but he stopped when she did. "We can leave if you want to."

Alyssa shook her head. "No. My dad would be really disappointed."

Dalton squeezed her hand. "Okay. Just know that you can talk to me. I don't want either one of us to have to pretend to be someone we're not. It's okay to be nervous about seeing your ex out in public, especially when you're on a date."

Alyssa's pulse slowed down a bit. "Thank you. Does it show? That I'm a little nervous?"

Dalton squeezed her hand again. "You wouldn't be normal if you weren't. I remember when Pam brought this other guy home with her for the weekend. It ate me up, even though I didn't want to get back together with her."

She squeezed his hand back and recalled what Alex had told her about Dalton and Pam's breakup. They hadn't been split up for much longer than she and Brendan. "Thank you," she said again as she took a deep breath. But her heart rate sped up again when she locked eyes with Brendan and he started walking toward her and Dalton.

The closer he got, the faster he walked. Until he was right in front of them.

# FOUR

Brendan wanted to shove Dalton to the ground and tell him to stay away from Alyssa. But he extended his trembling hand instead. And in the presence of someone like Dalton Landreth, the last thing a guy wanted was a shaky hand.

"Great day for this event." Brendan tried to stand taller as he made the comment, and he avoided Alyssa's eyes, fearful he'd burst into tears. Why did it have to be Dalton Landreth? The guy wasn't just great looking. He was also incredibly nice, someone Brendan had always liked. But right now he really wanted to hate Dalton.

"Yeah. It's a good day for it." Dalton's handshake was brief and a tad too firm. His other hand stayed intertwined with Alyssa's, and Brendan tried to calm his racing heart by taking a couple of deep breaths. This was bound to happen — Alyssa with someone else. But so soon?

"You look great, Alyssa." Brendan blinked a few times. *Please, Lord, don't let me cry.* Alyssa nodded and seemed to force a smile. He hadn't seen her in almost a month. Alyssa's boss, Jillian, had banned Brendan from the boutique, and Alyssa's father had recently paid Brendan a visit too. It took everything in him not to blurt out how sorry he was — again — then beg her to take him back — again. But apparently this was a date, with hand holding and all, so he tried to keep himself in check. Which turned out to be a total failure. "Alyssa, can I please talk to you alone?"

"No." She didn't even hesitate as she inched closer to Dalton. Alyssa looked up at the tall hunk of man next to her, and Brendan knew he couldn't compete with this guy physically, but he knew in his heart that Alyssa hadn't stopped loving him overnight. "I'm thirsty," she said as she batted her eyes at her date. "Maybe we can find some tea."

"Sure." Dalton turned to Brendan. "Maybe this isn't the best time to talk, Brendan. But we'll see you around, okay?"

Brendan took a step closer to Alyssa. "Please, Alyssa. I need to talk to you." He'd said it a hundred times, it seemed, but Alyssa had only given him one chance to

171

explain, two days after he left her at the altar. And he'd given her a version of the truth that hadn't won her back.

"Hey, man. I don't think she wants to talk right now." Dalton looked like he'd grown another foot as he faced off with Brendan. "Maybe another time." He coaxed Alyssa to come with him, and Brendan fought the urge to follow them.

Dalton handed Alyssa a plastic glass filled with sweet tea. "You okay?" He took a sip from his own glass, but kept his eyes on her. She was so beautiful, in ways he'd never even noticed before. He'd always been aware of her outward appearance — her gorgeous dark hair, tawny brown eyes, vibrant smile, and just enough curves to keep a man awake at night. But today he saw a transparency he'd never noticed before.

When Brendan showed up, there'd been no mistaking the hurt she still felt. Dalton saw it in her eyes, the way her lip quivered, the way her hand turned instantly clammy as she squeezed his. Alyssa felt things deeply, and as sorry as he was that she was hurting, he liked that about her. Pamela had never shown much emotion about anything, and that had bothered Dalton a little,

though the sex more than made up for it —
or so he'd thought. But maybe that's why
he'd cheated on Pam those times — because
he wasn't even sure she cared. With Alyssa,
he'd always know where he stood.

"Might as well face it — I'm going to run
into Brendan sometimes." Alyssa's voice
broke into his thoughts. She eased her hand
from his and cupped her glass with both
hands. "Thanks for being so great about it."

Dalton swallowed hard. "Um, you know if
you want to talk to him, it's okay with me."
A tiny lie, but Dalton had learned enough
about love to know it was something you
couldn't control. Either Alyssa would get
over Brendan or she wouldn't, and pushing
her too hard wouldn't help. But surely
Dalton could nudge her a little.

She shook her head. "What he did is
unforgivable. And not only that, he keeps
embarrassing me in front of the entire town.
He came into the boutique last month with
a violinist playing 'La Vie en Rose.' "

Dalton covered his mouth with one hand,
but she saw his smile. "Go ahead. You can
laugh. That's what the whole town is probably doing." Alyssa looked away, and Dalton
felt like a louse.

"I'm sorry. I wasn't laughing at you. I was
laughing at Brendan." He couldn't contain

his grin. "The guy is crazy in love with you to do that." He shrugged. "Gotta give him credit, I guess."

"No. He is keeping what happened fresh in everyone's mind. The more stunts he pulls, the more people talk about poor Alyssa, the girl whose groom ran out on her at the last minute. And all I want is for people to forget about it. I just want to move on."

Dalton touched her gently on the arm. "I get it. Really." He paused, trying to decide whether to put his own heart out there with hers. "I hope I can help you. Move on, that is." He eased his arm away, but when she smiled he wished he could hug her.

She gestured toward the crowd that had gathered by the sandstone monument. "I have to stay here for a while, at least until after the reenactment. But maybe we could leave after that?" She pushed back a ringlet of dark hair that the wind had blown across her cheek.

"I think that sounds great. And you pick where you'd like to eat. Anything is fine with me."

She smiled, and Dalton felt warm all over for the first time since he and Pam had broken up. He felt hopeful, and he was looking forward to spending some time alone with Alyssa.

Brendan dialed Rudy Schmutz's cell phone repeatedly. It had never occurred to him that Alyssa might have a date for the festivities, and something about the way Alyssa had looked at him just then seemed like a strong indication that the banner wouldn't go over well today. Maybe he had been doing too much. Maybe time was what Alyssa needed. He knew Rudy would keep the three hundred dollars no matter what, but going on with his plan would be really awkward. Everyone was already chattering about how Alyssa had shown up today with Dalton.

"Answer the phone, Rudy!" Brendan yelled in a whisper. But several more calls, and still no answer. He stuffed the phone into the pocket of his jeans, took his hat off, and ran his sleeve across a sweaty forehead. He put the Stetson back on his head and looked up to the sky. Then, out of the corner of his eye, he saw someone walking toward him.

"Hey, Mr. Pennington."

Alyssa's father folded his arms across his soldier uniform and frowned. "Hello, Brendan. Alyssa is here with Dalton, on a date." He paused, a strange expression on his face, and Brendan couldn't tell if Mr. Pennington was happy or upset about this. Brendan was well aware how disappointed Alyssa's father was in him. He'd said so several times, and Brendan regretted hurting him almost as much as he hated letting Alyssa down. The man had been like a father to him.

"Yes, sir. I saw them together earlier." He forced a smile, but Mr. Pennington knew him well enough to know it was fake.

"No trouble from you today." Alyssa's father pointed a finger at him. "And quit sending flowers and kittens and . . . whatever else to the house. We talked about this."

"Did she like the cat?" Brendan raised an eyebrow and waited. Alyssa loved animals. Surely he'd won a few points for that effort.

"She gave the cat to Glenda Hightower. We already have a cat."

"What? She loves cats. She wouldn't do that." Brendan kicked at the grass with his boot, then looked back up at Mr. Pennington. "She didn't want it because it was from me, right?"

Mr. Pennington put a hand on Brendan's shoulder. "Son, you have to let this go. At least for now. You're making everyone crazy, especially Alyssa. She just wants you to leave her alone. You're gonna have to give the girl some time to heal. Then maybe she'll want to talk to you after a while. I told you all this when we talked. This is the last time I'm going to ask you to stop pursuing her."

"Yes, sir." He sighed. "But what if I wait too long and she falls for Dalton? Then what?"

Mr. Pennington scratched his forehead, then stared long and hard at Brendan. "It is what it is, Brendan. If you're meant to be with Alyssa, then the good Lord will guide you back to each other. But if she's meant to be with Dalton, then that's that."

"You know she loves me, Mr. Pennington. And you know how much I love her."

He stared at Brendan for a long time before he answered. "I thought I did, son. I really did." Then he turned and walked away. Brendan felt like he'd been punched in the gut. He tried again — repeatedly — to get hold of Rudy.

Alyssa was sure that if anyone could mend her broken heart, it was Dalton. She'd always known he was a good guy, even though she'd mostly admired him from afar. Because he was Alex's friend, he'd shared plenty of dinners with her family, but Alyssa had usually left right afterward to go meet

Brendan, and of course Dalton had been with Pam. Everything seemed so different now, and she was going to keep an open mind. Maybe there was new love on the horizon?

When Dalton slipped away to the bathroom, she glanced toward Brendan but quickly looked away. She didn't want him walking back over and trying to start up a conversation again. Well, part of her did. Part of her wanted to hear every single word that Brendan had to say, yearned for him to make things right again. But she didn't believe he could ever make things right. Dalton might be an opportunity for a fresh start. At the very least he was sweet, easy on the eyes, and something to take her mind off of Brendan.

She cringed when she heard a plane overhead. They were close to the small airport in La Grange, but this plane was flying really low. She cupped her hands over her ears while she waited for Dalton to get back. Sherry and Monroe walked up beside her.

"Goodness me. That plane is so low. And it keeps dipping down on the other side of that hill over there, then coming back up again." Sherry covered her ears with her hands too.

"That's a Pawnee. Looks like Rudy's plane, but I don't think he's crop dusting." Monroe put a hand to his forehead, squinting from the bright sun. "When they tote a banner, they have to pick it up. They gotta swoop down within about five feet of the ground and pick it up with this special hook. The pilot can't get off the ground if he's already pulling the sign. I watched Rudy do it once a few years ago. It usually takes several tries, and Rudy's the only guy I know crazy enough to do that."

Alyssa glanced toward the bathroom, but no Dalton. She locked eyes with Brendan again, then tore her eyes away and willed him to stay where he was. She and Brendan used to do a lot with Sherry and Monroe.

The plane went out of sight again but quickly resurfaced. With a banner.

"Look!" Sherry bounced up on her toes. "I wonder if that banner says something about the reenactment. How cool!"

Cool isn't how Alyssa felt when she read the words on the banner as it swayed to and fro above their heads. *You have to forgive me, Alyssa. I love you. Please marry me.*

"Uh-oh." Sherry edged closer to Alyssa. "Try not to kill him. He does all this out of love."

Alyssa felt her nostrils flaring as she

179

clenched her hands at her sides. By the time she got to Brendan, she had tears streaming down her face.

# FIVE

Brendan opened his mouth several times, but there was no hope of getting a word in edgewise. He'd never seen Alyssa so mad.

"Why? Why can't you just leave me alone?" She swiped at her eyes, and Brendan took a step toward her, longing to hold her. But Alyssa took a step backward. "Don't touch me! Don't get near me!"

"I'm sorry. What can I do? I'll do anything." Brendan lifted his shoulders, then slowly lowered them. "I love you, baby. You know that. It's me. It's Brendan. I love you."

Alyssa stepped toward him again, her lip trembling, her cheeks bright red and stained with tears. "If you love me so much, then hear what I'm saying. I want you to leave me alone, Brendan. I am begging you to stop all these —"

The roaring overhead almost drowned out her words. Brendan hadn't factored in how loud the plane would be, and everyone was looking up as Rudy wove back and forth overhead.

"I know you still love me," he shouted over the racket. "And I did try to get hold of Rudy when I saw you with Dalton, to tell him not to fly over."

She put both palms out in front of her and eased back a few more steps. "Stay away from me." After a few moments, she put her hands at her side and stared at him. "I don't love you anymore, Brendan. I *don't* love you."

When she turned around, she fell right into Dalton's waiting arms, and Dalton shot Brendan a scowl that meant business. But Brendan couldn't move as he watched Alyssa bury her head in Dalton's chest. He watched as they walked out of sight. Rudy was still circling overhead. All Brendan wanted to do was to tackle Dalton to the ground.

Dalton led Alyssa into Las Fuentes Mexican Restaurant and pointed to a table in the very back. "Can we sit back there?" he asked the woman who greeted them.

After they were settled, he looked across the table at Alyssa. "I'm pretty sure there's no problem Mexican food can't fix." He smiled, hoping for a glimmer of happiness from his date.

She offered up a weak smile. "I'm not very hungry, but if anything can make me feel better, I guess it's Mexican food." She shook her head, then sighed. "I'm so sorry about all this. I'm sure you wished you'd never asked me out."

She blinked a few times, tears shining in her eyes, and once again Dalton wished he could hold her, comfort her. Her emotions were all over the place, and he loved that she was so transparent. He wondered if she would exceed his expectations in other ways as well.

"And I'm sure my dad is upset that I left right after I got there."

"I bet he understands, though. And don't be sorry. You can't control what Brendan does. I just feel bad for you, that he keeps doing these things that upset you." He reached over and touched her hand. "And I don't have any regrets about asking you out. None."

They both scanned the menus, then opted to share an appetizer tray and some *chili con queso*.

"Please tell me it gets easier." Alyssa leaned back against the seat and met his eyes.

Dalton took his hat off and put it on the bench beside him, something he should have already done. "Excuse my hat hair." He paused, scratched his chin. "Yeah, it definitely takes a while to feel normal again." He picked up a chip and broke it in half. "But, if it makes you feel any better, I can look back now, and I know that Pam wasn't the right person for me. I mean, don't get me wrong. I was devastated when she broke up with me. And, just like you, I was embarrassed, which only adds to the hurt." He shrugged as he dipped the chip into the little bowl of salsa. "But when the breakup is fresh like this, it's hard to see all the reasons that you really weren't meant to be together."

"Like what?" Alyssa bit her bottom lip. "Is that too nosy? It's okay if you don't want to say."

"She never cried." He blurted it out, then instantly wished he hadn't.

Alyssa closed her eyes and leaned her head back. "Well, I'm certainly making up for that today." She looked back at him and sighed. "Sorry."

"No. Don't apologize. It just shows that you're human, that you get sad and feel things. When I say Pam never cried, I mean *never.* I'd be struggling not to choke up during a sad movie, and she never even came close. Now that I think about it, I never saw her cry the entire three years we dated, and that kind of bothered me. Plus, she was a vegetarian and spent a lot of time trying to get me to convert." He smiled. "The thought of being with her the rest of my life without a cold beer and burger on my back porch, well . . ." Shrugging, he added, "But I loved her, and I would have stayed with her — oh yeah, and, she only wanted one child. I want a big family. There were just a lot of things I pushed to the side while we were together, thinking that love was all we needed."

Alyssa waited as the waitress put the bowl of spicy cheese dip and the appetizer plate on the table. "That was one thing I loved about being with Brendan. We wanted exactly the same things. We both wanted to live right here in Fayette County, in La Grange. Brendan wanted a place in the country, and the little house he'd put a deposit on was a step in that direction. We were both taking online college classes. We both wanted a big family." She waved a hand in the air. "I could go on and on." Her smile was sad. "He was my best friend too."

Dalton could almost feel the love Alyssa

had for Brendan radiating from her. He didn't think Pam had ever loved him like that. "He was a lucky man." Dalton paused. "Maybe you're making a mistake by not trying again with Brendan." He held his breath, but let it out when Alyssa started shaking her head.

"A part of me will always love Brendan, I guess. But I was so sure about us. About everything. I never doubted that he loved me. I thought we were so perfect, that we knew each other so well. I could have never imagined we would spend a year planning a wedding and then he'd do what he did." She avoided his eyes as she dipped a chip in the *queso.* "I don't trust him anymore."

Dalton didn't have an answer for her. He reached for a nacho and tried to think of something intelligent or comforting to say. "Maybe this isn't the right time to say this, but . . ."

She raised her eyebrows as she munched on a chip.

"I've always had a crush on you, but I got bad vibes from Alex whenever I mentioned that to him. I don't think your brother thought I was good enough for you."

Alyssa let out a light laugh, which was nice to hear. "He was like that about Brendan in the beginning, and . . ." Then she looked up, a twinkle in her eye. "You had a crush on me? Wow. I always had a crush on you too. But I didn't think you noticed me."

Dalton couldn't help the warm feeling that wrapped around him, but he told himself to be careful. He knew how much Alyssa and Brendan had loved each other. And though he hadn't had that kind of relationship with Pam, she'd hurt him just the same. He planned to stay one up on this situation. If a relationship developed with Alyssa, he needed to protect his heart.

"Really? I had no idea." He searched for the right thing to say, but instead he just blurted out what came to mind. "Are you afraid of getting hurt again?" He laughed. "Dumb question. I guess I worry about that. I know I'm a guy, and I'm supposed to be all tough and everything, but I don't think my heart could take another blow." He tried to make light of the comment, smiling even though it was true. His heart couldn't take it . . . nor his ego.

"I definitely feel that way." She was smiling now too. "So what are we doing here together? Why'd you ask me out?" She held up a finger, then went on. "And why did I accept? If we're both so afraid of getting hurt again, then why put ourselves out there?"

Dalton picked up his hat, put it on his head, and slid out of the booth. "Yeah, you're exactly right." He tipped his hat at her. "I'm sure you can find a ride home." He took about three steps before he turned back around to see the look on her face. Then he burst out laughing as he slid back into the booth and took his hat off. "Gotcha."

Alyssa laughed, a good hearty chuckle, and Dalton reached across the table to put his hand on hers. "No matter what happens, laughter's good for the soul. Let's just laugh, have a good time, and take things one small step at a time."

She smiled. "I'm totally good with that."

Brendan thumbed through photos from the past two years with Alyssa. She was a stickler for actually printing out the pictures as opposed to just keeping digital versions on their phones or a computer. "Someday our children will want to look through photo albums, and no one puts pictures in albums anymore," she'd said.

He picked up a picture from their first trip to Galveston. They were standing on the beach with the ocean behind them and huge grins on their faces. Brendan's face looked out of proportion because he'd had his arm outstretched to take the picture himself. But it had been a great day, the first of many beach trips. Alyssa used to roll down the car windows to smell the ocean before they could even see the coast.

In those days he would never have predicted he would be alone in his room, pining away for what was.

As he flipped through the photos, he wished he could go back in time. For the past couple of months, he'd believed his over-the-top stunts would make her see how much he loved her, how sorry he was, how they belonged together. But today for the first time he'd seen it in her eyes — she was done with him. And the sting of seeing her with Dalton had only added to Brendan's misery. He'd spent every extra dollar he had and every spare minute trying to make up for hurting her and to get her back. But today he'd embarrassed her and hurt her even more.

"Brendan?" His mother knocked on the door, then walked in before he could put the pictures away. "You okay in here?"

He'd told her plenty of times not to just walk in. "I'm fine, Mom." He started putting the pictures back in the box, each one reflective of the life he could have had with Alyssa.

"You've got company. Alex Pennington is here."

Brendan took a deep breath. "Tell him I'm not here."

His mother stepped to one side as she pushed the door open to make room for Alex. "Sorry, hon." Mom shrugged as she closed the door behind Alex.

"If you came to yell at me about the plane, save your breath. I already know it was a stupid thing to do." Brendan swung his legs over the side of the bed as Alex took a seat in the chair against the wall. Alyssa's brother had the same dark hair and eyes as Alyssa, but his features were sharp and defined, unlike his sister's softer ones.

"Yeah, you've done a lot of stupid stuff." Alex grinned. "But, I'm here because we need to do something about Dalton before this thing with him and Alyssa takes off."

"What?" Brendan sat taller. "Dalton's your best friend. I figured you'd be thrilled to see him with your sister."

Alex frowned. "Yeah. He's my best friend. And I love the guy. But I don't want him with my sister." He sighed. "He'll end up hurting her. And besides, everyone knows she still loves you."

Brendan hung his head. "I don't know about that, Alex. Today Alyssa told me straight out that she doesn't love me anymore."

They were both quiet for a few moments, then Alex smiled. "A woman's heart is a funny thing." He pointed a finger at Brendan. "And you are doing everything wrong to win her back. Right now, Alyssa *knows* she can have you back. What if she thought she couldn't? What if she thought you were moving on the way she thinks she is with Dalton?"

"I'm not gonna play games with her, Alex. She's the only woman I've ever loved, ever wanted."

Alex threw his hands up. "Then why did you back out at the very last minute? It had to have been more than just cold feet." He dropped his hands and stared at Brendan. "Look, I was at the bachelor party, and as bad as some of the guys were talking about their wives, that wasn't it. I know how much you love my sister. And I know about, uh — about your family situation. There was something else that caused you to freak out."

Brendan sighed as he recalled his and Alyssa's wedding day, how beautiful she'd looked as she walked toward him. But if he told Alex what he'd seen that day, it might wreck other lives.

"Just really bad cold feet," he finally said as he avoided Alex's eyes.

"Everyone says that's normal. But I gotta say, I never expected that from you." They were both quiet. No one could make Brendan feel any worse than he already did.

"What do you want me to say, Alex? I messed up. And I can't control who Alyssa goes out with."

"Well, that's a shame. Because Dalton uses women. I've seen it."

Brendan frowned. "He was with Pam Herring for years. That doesn't sound like a guy that bounces from woman to woman."

Alex shrugged. "Pam looked good on his arm, and she was good in the sack. But Dalton wasn't faithful to her. I know of several times when he cheated on Pam." He grimaced as he scratched his head. "Look, Dalton is basically a good guy, and he's my friend, but well, you know." Alex shrugged. "I just don't trust him to date my sister."

Brendan would have preferred for Alex to plead his case based on Alyssa's love for him instead of just focusing on the negatives about Dalton. But he couldn't stand the thought of Dalton touching Alyssa — especially since he knew that Alyssa was waiting until she got married. At least that had been the plan, and they'd both been committed to it. But was Dalton handsome and persuasive enough to change her mind?

Brendan's stomach churned, knowing he wasn't done fighting for her.

# Six

Alyssa gently cradled little Monroe Broderick Modenstein Junior. Nine pounds, two ounces, twenty-two inches long. And with a full head of dark hair like his father.

"I can't believe how gorgeous he is." Alyssa passed the baby gently to Dalton, then moved closer to Sherry. "Where's Monroe?"

"He left right before you and Dalton got here. He was hungry." Sherry blew a strand of hair from her face. "I don't know why he's so famished. I did all the work. Twenty-six hours of labor." She made the sign of the cross. "Thanking my almighty God and Father for every drug given me throughout this ordeal."

Alyssa glanced at Dalton. He looked so natural holding little Monroe as he rocked him back and forth in his arms. Then she turned back to Sherry and grinned. "I thought you weren't going to have any drugs?"

Sherry reached for her purse, which lay on top of the bed covers, and began digging around in it. "They forced me to take something for the pain." She shook her head. "I didn't want to, but they made me."

Alyssa stifled a smile. From the waiting room they'd all heard Sherry wailing and begging the nurses to fetch the doctor and bring her something for the pain.

Sherry pulled out a compact, opened it, and frowned at her reflection before she turned to Alyssa. "Some kind of friend you are. Why did you let me eat myself into a fat person while I was pregnant?"

Alyssa didn't understand why this revelation was presenting itself now, but she just shrugged. "You're right. I should have pried those double cheeseburgers from your hands. And the double orders of fries, the chocolate shakes, and —"

"Enough." Sherry held up her palm to Alyssa, then turned her hands over and wiggled her fingers. "Now, give me my precious little boy."

Dalton eased the baby into Sherry's arms. "He's not that little. Bet you've got yourself another football —"

"Hey, babe. Got your food." They all

turned as Monroe walked into the room. He put the carry-out bag on the bedside table and began to unpack it. "Double cheeseburger, double fries, chocolate shake, just like you ordered."

"As always, my beloved, your timing is perfect." Sherry turned to Alyssa and raised an eyebrow. "Not a word from you, missy."

Alyssa bit her lip to keep from laughing.

"We should probably go and let you eat." Dalton reached for Alyssa's hand. They'd been going out every weekend for the past month. Today they'd decided to spend the entire day together.

Alyssa hadn't seen Brendan since the day at Monument Hill, and even though she would have never admitted it to anyone, she'd frequented a few places she knew he went, hoping to just bump into him. But Dalton had been keeping her distracted, and she hoped that with each day she would think less and less about Brendan.

Each of their outings had ended with a hug and a quick kiss, mostly because Alyssa hadn't been ready for anything more. But something about a man and a baby . . . Watching Dalton handle Monroe was bringing on some unexpected feelings.

"What do you feel like doing?" Dalton opened the door of his truck. Alyssa eased

196

herself up on the seat and slid closer to him than she usually did.

"Hmm." She tapped a finger to her chin as he started the engine. They'd been doing the dinner and movie thing the past few weeks. "I don't know."

"We could, uh, go to my house, watch some TV or something." Dalton put the truck in reverse, then glanced her way. He'd mentioned it before, but Alyssa had always had an excuse.

She pulled her hair loose from its clip and let it fall below her shoulders before she rolled down the window and closed her eyes. The chilly breeze slapped at her cheeks as Dalton shifted gears and picked up speed.

Dalton was everything she'd ever wanted in a guy — good looking, charming, and polite. Everyone loved him. And he'd been so patient. He really seemed to understand what she was going through. Maybe it was time to loosen up a little — with some ground rules in place, of course.

"Sure." She slowly opened her eyes and turned toward him. "I'd love to see your place."

Fifteen minutes later Dalton turned onto a gravel road and then, almost immediately, into a long driveway. Alyssa's emotions swirled and skidded as they bounced toward a tiny farmhouse and pulled up in front.

She pulled her pink cardigan snug as Dalton helped her out of the truck. It was unusually cool for October. Dalton put an arm around her as they walked up the porch steps. After he unlocked the door, he pushed the screen door open and stepped aside for her.

"Wow. I'm impressed." Alyssa had been inside this house before, back when Mr. and Mrs. Shelton owned it. But it didn't look at all the same. The clapboard walls were painted a light tan, and the red couch really made the room pop. There was a plaid recliner in one corner next to a small table, and a big flat-screen dominated the opposite corner. For an old farmhouse, the place had a really modern feel to it.

"Thanks," he said. "I did the work, but I guess I have to give Pam credit for the decorating. She'd come from school and stay with me on the weekends." Dalton put his keys on the coffee table as if what he'd just said didn't have an ounce of meaning. But for Alyssa it was confirmation that Dalton and Pam had done a lot more than she or Brendan ever had. She tried not to think about it as Dalton pulled her into his arms.

The feel of lips brushing against hers

wasn't something new. There'd been other guys, other kisses, even before Brendan. But for the past two years, it had been only Brendan, and one thing her former boyfriend had excelled at was kissing.

There was an urgency in the way Dalton kissed her, and Alyssa waited for the tingling in her stomach to spin into a wild swirl of passion, for her pulse to pound in her chest, for her knees to go weak as they did when Brendan kissed her. But as Dalton pressed against her with a hunger she wasn't familiar with, something just felt off.

Assuming it was her and not him, she tried to kiss him back with the same passion. But as he pulled her closer, it was becoming obvious that he hadn't brought her here just for a few kisses.

Dalton could feel himself trembling as he pulled Alyssa closer, kissing her the way he'd only dreamed about. He longed to go further, but she eased away from him. "Sorry," he whispered before he drew her back to him. He would have to take things slow with Alyssa, but he couldn't help but wonder how long Brendan had waited before he'd slept with her. Dalton didn't want to push her, but he'd wanted her for a long time, and it would be hard to wait too long. He forced his mouth from hers, pushed back a strand of her hair, and waited until his pulse got back to normal before he said anything.

"I've wanted to do that for a long time." He wondered if she was thinking about Brendan, but he didn't want to spoil the moment and ask. Pam had certainly crossed his mind, but he assumed that was normal. He'd been with Pam for a long time. Alyssa was the first person he'd kissed since he and Pam had broken up, and the kiss was every bit as good as he'd suspected it would be. He leaned forward and covered her mouth with his again, and even though she responded to him, he could feel hesitation.

He forced himself to pull back again. He brushed a kiss across her forehead, then another one on her cheek. As he gazed into her eyes, he made another mental note to take things slow with her. "First kiss since Brendan?" He held his breath for a few moments, wishing he hadn't asked, but hoping she would throw him a bone, tell him how great a kisser he was — the way Pam always had.

She just nodded. "Yes."

"I'm willing to go as slow as you want, Alyssa." He reached for both her hands, then guided her to the couch. After they sat down, he brought her hand to his lips and kissed her palm. Just that simple act made him want to lay her down right there. Sex had certainly been the highlight of his relationship with Pam, and he yearned to make it part of his life with Alyssa. She was sweet, emotional, and sensual — not to mention gorgeous. Sex with her was bound to be amazing. But he truly cared about Alyssa, so he was willing to wait.

But not forever.

# SEVEN

Brendan sat on the side of his bed opening and closing the little box that housed Alyssa's engagement ring. It wasn't the biggest and most expensive ring in the world, but the expression on her face when Brendan gave her the diamond was forever etched in his mind. "It's perfect," she'd said through her tears.

A week after the wedding date, Sherry had shown up at his work with the ring. "Alyssa said to get your money back," she'd told him. But as tight as things were, he'd never been able to bring himself to do that. And he was still kicking himself for all the money he'd spent trying to woo her back. At the time he would have done anything to have her back in his arms. But now that she was with Dalton, he'd quit wasting his money and time over the past couple of months. Brendan knew that the money he could get for the ring would help his mother with prescriptions that weren't covered by insurance.

He put the ring in his pocket, then walked through the living room past the Christmas tree. Brendan wasn't in the spirit of the holidays, but his mother had wanted a tree, so Brendan had brought one home and decorated it for her. He stopped at the door to his parents' bedroom and tapped lightly on the door. "Mom?" His father opened the door. "I'm off work today, but I'm leaving to run some errands. How's Mom?"

"Not so good today." Dad rubbed his eyes. "That last round of chemo really took it out of her."

Brendan had noticed some changes in his father over the past couple of months. It was like his mother's cancer had snapped him into being a better man. Things were far from perfect, but he'd slowed way down on the drinking when Mom quit completely. She'd done it when she started the chemo treatments, said it made her sick to her stomach. But Brendon suspected there was more to it than that. Maybe thoughts of her own mortality had fueled the decision to quit.

Dad looked up, and Brendan saw fear in his eyes. For all their fights, all their faults — his parents truly did love each other. It was a shame it had taken something like this for them to start making changes.

"Do you need me to stay home or stay with her?"

"No. I'm here if she needs anything."

Brendan stuffed his hand into his pocket and fumbled with the small box. "Okay. I'm going to go return Alyssa's ring. You can use the money I get to help with Mom's bills."

His father rubbed his eyes again. "You take that money and do something for yourself. Buy yourself something for Christmas. We'll make do. And don't be gone too long. Storm's supposed to hit this afternoon." His father closed the bedroom door.

Brendan stood there for a few moments, still shocked at his father's change of behavior. Maybe fear does that to a man. Fear had certainly wrecked Brendan's life. As for buying himself something, he couldn't think of anything he needed or wanted.

Except Alyssa.

He plucked his coat from the rack by the front door and buttoned it up on the way to his truck. It had been unseasonably cold the past week, and now they were under a winter storm watch. Folks in town were saying they might even have a white Christmas.

Brendan doubted that. Snow was rare in Texas, especially this early into the winter. But things could definitely get icy, and that's what they were predicting for later today — frigid temps, high winds, freezing rain, and sleet. That could pretty much shut down the town, since no one knew how to drive in that kind of weather. He remembered his uncle from Minnesota laughing when Brendan's father said they couldn't leave the house because there was ice on the roads.

So far the roads were okay, though. He turned the corner into the town square, wondering if he'd run into Alyssa. The jewelry shop was right next to Jillian's Boutique, where she worked. He eyed the lampposts and the shop windows all decorated for Christmas and thought about the holidays last year with Alyssa.

*We were so happy. Why did I have to mess things up?*

He'd seen Dalton and Alyssa in Dalton's shiny red truck a few times, but he'd managed to avoid any direct contact since that disastrous encounter at Monument Hill three months ago. He'd heard through the small-town gossip loop that things were getting serious between her and Dalton, so he'd tried to avoid the places where they might be — including church. He'd started going to a church in Schulenburg, about fifteen miles from La Grange — just far enough away that no one knew his story. His parents had even gone with him a few times. At times Brendan almost felt like they were a normal family.

As he pulled into the parking lot, he spotted Alyssa's car right away, and an overwhelming desire to see her overtook him. Getting out of his truck, he walked toward the glass window that ran the length of the boutique. A guy Brendan didn't recognize was pouring kitty litter on the sidewalk in front of the jewelry store. Brendan was pretty sure you did that after the ice formed, not before.

As he passed the boutique window, he leaned in close to the glass, looking for Alyssa. There she was. And there was Dalton too, kissing her. Brendan forced himself to watch. It was his own self-inflicted punishment for letting her get away. But he should have pried himself from the scene before Dalton came out of the shop.

"Brendan." Dalton stopped in front of him, frowning. "You're not here to bother Alyssa, are you?"

"Nope." Brendan wanted to punch Dalton

in the gut, just because. But instead he nodded toward the jeweler's. "I have business next door." He tipped back the rim of his Stetson. "I was just wondering if Jillian and Alyssa were, uh, ready for the storm."

Dalton stuffed his hands in the pockets of his coat, teeth chattering. "Jillian already left, and Alyssa is getting ready to close up shop so she can get home before it gets icy. I've gotta go home and wrap my pipes before Alyssa and I get together tonight."

Brendan nodded. If Dalton had meant the comment to sting, it did.

"Listen, you should probably know that, uh, I asked Alyssa to marry me, and she said yes."

Brendan felt the breath rush from his lungs as his knees went weak. "After three months?" *Who gets married after dating for three months?*

"Well, it will be ten months by the time we get married in July, and we don't see any reason to wait. We've known each other since we were kids, and we both know what we want." He paused and took a deep breath. "I just didn't want you to hear it on the streets."

*Alyssa will have her July wedding after all.* Her mother had gotten married in July, and so had her grandmother and great-grandmother. And if Brendan hadn't blown it, Alyssa would have married him in July.

He opened his mouth to say something, but nothing would come out. He sighed, but then forced himself to meet the eyes of the man who would be sharing his life with Alyssa. He held out his hand. "Congratulations."

"Thanks. Hey, how is your mom doing?"

Brendan was still trying to picture Alyssa married to Dalton. "Um, the chemo's been rough, but she's almost done, and the doctor says things are going pretty well."

"Good news. Give your parents my best." Dalton gave a quick wave and headed down the sidewalk, but he looked back several times, probably to make sure Brendan didn't go into the boutique. Brendan was tempted, but he made himself walk on. In light of this news, there was definitely no reason to hang on to Alyssa's ring. He edged past the guy pouring kitty litter everywhere, and hurried inside the jewelry store.

Charlie Wetherall was behind the counter. Normally Brendan looked forward to any visit with Charlie. The old-timer was full of great stories about La Grange, including first-hand tales about the notorious Chicken Ranch — the illegal (but tolerated) brothel that used to operate a couple of miles outside of town. Some news reporter from Houston had gotten it shut down back in the seventies. But since then there had been a movie about it starring Dolly Parton, and "La Grange," the song about it by ZZ Top, still got a lot of play on local radio stations. But not many people remembered the place like Charlie did, because he'd done odd jobs on the property. Or so he said.

Brendan usually found the old guy's stories fascinating, but not today. He just wasn't in the mood. His heart was heavy as he pulled the small box from his pocket, opened it, and put it on the counter.

"I was just wondering if I could return this." He held his breath, tempted to grab the box back and run out of the store. Or run next door and beg Alyssa not to marry Dalton. But he kept his feet rooted to the floor while Charlie inspected the half-carat diamond in its dainty white-gold setting. Dalton had probably gotten Alyssa a much larger ring.

"You sure about this?" Charlie drew his thick gray eyebrows together.

Dalton nodded. "Yes, sir. I have the receipt if you need it."

Charlie picked up the ring and looked it over. "I don't think that will necessary. Be right back."

As Brendan waited, the kid who had been scattering kitty litter on the sidewalk came inside, his teeth chattering. "Hey," he said as he walked around to where Charlie had been standing. "Can I help you with something?"

Who was this kid anyway? He didn't look like he could be over fifteen or sixteen, and Brendan didn't remember seeing him before. "Are you new here?"

"I'm Charlie's nephew. I'm just here for the Christmas holidays." He extended his hand. "I'm Jeremy."

"Nice to meet you." Brendan shook his hand and looked past him, hoping Charlie would hurry back.

"I was just trying to get ready since they say we're gonna get pounded. Bastrop is getting hit right now. Lots of rain and sleet and real bad winds. We heard on the radio that people are sliding all over the road. Lots of wrecks."

Brendan turned around and looked outside. Though the gray clouds seemed lower than when he'd walked in, it was eerily still. But Bastrop was only about thirty miles from La Grange. "You sure? I thought we weren't going to get the brunt of it until later this afternoon or this evening."

"That's what we thought too, but this storm is crazy. You see on TV what it did in Oklahoma last night?"

"Yeah, but I don't think it will get that bad here. I hope not anyway." Brendan was wondering if he should go back home and check on their house. But the place had been around for over a hundred years. Surely it could weather an ice storm.

Charlie came from the back room. "I see you met my nephew?"

Brendan nodded as Charlie handed him an envelope. "Here you go, son. I'm sorry things worked out the way they did. I've refunded all your money."

Brendan hadn't expected to get all the money back. "Thanks, Charlie. I appreciate it." He glanced over his shoulder again toward outside. "Jeremy said the storm is already in Bastrop."

"That's what I hear. We're getting ready to close up and head home. We've done all we can do here. Pipes out back are wrapped, and I want to be home with Evelyn before the streets get icy." He pointed toward the back. "Jeremy, go make sure the coffeepot is turned off. Then let's head to the house."

Jeremy shuffled to the back. "He's a good kid," Charlie said. He smiled, then whispered, "Not the sharpest tool in the shed, but then neither is my brother." He chuckled, and for a few seconds, Brendan worried Charlie was leading into another story about the Chicken Ranch. He quickly stuffed the envelope with the money in his back pocket.

"Thanks again, Charlie." He waved before he turned and walked out the door. Small drops of icy rain began to splat around him as he crossed over to his truck. But he sat there a while, hoping to catch a glimpse of Alyssa. He really needed to talk to her now, hear the news of her engagement from her own mouth. He was still sitting there when Charlie and Jeremy locked up the shop and headed to their own vehicle. Brendan finally talked himself into leaving and had just put the truck in reverse when his cell phone rang.

"Dad, is Mom okay?" His heart raced because his father rarely called him.

"Yes, but I was calling to tell you to stay off the roads. I just heard on TV that there's ice on the bluff. Two cars slid over the side already. The weather alert system is going off continuously, and the storm isn't even here yet."

Brendan didn't like driving the bluff when it was raining, much less covered in ice. It was a narrow part of the two-lane highway with several hairpin turns. And it was the only way home without going many miles out of the way. "Okay," he said, still adjusting to his dad behaving like a dad. "Do you think you and Mom will be okay?"

"I think so. We'll hunker down and stay off the roads. I don't remember a storm like this in years."

*Thank you, Lord, for keeping my dad sober so he can take care of my mother.* Brendan had thanked God every day since his father had eased up on the drinking. "Okay, I'll stay somewhere in town, and I'll see you when it clears up."

Brendan hung up and was thinking about where to go when the door of Jillian's Boutique flung wide. Alyssa removed the big wreath from the door and took it inside. Brendan hurried out of the truck. But he found he needed to walk carefully because it was beginning to sleet, and ice had already formed in a few places on the sidewalk. He made it to the boutique just as Alyssa was locking the door.

"Hey."

Alyssa spun to face him. "Brendan." She brought a hand to her chest. Her left hand. The one with a big giant rock on her third finger. "What are you doing here?" she asked him.

She glanced at her watch and avoided his eyes. "I have to go. I'm late, and . . ." She put her hands in the pockets of her coat, then stepped around him. He grabbed her arm, but she shook loose.

"Brendan, I have to go."

"My dad just called, and two cars went over the bluff. It's covered in ice and that's your only way home too. The storm is coming through faster than we thought."

She peered out into the wet street. "I'll drive really slow." She took two steps, then turned back around. "Do — do you know who went over the edge? Dalton just left here, and . . ."

Brendan saw worry etched across her beautiful face. "I don't know. But Alyssa, please don't get on the road right now."

"I'll be careful." She stepped over the curb. And down she went.

Brendan slid across the patch of ice and offered her his hand. "Are you hurt?"

She huffed. "No. But I'm supposed to meet Dalton." Her teeth were chattering, and Brendan's cheeks burned from the frigid air.

"Can we please go back into the boutique and warm up? Maybe a cup of coffee? We don't need to be driving, and I really want to talk to you."

■ ■ ■ ■

Alyssa had missed Brendan more than she'd ever admit to anyone, and knowing that left a sick feeling in the pit of her stomach. She didn't want to miss him. Or care one little bit about him. She had a wonderful man now, someone she trusted not to hurt her the way Brendan did. Someone who wouldn't walk away from her in front of the entire town.

"Here." She led him into the little break room in back of the store and busied herself with filling the coffeepot. "What do you want to talk to me about?" She wished she had a button she could push, an invisible shield of sorts — something to protect her heart from whatever he had to say. He sat down and motioned for her to join him at the table.

Before she could take a seat, Alyssa felt her phone vibrating in her coat pocket just as Brendan's phone started ringing. She recognized his ring tone — "Kokomo," by the Beach Boys. Brendan loved the beach as much as Alyssa did, and as her phone continued to vibrate, she thought of the many trips they had taken to Galveston, Freeport, and Port Aransas. She was lost in memories when she finally reached for her phone. It had already gone to voicemail. When she looked at Brendan, she knew something was wrong, so she waited until he hung up.

"What is it? What's wrong?" Alyssa took a step closer to him. "Is your mom okay?"

Brendan stood up and paced the small room. "That was my dad again." The color had drained from his face. "Two people have already died in car accidents between here and Bastrop."

Alyssa checked her voicemail as her heart pounded in her chest. How could she have missed a call from Dalton? She was mad at herself for allowing Brendan to distract her. But relief washed over her when she heard Dalton's voice. He told her not to get on the road at all. Begged her not to. He said he was sliding all over the place.

She hit End on her phone and put it in her pocket. When she looked up, Brendan was staring at her. She met his gaze, then quickly looked away.

How long could she stay cooped up with Brendan before he saw right through her?

# EIGHT

Dalton did his best to keep his truck from sliding on the ice, but it was like bumper cars on Highway 77. He'd never heard the term black ice until yesterday, when everyone was talking about the weather in Oklahoma. But when he tried to steer into a skid the way he'd always heard, he just kept sliding. He cringed as he sideswiped another truck. Not a minute later, someone slammed into him. This was insane, and the sleet was coming down hard now. He pulled into a grocery store parking lot along with a lot of other people who were getting off the icy highway.

He managed to park, then pondered his next move. First priority was to make sure Alyssa was okay since she hadn't answered her phone. He was relieved when she picked up after the first ring. "You okay? Where are you?" he asked.

"I'm still at the boutique. I think the bluff

is too slick for me to get home."

"Oh man. I shouldn't have left until you were ready. And I didn't even make it home to wrap my pipes. It's crazy on the roads. I can't even see, it's sleeting so hard. You're better off staying put. I'm sorry you're by yourself, though."

Silence.

"Alyssa. You okay?"

"Yes. I'm fine. But I'm not alone." There was a long pause. "Brendan is here."

Dalton's chest tightened. "I knew he was there to bother you. Hold on — I'm coming back to get you."

"No. Listen to me, Dalton. This thing is bad. People have died in Bastrop."

He cringed as he watched a woman fall down in front of the store. But once she was up, he refocused on Alyssa. "I'm in the HEB parking lot. That's not very far. I can get there okay."

"No! Please, Dalton. Just go inside the store like everyone else. No one here knows how to drive in this."

"Okay, you win." He stifled a string of curse words on the edge of his tongue, then climbed out of his truck and started taking slow, careful steps toward the store as the sleet pounded his cheeks.

"I love you, Alyssa." He couldn't hear

whether or not she responded, and by the time he got inside he'd lost service. He couldn't stand the fact that Alyssa was with Brendan, but that was better than her being alone. And Dalton knew how much Brendan loved Alyssa. He wouldn't let anything happen to her. And right now that was the most important thing.

Brendan breathed a sigh of relief when Alyssa ended her call with Dalton. It was hard to hear her worry about another man, but at least she hadn't told Dalton she loved him. Brendan had been able to hear Dalton almost yelling into the phone about the ice and sleet, and he'd heard him tell her, "I love you." She hadn't said it back. Surely that meant something.

"Call got dropped." She gave a little growl of frustration as she punched at her phone. "And now he's not answering." She sat down in one of four chairs surrounding a square table in the back room and peered at the screen. "I've got to call my parents."

That news blew a hole in Brendan's theory. She'd gotten cut off from Dalton before she could say "I love you." But she did love the guy. Of course she did. She was planning to marry him.

Brendan pulled out his own phone while

Alyssa tried repeatedly to call her parents. "I can't get through," she said. "I keep getting a message that all the circuits are busy."

"I can't even get a text through to my dad. This is what happened with the cell phones last year when those tornadoes came through. Remember? I guess so many people are using their phones, it just overloads the system or something." Brendan sat down in the chair across from Alyssa. "I can't get my weather stuff on the phone either. Is there a radio or TV back here?" He glanced around the small room.

"I don't think so." Alyssa stood up and walked to a row of cabinets that ran the length of the wall to the right of a small sink. "And if the power goes out, it's going to be pitch black in here." She squatted down in front of one of the cabinets and started rummaging around. When she got back to the table, she had four pillar candles. "I know there's a flashlight here somewhere." She went back to the row of cabinets and eventually returned with a flashlight and a book of matches. "Just in case."

Brendan thought about his parents and hoped they would be okay. Especially Mom. When he finally pushed the thoughts aside, he looked up, and Alyssa was staring at him.

He locked eyes with her. "What? Why are you looking at me like that?"

"You have the worry look on your face. I'm guessing it's about your parents."

He nodded. "You know me so well."

She looked down and sighed before she looked back up at him. "I thought I did."

Brendan stared at her for a while before he asked, "Do you really love him?" He blinked a few times. "Because if you really love Dalton — and you will really be happy with him — then I will pray for all the happiness in the world for you." He glanced down at her hands and forced himself to study her ring. Dalton would be able to give her more than he could.

Her bottom lip started to tremble and he felt hopeful for a moment. Then she said, "Yes," and Brendan was sure he could feel the crack in his heart deepening.

"Okay," he said softly.

Alyssa couldn't pull her eyes from Brendan's as she waited for any hint of regret in his voice, but he held on to the stony expression and was quiet. She stared into his eyes, hoping to see his soul, to understand why he'd ruined everything for them. "Why did you do it, Brendan?"

He closed his eyes, took a breath, and

leaned back in the chair, slouching as he folded his arms across his chest. "I told you. I told you what happened. I've tried to tell you over and over how wrong I was and why I freaked out."

"Tell me again." Maybe she could make sense of it now that she was detached from the situation and planning to marry someone else.

"Will it make any difference? Is there anything I can say to keep you from marrying Dalton?"

The room went black just as she shook her head. In the dark, her heart pounded in time with the rattle of sleet on the tin roof a story up. She knew all Brendan's reasons — lame as they were. But she also knew she'd pushed Brendan into marriage, even if it was only a little bit. She wasn't sure she'd even realized it until she was on the other end of the scenario — with Dalton being a little pushy about tying the knot.

A lit match brightened the table between them. Brendan touched it to a candle wick, then went on to light all four candles. Alyssa turned the flashlight on and pointed it toward the ceiling.

*I'm so lucky and blessed to have Dalton.* She planned to keep that thought in the forefront of her mind. Things had been good between her and Dalton these past months. Different than with Brendan. Much safer on her heart, even if she did have to keep a rein on Dalton's physical advances. She was determined to wait until after she was married to have sex. It was a vow she'd taken when she was young. But sometimes she wondered if that's why Dalton was in such a hurry to get married.

"I messed up, Alyssa." Brendan slouched back down into the chair again.

*Aren't you even going to try? Can't you offer up something that makes sense?*

Brendan kept his eyes down, but she saw him take a deep breath in the semidarkness. "It won't take long for it to get really cold in this room without any heat."

Alyssa nodded. The floors in the shop were concrete that Jillian had stained a light beige, so it was hard to keep the place warm even with the heat on. And it was probably just as well that Brendan changed the subject.

"Do you think we'll be okay in here?" She thought about the people who'd died in the path of the storm. She silently prayed for them and asked God to keep her and Brendan safe. And their families. And Dalton.

"I think so. The main danger is out on the roads."

Brendan sounded confident, but she knew he would, even if he thought the storm was going to level the building.

They were quiet for a while, listening to the howl of the wind outside, but memories of her and Brendan kept flashing in her mind. She tried to focus on the memories she'd be making with Dalton after they were married. But Brendan's eyes shone like beacons in the darkness, and she couldn't help thinking about all the times she'd imagined them making love on their honeymoon night. Now that experience would be shared with Dalton. Would she wonder for the rest of her life how it would have been with Brendan?

"Thank you for stopping all the antics to win me back." *Which is what I thought I wanted.* Now it was so over. Ended. Done.

"I never meant to hurt you."

"Well, you did."

They were quiet again, and Alyssa wished she knew what was going on outside. The winds seemed to be a little quieter, but there was a steady pelting of rain or sleet on the roof. Maybe they should talk about something else.

"Have you seen Sherry and Monroe's

baby? Little Monroe Junior looks just like his father. They'll be great parents." She forced a smile, but Brendan rolled his eyes. "What was that for?"

Brendan shook his head. "Nothing."

Alyssa knew Brendan, and his expression was not indicative of *nothing.* Maybe he was deep in regret that he and Alyssa would never have children. "Sherry has a lot of baby weight to lose, but I don't think Monroe cares about that. He just adores her." Brendan grunted, and even in the dimly lit room, Alyssa saw him roll his eyes again. "Why are you doing that? Rolling your eyes — and grunting?" She folded her arms across her chest, too, and they faced off. The candles cast shadows across Brendan's face. Shadows that mirrored Alyssa's heart.

"Things aren't always as they seem." Brendan turned toward the door. "I should probably go check on things. It sounds like maybe it's letting up."

Alyssa wasn't about to give up on this conversation thread. "It's still really cold, so it's going to be icy for awhile. So what do you mean, things aren't always as they seem?"

Brendan avoided her eyes as he shrugged. "I'm just sayin'." He shrugged again.

Alyssa frowned and tapped a finger to her chin. "I don't know of anyone who loves their spouse as much as Monroe loves Sherry."

"Well, you should know." Brendan still wasn't looking at her. "She's your best friend."

"Yes, I do know. And Sherry loves Monroe just as much." Alyssa realized she was hoping for a fight. And she didn't really care what it was about. She just wanted to yell at Brendan. Hurt him. "And I actually thought you loved me like that too. But how wrong I was."

Brendan finally locked eyes with her. "Guess it doesn't matter now anyway."

Alyssa knew with every inch of her being that it shouldn't matter, but somehow it did. And she wanted to make sure that Brendan felt at least some of the pain she'd been toting around like luggage weighing her down.

"You're absolutely right." She sat taller and smiled. "Doesn't matter at all."

But suddenly nothing had ever mattered more. She wanted Brendan to revert back to the desperate guy who'd been begging her to come back to him. If he did, would she? Could she give up Dalton, a man so perfectly suited to her that God had surely blessed their future? And she trusted

Dalton. He'd never hurt her.

"Just for the record . . ." Brendan met eyes with her again. "I loved you with all my heart. I will love you forever. That is never going to change for me. Never."

Alyssa fought the urge to run around the table and dive into his arms. She was engaged to someone else, but it took everything she had to keep her behind in the chair. "You don't hurt the people you love."

Brendan cocked his head to one side, his expression stony again. "Of course you do. When the love is real and deep, you have the capacity to hurt someone more than you ever thought. People who love that deeply hurt each other, even though they don't mean to."

Alyssa couldn't argue, but she would have spent the rest of her life wagering that she and Brendan would have kept the hurt to a minimum, relying on their love instead. She stayed quiet, thinking how much easier life was going to be with Dalton. Brendan was complicated.

"I guess," she finally said. "But I think that Monroe and Sherry could be the model for what a good marriage can be."

"If they are, it's a sad day in La Grange, Texas."

Alyssa tapped the table with her palm. "Quit talking in code, Brendan. If there's something you want to say about Sherry and Monroe, just spit it out."

Brendan narrowed his eyes and stared at her from across the table. "Marriage ruins things for people."

Now it was Alyssa rolling her eyes. "What are you talking about?"

"I thought Monroe and Sherry were the happiest couple I've ever known. They seemed proof positive that marriage could be the most beautiful experience. It was partly because of them that I believed two people could really love each other that much and make it work." He held up a palm toward her as he always did when he didn't want to be interrupted. "My parents really struggled with being married. I'm actually amazed that they're still together. And I've heard lots of guys bashing their wives — way more than just at the bachelor party. So I was terrified that marriage would ruin us." He looked at Alyssa and blinked a few times. There was no mistaking the tears in his eyes.

"But when I saw Monroe kissing another woman the morning of our wedding, I lost faith in everything. Even us."

■ ■ ■ ■

Alyssa couldn't breathe. She started trembling, and she wasn't sure if it was because of the cold or this news. "What?" was all she could manage.

Brendan sighed. "I left the room where all the groomsmen had gathered. I wanted to make sure Monroe had the ring in his pocket, and I hadn't seen him in a while. I looked everywhere, and when he wasn't in the sanctuary or outside where a few people were hanging out, I headed toward the kitchen. I figured Monroe was looking for something to eat since we were hours away from the reception."

Alyssa held her breath as she waited for him to go on.

"He was in the corner with . . ." Brendan blinked again. "Amy Shanks."

Alyssa started shaking her head. If there was a second-place winner for happiest couple alive, it would have to be Amy and Bob. She recalled seeing them when she walked down the aisle, both smiling, and so proud of Raelyn and Joshua as flower girl and ring bearer. "If they were hugging or something, then . . ." That was all Alyssa could allow herself to believe.

"No, Alyssa. They weren't hugging or talking. They were making out. Full-blown making out. And it wasn't the first time. Monroe finally 'fessed up when I confronted him. He and Amy slept together."

Alyssa's left hand had joined her right hand across her chest as she tried to figure out which part of this awful picture upset her the most — that Monroe would do this, or that Amy would. But she hadn't even processed the thought when she thought about Sherry. And their new baby. "Why didn't you tell me?"

Brendan took a deep breath. "Sherry is your best friend."

"Even more reason."

"Maybe. I don't know. Anyway, I couldn't go through with the wedding after I found that out. Monroe said they'd only actually been together once and they were sort of saying good-bye when I caught them. Said he'd been freaked out about being a father and a whole bunch of other stuff, and . . ." He stopped. "But it just shook me so hard. I could almost see you with some guy somewhere down the line. I was afraid our love wouldn't be strong enough, that we'd end up all messed up like everyone else I know."

"I would have never done that, Brendan.

230

And I know you wouldn't have either. Our love would have lasted forever."

Brendan smiled, but it was a thin-lipped smile. "Really? Because it didn't take you long to hook up with Dalton and accept his proposal. So clearly, what we had wasn't real at all, and I'm thankful I realized that before we went through with the deed."

Alyssa trembled. "The *deed*? Is that what we're calling it now?" A tear slipped down her cheek as she glared at him. "Thank God I am marrying Dalton."

"Yeah. Thank God."

# NINE

It was eerily quiet in the dark room, and Alyssa was pretty sure the worst of the storm was over. But as darkness settled on her heart, she wondered if Brendan was right. Would their marriage have been doomed from the start, if for no other reason than Brendan didn't have faith in them? And why was she marrying Dalton so quickly after her breakup with Brendan?

Good questions. And she had no answers. But heaviest on her heart was Sherry.

"I'm sorry." Brendan hadn't moved from the chair across from her. "I really am. I can't stand to see you cry."

She lifted her chin. "I'm fine."

"Are you going to tell Sherry?"

She'd been thinking about that, reversing the situation and knowing she would want Sherry to be honest with her. "I think I have to."

"I shouldn't have told you."

Alyssa wished that too. She wondered what she would have done if she'd caught Monroe and Amy together.

"Amy came up to me that same afternoon and asked if I was going to tell Sherry and Bob. She swore to me that aside from a few kisses here and there, they'd only been together once. He was trying to end it, but they got caught up in the moment."

Alyssa poured the buildup of melted wax from one of the candles onto the paper plate it was sitting on. "This will destroy Sherry."

"Maybe don't tell her."

Alyssa was quiet. She didn't want to be responsible for wrecking a marriage and family, but she wasn't sure this was a secret she could keep. "I don't know. I'll have to think about it. Sherry has a right to know that her husband was unfaithful." She poured the wax from the other three candles onto the plates beneath them as she tried to envision Sherry's reaction to this sad news. She checked her phone for cell service, and when she saw three bars, she tried her mother's cell. "It still says all circuits are busy."

Brendan checked his phone. "I don't have any service at all now."

Alyssa knew this might be the last time she'd be alone with Brendan. She didn't want to remember their last conversation as being so ugly.

"I'm sorry, too, Brendan." She kept her eyes on his, not wanting to miss his reaction. He frowned.

"For what?"

"Maybe I pushed too hard about getting married. And I know how deeply you feel things, how much you wanted to be sure our marriage would work despite all the broken relationships around us. But Brendan, there are never any guarantees."

Brendan kept his eyes on hers. "I know. But somehow in my mind I was sparing you further hurt down the line. Sparing both of us."

Alyssa put her elbows on the table and cupped her cheeks in her hands. "Then what changed your mind? It was only a few days later that you started sending flowers." She grinned. "And kittens."

He smiled. "I can't believe you didn't keep the cat." He shook his head. "Anyway, it was actually Monroe that changed my mind. I mean, not just Monroe. I was already panicked when I realized I'd really lost you. It wasn't like I could take a couple of weeks, get my bearings, think it all through. You hated me, wouldn't talk to me, and the void was overwhelming. So, I talked to Monroe."

Alyssa waited. "Why Monroe? I know he was your best man, but once you knew, why talk to him?" She pictured Monroe standing to Brendan's left with the other groomsmen and Sherry on the other side with the bridesmaids. Sherry had been oblivious.

"I had to know if he still loved Sherry." He paused, a faraway look in his eyes. "He said he'd made a horrible mistake and that it didn't change the way he felt about Sherry. And then he asked me if I would be happier with or without you. It was such a simple question, and I told him I can't imagine not having you in my life. I just didn't want to be the guy responsible for hurting you somewhere down the line."

Alyssa was quiet. The electricity came back on, but neither one of them moved.

Dalton jiggled the doorknob of the boutique, then pounded on the door, his heart racing. All the way over, as he maneuvered the slick streets, he'd had awful visions of walking in and finding Alyssa and Brendan together in a way that would have rocked his world. Alyssa was going to be his wife soon, but he constantly felt like he was still vying for all of her, like there was a part of her longing to be back with

Brendan. But when she unlocked the door and ran into his arms, his pulse started returning to normal.

"Thank goodness you're all right." She leaned up to kiss him.

Brendan was behind her.

"Are you okay?" Dalton gently grabbed her arms and eased her away.

"Yes. We're fine." She pointed a finger at him. "But you weren't supposed to drive. I asked you not to."

Dalton sighed. "I had to know you were okay." And he hadn't wanted her to spend one more minute with Brendan. He looked past her at Brendan. "Thanks for taking care of her."

Brendan shrugged. "I didn't do much."

"There's still ice on all the roads, but it's not sleeting anymore, so it's easier to see. And they've got trucks out putting sand on the bridges and overpasses. I think it's okay to take the bluff now. There was a generator at the HEB, so we never lost power, and they had a radio going. They're broadcasting which routes not to take."

"I gotta go." Brendan eased his way around Dalton and Alyssa and rushed out the door. He had his head down, but Dalton saw the tears in his eyes. Dalton turned to Alyssa, but she didn't see him. Her eyes were on Brendan, and Dalton wondered if she was going to sprint out the door after him. She didn't, but her eyes stayed on her ex until he was in his truck. When she finally looked at Dalton, she had tears in her eyes too.

"Glad everyone is okay," she said softly. But Dalton was pretty sure her tears weren't tears of joy. And he wondered if everyone really was okay.

Alyssa waited a few days before she went to visit Sherry. She had almost decided not to tell her friend at all. But then her mother had told her Bob Shanks had asked Amy for a divorce. What if the whole story got out? Alyssa wanted Sherry to hear it from her, not from local gossips. So she showed up at the door with two lattes and a bag of donut holes.

After she'd cuddled with little Monroe for a while and admired the little elf onesie Sherry had bought for him, she handed the baby back to Sherry. "I got stranded with Brendan during the ice storm."

Sherry's eyes grew wide. "You're kidding. And why are you just now telling me?"

"Nothing happened. We just stayed in the room in the back of the boutique until it stopped sleeting and the trucks got sand on the roads."

"And?"

Alyssa bit her bottom lip and shrugged. "And we talked." Sherry pulled her baby close, then reached for the latte on the table beside her. "And?" she asked again.

Alyssa had recalled her time with Brendan over and over during the past week, and she'd analyzed the whole thing repeatedly. "Apparently Brendan was afraid he'd end up hurting me if we got married. Maybe I pushed too hard about getting married." She shrugged. "And there's his parents, their messed-up relationship and all, and . . ." She stopped, took a deep breath. This was harder than she'd thought. "I don't know. It's probably still a cop-out. People hurt each other. That's life."

Sherry scooted to the edge of the couch and got up. "Let me go lay Monroe Junior down. I'll be right back."

By the time Sherry returned, Alyssa had talked herself out of telling Sherry.

"People do hurt each other." Sherry plopped down on the couch beside Alyssa. "It's what we do with those hurts that defines us and our future."

Alyssa nodded, wondering if Sherry would feel the same way once she found out about Monroe and Amy's little indiscretion.

"Do you think I'm doing the right thing by marrying Dalton? Am I rushing into this because I'm trying to hurry the healing process?"

Sherry smiled. "I'm not the one marrying him. It's what you think that matters."

"Dalton loves me. I know he does. And I love him."

Sherry put a hand on Alyssa's leg. "Who are you trying to convince? Me or you?"

"I don't need convincing. He's the perfect man for me."

"Then marry him." Sherry flung her pigtails over her shoulder. "But just know that once the newness wears off and you truly settle in as husband and wife, there better be enough there to sustain you. Because marriage is hard. Everyone looks at me and Monroe and constantly comments about how happy we are. But we work at it all the time, each and every day."

*Oh, Sherry.* If her friend only knew what was coming. How could Alyssa not tell her and let her hear it from someone else?

"Sherry, there's something I have to tell you." She gazed into her best friend's eyes. "Something Monroe told Brendan."

Sherry hung her head for a few moments, then looked back up with a little smile. "No. There's nothing you need to tell me."

"Yeah, there is. It's about Monroe." She put a hand on Sherry's leg, but Sherry placed her hand on top of Alyssa's and shook her head.

"It's what we do with the hurts that defines who we are and our future," Sherry said again. "And I choose to forgive."

Alyssa swallowed the lump in her throat. "You know?"

Sherry nodded. "I know that Bob left Amy because she and Monroe slept together."

Well, that confirmed what Brendan had told Alyssa.

"I can't control Bob and Amy's future, only mine and Monroe's."

Alyssa didn't know what to say.

"People hurt each other." Sherry's voice was gentle. "You can forgive, or you can let the hurt wrap around you until it sucks the life out of you."

"I admire you, Sherry." Alyssa was sure she was missing the forgiveness gene, at least when it came to Brendan. She wanted to ask her friend what her secret was. *How do you forgive so easily?*

"Uh, don't admire me. I'm human, and I reacted accordingly. There was crying and screaming. And fear — lots of fear."

Alyssa's thoughts about her own life were all over the place. Was her inability to forgive

Brendan defining her future?

"I was absolutely terrified that we couldn't get past it," Sherry added. "But we are. We are getting past it. Things aren't perfect. But we both believe our marriage is worth it." She scowled. "Though I admit I still have moments when I want to take a baseball bat to his head." She nudged Alyssa with her shoulder. "Pray about it."

"I am. I just hope I'm doing the right thing."

"Only you know the answer, sweet friend." Sherry leaned closer and put her arms around Alyssa's neck. "I'll be praying too."

"You better, because I'm sure not getting any answers."

*Please, God, show me a sign.*

Alyssa walked up the sidewalk with a heavy heart. Her father came out of the house and onto the porch. He put his hands on his hips and shook his head.

"That boy is up to his old tricks again."

Alyssa felt a bit lighter all of a sudden. "What?"

"Brace yourself. Once again, it looks like a funeral home in there." Her father scowled. "Let me know if I need to have another talk with him. I know how much it upsets you."

Alyssa rushed past her father and ran into the living room. There were seven vases, each filled with a dozen red roses.

"That boy is never going to give up," her mother said when Alyssa walked into the living room. "And roses are expensive."

Alyssa wanted to be as upset as her parents, but she was having a hard time controlling the burst of joy she felt that Brendan hadn't given up.

"There's the card." Mom pointed to the vase on the coffee table.

Alyssa fumbled with the small envelope. *God, is this the sign I've been waiting for? Does this mean I should be with Brendan instead of Dalton?*

She eased the card out and read:

Dear Alyssa,
   You are the light of my life, the woman of my dreams. I want to spend the rest of my days loving you. I hope these flowers brighten your day.
   I love you very much.

                              Dalton

Alyssa swallowed hard. She'd asked the Lord for a sign. And there it was — scrawled at the bottom of the card.
*Dalton.*

# Ten

Brendan looked out the window on Christmas morning and smiled. Everything was covered in snow, and he would have done anything to share this experience with Alyssa. She'd always dreamed of a white Christmas. Pushing aside the vision of her and Dalton having Christmas dinner together with one or both of their families, he walked to the kitchen to check on the turkey. He breathed in the aroma, then pulled his phone from his pocket and held it for a few moments, tapping it against his hand.

"Smells good in here." Brendan's father walked to the far end of the kitchen counter where he kept all of his mother's medications, and he poured Wednesday morning's pills into his hand. "Merry Christmas." His dad smiled. "Mom is having a good day." Then he filled a glass of water from the sink and went back to their bedroom.

His mother was finally done with her chemo, and the doctors said her prognosis was good. Brendan was thankful for that on this cold Christmas morning. He was thankful for his parents' renewed relationship too. It was far from perfect, but things were a lot better. And today he was going to try to keep the cup half full and remember all that he'd been blessed with. Even if those blessings didn't include Alyssa.

He put on his jacket and walked out onto the porch, gazing out over the covered pastures. For Texans who rarely saw snow, this was a real treat, especially on Christmas Day. He pulled up the contact list on his phone and scrolled down until he got to Alyssa. She used to complain that he never texted her. And that was true. He'd always wanted to hear her voice as opposed to a text. But in light of their new situation, a text seemed more appropriate.

Your prayers were answered. Enjoy the snow, and Merry Christmas.

His finger hovered over the Send button for a while. He hadn't seen or talked to Alyssa since they'd been stranded together.

He jumped when his phone buzzed in his hand.

244

> Merry Christmas to you too. xo

His pulse picked up when he saw her text, especially the *xo* — meaning "hugs and kisses." But that was just Alyssa, and Brendan figured she probably sent that with all of her holiday greetings. Or did she? In celebration of the season and the day, he was going to allow himself to read just a little bit of meaning into it.

Alyssa sat on the edge of her bed and typed in "I miss you" on her phone. Then she erased it. Then she typed it out again. And erased it again. She wondered if Brendan had caught the *xo* and if he had attached any meaning to it. She knew she was on the right path, and things were great with her and Dalton, but she was praying every day that God would take away the lingering hurt she still felt about Brendan.

> I hope you and your family have a blessed day. I was glad to hear that your mother is doing better.

She hit Send before she changed her mind. Then she went downstairs. When she heard Dalton's truck coming down the road, she tossed her phone onto the couch and went out to meet him. He got out of the truck, kissed her, then gathered up several wrapped presents from the seat beside him.

"I thought my ring was my present," she said as she playfully ran her fingers across the top of one of the boxes.

Dalton eased the gifts away from her. "Who said these were for you?"

She smiled, then pointed toward the snow-covered yard. "I've waited for this my entire life — a white Christmas. Isn't it beautiful?"

"Not as beautiful as you." With his hands full, he leaned down and kissed her again. Then they walked into the house.

"Your phone is buzzing on the couch." Her father nodded toward the couch as he walked over to Dalton. "What have we here?"

"From Santa," Dalton said as he stowed the gifts under the tree. They shook hands, and Alyssa picked up her phone. There was another text from Brendan. She knew she was venturing into dangerous territory, but it was Christmas, and she felt more sentimental than usual.

Thank you. Everything is going good. Mom is better, but not drinking. Dad only drinks a little. So, I have lots to be thankful for.

Alyssa excused herself and took the phone with her to the bathroom. She sat on the edge of the tub and stared at the screen. She typed out "I miss you" again, and hit Send before she chickened out again. Maybe she was challenging the Lord's plan for her, but she still tossed and turned a lot of nights, thinking about Brendan.

She stayed in the bathroom as long as she could get away with but she didn't hear back from him. She had to consider the fact that it really was over, that Brendan had moved on.

And that was as it should be.

Dalton took an extra helping of turkey and dressing even though he was stuffed. But this had been Alyssa's first year to make the dressing herself, so he wanted her to know how much he loved it.

"This time next Christmas, you'll be celebrating as husband and wife," Alyssa's mom remarked as she refilled everyone's tea glasses and put a pumpkin pie and chocolate pie in the middle of the table.

Dalton smiled at Alyssa. She seemed quiet today, but maybe it was because she'd gotten up early to start on the dressing. It wouldn't have been a deal breaker, but Dalton was glad that Alyssa was a good cook. She was everything he wanted in a wife, in fact. It had been really hard to live within the boundaries that Alyssa had set for them physically, but come July, he'd be able to really show her how much he loved her. July seemed like a lifetime away, though.

While the women cleaned the kitchen, Dalton and Alex got more firewood from outside and built up the fire while Mr. Pennington got comfortable on the couch. Then Dalton joined Mr. Pennington on the couch, Alex settled into the recliner, and it was finally football time. It was times like this when he was glad he was a guy — though he'd never dare say anything like that in front of Alyssa.

Before the women joined them, Dalton felt a buzz next to his leg. He glanced down and saw Alyssa's phone. He waited to see if his team scored before he picked it up to take it to her. He stood up with the phone in his hand, his eyes still on the game, but when the quarterback totally missed his mark, he headed toward the kitchen. He glanced down as he got to the doorway, and his chest tightened when he saw the text was from Brendan. He put the phone in his pocket and took a detour to the bathroom.

His chest tightened even more when he read the entire conversation from that morning. There was something about the snow, then Alyssa wishing him a Merry Christmas. Dalton could understand that, but was the *xo* really necessary? Then came a couple of generic texts — her wishing his family well and him thanking her.

But it was the last text from Alyssa that caused Dalton heartache: "I miss you." Then he read Brendan's response.

I miss you too. I would spend the rest of my life making up for what I did on our wedding day if you just gave me half a chance. You are my forever love. If Dalton is what you want and you really love him, then I have no choice but to let you go. But if there is any chance for us, please let me know, Alyssa. I'll spend eternity loving you. xoxoxoxoxo

Dalton closed the lid on the commode and sat before he fell down. He didn't think of himself as a bad person, but he sure felt like one when he deleted the entire text from Brendan.

Alyssa kissed Dalton at the end of the day and sent holiday greetings to his family, and they talked about how great it would be to have both of their families together at their house next Christmas. It all sounded picture perfect, but to Alyssa it was like a photo negative that might not ever get developed. Whether she wanted to admit it or not, she was waiting for Brendan to text her, to change her life, to alter what had been set in motion. But by eleven that evening, she decided it wasn't going to happen. She'd told him she missed him, and he hadn't responded.

She was far from sleep when Alex knocked on her door.

"Come in."

Her brother walked in and sat down on the edge of her bed. "You okay?"

"Yeah, why?"

Alex shrugged. "I don't know. You were kinda quiet this evening."

Alyssa smiled. "I'm okay."

Alex glanced at the little collection of stuffed animals on the top of her dresser. "I think those will have to go when you get married."

She rolled her eyes. "I know that, Alex." She wasn't sure if Alex was referring to the fact that she'd outgrown stuffed animals or remembering how Brendan had won all of those for her at the county fair year before last. Either way, she was a grown woman making grown-up choices, and the stuffed animals would eventually get packed away in the red suitcase under her bed along with her other keepsakes.

"You can change your mind, you know."

Alyssa frowned. "What are you talking about?"

Her brother ran a hand through his hair and sighed. "It's never too late to go back to Brendan. That's all I'm saying."

"Wow. That's a terrible thing to say, especially for someone who is supposed to be Dalton's best friend." But even as she spoke, she glanced at her phone. Still nothing from Brendan.

So be it. In seven months she would marry Dalton. And Brendan would go on with his life.

Alex stood up and headed toward the door. "Just be sure you're doing the right thing," he said over his shoulder. Alyssa sensed a heaviness in her brother's heart, as if he thought she was ruining her life, making a huge mistake.

*It's not a mistake.*

After the door closed behind Alex, she picked up her phone and deleted Brendan as a contact. Then she blocked his number, determined to go forward with her life. With Dalton. The way God intended.

# ELEVEN

Alyssa stood next to her father in back of the church. Again. Everything felt eerily familiar, except that she had on a different wedding dress and the aisle looked much longer than the first time she'd been here. The pews were decorated with white bows and greenery, and even the guests seemed to be seated in almost the same spots. Sherry, thirty pounds thinner, was back in place as matron of honor, but this time Alex was best man and Monroe stood beaming in a pew near the front, holding his son. So many of the same players, with one significant exception.

She'd chosen red roses for her bouquet this time. And once again she was a July bride, following in the footsteps of her mother, grandmother, and great-grandmother.

Raelyn and Joshua performed their flower girl and ring bearer duties perfectly, even though their parents sat on different sides of the aisle this time.

Alyssa's father told her he loved her as she looped her arm through his. And when Mrs. St. Claire started to play the wedding march, Alyssa reached down to squeeze her father's hand three times. He squeezed back. Then they took their first small step together toward Alyssa's groom.

Glenda Hightower had done Alyssa's hair that morning, swept it into an updo that was both lovely and practical for a hundred-and-four degree day in La Grange, Texas. The church had air conditioning, of course. But someone must have forgotten to turn it on soon enough that morning, because Alyssa could feel beads of sweat accumulating on her forehead.

Dalton in his white tails had never looked more handsome. Alyssa fought the memories as they assaulted her, doing her best to shove them behind her.

Dalton would be a good husband, and any girl would be lucky and blessed to have him.

Brendan stood outside the church peering through the glass door as Alyssa walked down the aisle alongside her father. He was surprised she hadn't posted a guard or something to keep him out.

He'd fantasized for months about how this would play out. All he had to do was rush into the church when Pastor Dean asked if there was any reason why this man and woman shouldn't be joined in holy matrimony.

"I object," he would say. "Alyssa, you can't marry Dalton. You have to marry me. I love you with all my heart. We belong together."

Then she would turn around, bring her hands to her chest, and call out to Brendan. "Thank goodness you came before I made a terrible mistake. I love you, too, Brendan!"

She would run to him, and he would sweep her into his arms and carry her out of the church. Then they'd scurry into his old white truck and flee the scene.

But as he watched her father lean over and kiss her on the cheek, his feet stayed rooted to the cement beneath them. He pressed his ear against the door, and after Mrs. St. Claire stopped playing the organ, he faintly heard Pastor Dean ask the question he'd been hearing in his mind every hour, waking and sleeping.

Now was his chance. It would be dramatic, like out of a movie. Alyssa would be thrilled Brendan had saved the day. Saved her from making the biggest mistake of her life.

Or would she?

He couldn't move as Pastor Dean scanned the attendees for any objection. As expected, no one had any problem with Alyssa and Dalton getting married. Why would they? Alyssa deserved a great guy like Dalton, and no one was going to ruin Alyssa's perfect day for a second time. Not even Brendan.

"Don't do it, Alyssa. Don't do it," he whispered as he squeezed his eyes closed, willing her to feel how much he loved her. "Please, don't do it."

They'd run into each other a few times since Christmas, but Brendan had respected the fact that Alyssa had never texted him back that day. He had tried to text her several times since then, with no response. But he was here just the same, praying that she wouldn't go through with this wedding.

Dalton didn't think he'd ever seen anyone as beautiful as Alyssa in her wedding dress, standing before him, about to become his wife. He was a blessed man, and he would spend the rest of his life loving her. He would be faithful — he knew he could do it. He would never let her down.

Visions of their wedding night swirled in his head. He'd waited a long time. The waiting was almost over.

There'd been a scary moment after the

rehearsal dinner the night before when she'd accidently called him Brendan. Luckily she'd made the slip while they were walking to his truck, so no one else had heard it. He could still recall the sting, but Alyssa had apologized profusely. She'd never done that before, so hopefully it wouldn't happen again.

When Pastor Dean asked if anyone objected to them getting married, Dalton held his breath. He knew it only happened in movies, but he halfway expected Brendan to come rushing through the doors to stop the wedding. Pastor Dean did seem to be waiting an unusually long time for someone to object. Did the pastor expect such an outburst too? But all was quiet, and Dalton tried to keep such thoughts from his mind. He was about to marry Alyssa, and he was the happiest man in the world.

But then he noticed Alyssa's lip trembling, the sweat beading on her forehead, the tears forming in her eyes. *She's not going to go through with it.*

As they faced each other, Dalton stared into her eyes. Her beautiful eyes. The eyes he wanted to wake up to for the rest of his life. He whispered, knowing Pastor Dean would hear, but he didn't care. "Are you okay?"

She smiled as she nodded. "Just nervous."

Dalton knew that was normal. He was nervous too. He reached for both of her hands, and finally it was time.

"Do you, Dalton . . ."

Alyssa eased one of her hands from his and dabbed at her forehead, but she was too late to catch the trails of water that started running down the sides of her face. It seemed odd that she'd be so warm in the cool sanctuary. Dalton had made sure the air conditioner had been running since early morning.

*Maybe it's the dress.* He tried to stay focused on Pastor Dean so he wouldn't miss his cue, but he couldn't seem to take his eyes from Alyssa's. And it was impossible not to see the fear in her expression. The girl never could hide what she was feeling.

Alyssa felt like she was standing under a faucet. Being a jilted bride had been awful. But if she didn't get control of her nerves soon, she would be forever dubbed as something equally unflattering. *Sweaty bride* came to mind.

And it wasn't just the perspiration. Her heart was beating way too fast, and all she could see was Brendan's face. But she had to trust that this was God's plan for her.

"Do you, Dalton, take this woman to be your wife? Do you promise to love, honor, and protect her for as long as you both shall live?"

Alyssa swallowed hard. This was it. She waited. Then she waited some more.

*Dalton?*

Alyssa was sure you could have heard a pin drop. Everyone was waiting for Dalton to say the two magic words. But Alyssa wasn't even sure he was breathing as he stared at her. Finally he spoke.

"I can't do this," he whispered. "I'm sorry."

Alyssa held her breath, and she planned to hold it until she passed out and died. There was no way this was happening again. *No way, no way, no way.*

"I'll always be number two. I can't live with that. I love you enough to . . ." Dalton paused as tears welled in the corners of his eyes. ". . . to let you go."

Alyssa couldn't say a word. She hadn't passed out, and she hadn't died. But why did the men in her life have to wait for this exact moment to reveal their true feelings? She didn't cry as she lifted her dress and ran down the aisle toward the back of the church.

Instead relief washed over her, and she

might have kept running to the county line if she hadn't run right into Brendan.

"I've got the truck running," he said, breathless, as he scooped her up in his arms. He tripped twice and almost dropped her, but eventually they were in the truck and speeding away.

Alyssa didn't look back.

# TWELVE

Alyssa wiggled her toes in the sand and breathed in the saltiness of the warm breeze on Galveston Island. She'd chosen a flowing white dress that hung just below her knees, with a scooped back and dainty straps. Instead of a fancy updo, she'd chosen to leave her dark curls loose, pinned up on one side with a single white rose. As the sun set against a blue sky, a pink horizon was the backdrop for this special gathering.

"You look beautiful." Brendan stood across from her in white slacks and a loose white shirt. He, too, was barefoot. And the perspiration that dotted both their foreheads was due to the July weather, nothing more.

"Thank you."

Pastor Dean, both sets of parents, and Sherry and Monroe stood with them on the beach as they prepared to read their vows to each other. They had left little Monroe with Sherry's mother back in La Grange, and it warmed Alyssa's heart to see Sherry and Monroe holding hands and smiling.

Brendan's father sat with his arm around his mother, and Alyssa smiled when she saw him kiss her gently as she leaned into his side. Though Nina's hair had started to grow back from the chemo treatments, it was still thin and wispy. But Alyssa had heard Brendan's father earlier in the day tell Nina how beautiful she was, and Brendan had said his parents had been gifted with some sort of awakening throughout the course of his mother's illness. Sitting to their right was Brendan's brother, Craig, and his wife. Brendan's father had reached out to them, and their presence seemed to make the sun shine bigger and brighter on this blessed day.

Alyssa knew that she and Brendan would hurt each other. It was part of life, part of loving someone. But she trusted him, and she knew that she was exactly where she was supposed to be.

Pastor Dean started the ceremony, and when he asked, "Who gives this woman to this man," her father answered, "Her mother and I. *Again*." Everyone laughed, and Alyssa found herself beaming. This casual and comfortable atmosphere suited her and Brendan perfectly. She had spent so much time dreaming about her perfect formal wedding. But now that she was here, she knew this was exactly the wedding she was meant to have.

Brendan slid a simple gold band on Alyssa's finger and intertwined his hand with hers as he read the vows he had written.

"Alyssa, our love is a gift to cherish without fear, no matter the hurts that will come. With you I feel renewed and alive. It's like a swim in the ocean after taking a dive, crisp and refreshing. But it's so much more than that. It's the sound of my heart as it goes pitter-pat."

Alyssa smiled as she blinked back tears.

"My feelings for you are pure as a new baby's soul, and once I was lost, but I now have a goal. To be the best person I can be while loving you for all eternity." Brendan looked up with tears in his eyes. "I promise to love, honor, and cherish you for as long as we both live."

Sherry let out a tiny laugh. "Good luck topping that, Alyssa."

Alyssa smiled as everyone chuckled, knowing they were right. It was the perfect moment. The perfect wedding. She unfolded the piece of paper in her hand and read.

"My dear Brendan, God gives us the free will to choose whom we will spend our lives with, but sometimes we step off of His intended path. I'm thankful to Him for guiding us back to each other." She paused and swallowed back the lump forming in her throat. "You are my soul mate, my best friend, and the love of my life. I promise I will love, cherish, and honor you until death do us part."

Pastor Dean closed his Bible. "By the power vested in me, I now pronounce you husband and wife."

Sherry threw both hands in the air and jumped. "Thank goodness!"

Brendan smiled before he moved closer and cupped Alyssa's cheeks in his hands.

They'd gone full circle, but one thing remained the same. A wonderful shiver ran through her as her husband's lips met hers. A wild swirl of passion sent her pulse pounding in her chest and made her go weak in the knees.

*Life is good.*

# ACKNOWLEDGMENTS

I'm honored to be included among the fabulous authors who all contributed to this collection — *A Year of Weddings*. Who doesn't love a wedding? And this was such a fun story to write.

As always, God gets the glory for each and every story He gifts me to share. But it would be hard to stay focused without my wonderful family and friends, so another huge thank-you to all of you. Especially to my husband, Patrick, who has to live with me when I'm up against deadlines. Love you, dear.

Special thanks to my editor on this project, Ami McConnell, and the entire team at HarperCollins Christian Fiction. Ami, you push me to be a better writer, and I don't ever want to stop growing in this wonderful, challenging profession. So keep doing what you're doing. I can take it, lol. I think you're awesome.

And I have a fabulous agent — Natasha Kern — who continues to teach me about the industry (which seems to be changing daily). Natasha, you provide me with spiritual insight that inspires and educates me. You also wear so many other hats — lawyer, physician, financial advisor, estate planner, reviewer, consultant . . . and the list goes on. Best of all, you are a trusted friend.

Janet Murphy, you continue to rock! Four years into this amazing journey, and you did what you said you would — made yourself irreplaceable to me. Love you much.

It's an honor to dedicate this book to one of the finest men I've ever known, my father. A romantic at heart who was married to my mother for fifty-four years. Rest in peace, Daddy. I miss you every single day.

# DISCUSSION QUESTIONS

1. If Alyssa had married Brendan the first time, what life experiences would both she and Brendan have missed out on that ultimately gave them insight as to what a good marriage can be?
2. How much do the relationships around us influence our own marriages and/or relationships?
3. What if Alyssa had married Dalton? Do you think she would have held him in second place, as Dalton had feared? Or did they have a foundation in place that had room for them to grow as a couple? Or does true, real love — like Alyssa had with Brendan — never die?
4. Sherry chose to forgive Monroe. Not an easy task in that situation. Would you be able to rise above infidelity and forgive? If not, why?

God forgives us. Shouldn't we follow His lead?

5. Brendan's parents changed during his mother's cancer treatments. Do you think this happens sometimes when a couple is faced with a life-threatening disease? Was this a wake-up call? Or do you think alcoholism is a pattern that isn't easily cured — and that Brendan's parents will eventually slip back into their cycle without professional help?

6. Dalton cheated on Pamela. Once a cheater, always a cheater? Or do you think that Pamela's lack of emotional intimacy justified him seeking out other women? He wasn't married to Pamela, but committed to her. Do you think that Dalton would have eventually cheated on Alyssa?

# ABOUT THE AUTHOR

Award-winning, bestselling author **Beth Wiseman** is best known for her Amish novels, but her most recent novels, *Need You Now* and *The House That Love Built,* are contemporaries set in small Texas towns. Both have received glowing reviews. Beth's highly anticipated novel, *The Promise,* is inspired by a true story.

# AN AUGUST BRIDE

DEBRA CLOPTON

*Kyndall Paige — the newest
joy of my heart —
what fun adventures we will have . . .*

# ONE

Kelsey Wilcox hated weddings.

But she loved her cousin. Loved her enough to endure a weekend of wedding torture.

Leave it to Tiff, though, to drag out the agony, opting for two days of wedding "fun," starting with this fancy rehearsal party, complete with music and dancing. And romance.

Fun — *like a toothache.*

Kelsey tugged at her gold sequined dress and struggled to readjust her attitude — the floor-length dress wasn't helping. She'd found it on the seventy-five-percent-off rack, refusing to pay more for something she'd never wear again. The thing itched, weighed a good ten to fifteen pounds, and was totally *not* Kelsey.

But Tiff had loved it.

So, here Kelsey stood, feeling like a total fake.

*Come on, Kels, attitude adjustment, remember.*

Right. Kelsey fixed her gaze on the vivid orange sun beginning to lower over the sparkling blue Corpus Christi Bay. She loved balmy August evenings.

Loved walking barefoot across the beach, the touch of the fading sun on her skin and the soothing sensation of warm sugar sand sifting through her toes. She drew on that now — needing every ounce of calm she could find before heading into the wedding party.

*Good girl — calm, relaxed. Better, much better.*

Her fingers tightened around the strappy heels dangling from her fingertips. "You can do this, Kels. For Tiff," she said aloud to the seagulls playing on the breeze without a care in the world.

Determined, she hoisted the tail of her dress out of the sand, forced down the lingering jitters, and struggled to let the perfection of the setting sun settle more securely around her. This incredible beach had always been her haven. Her place of refuge. Tiff had understood this. She shared Kelsey's love of the beach just as much. Her hope had been that this destination wedding, here where Kelsey had started her new

276

life a couple of years ago, would help Kelsey. Even on Tiff's special weekend, she'd been thinking of Kelsey's feelings . . .

It was all the more reason for Kelsey to force a smile and be supportive. And she really was happy for her cousin. Steven Lucas was a great guy. Unlike —

*Nope, you are not going there.*

Only fifty yards or so down the beach that stretched out between her bungalow and the hotel, she paused and studied the very new addition to the Corpus Christi skyline. Like the boardwalk that housed her bistro and several gift shops, the Castle Hotel was only a few years old. It had been created to be a destination-wedding showplace. With its white gleaming walls and endless glass windows and stairways that flowed down to the sand, the Castle Hotel had succeeded. It was almost impossible to see where the white stairs ended and the white sand began. Looking at it, Kelsey half expected to see Cinderella and her prince embracing on the landing.

She thought of Tiff and her prince, and knew she could get through this. Inhaling one last calming breath, she headed across the sand toward the stairs.

"Yoo-hoo, Kelsey!"

Kelsey swung her gaze away from the

hotel and a little farther down the beach. Instantly, her insides tensed.

*The "posse" had arrived.*

Yup, there they were — her redheaded aunt Esther Mae Wilcox and her two best pals, Norma Sue Jenkins and Adela Ledbetter Green. All three ladies waved wildly at her from the ocean's edge. Their excitement made her smile, despite her misgivings. Millie, one of her aunt's tiny black Yorkiepoos, dashed back and forth beside the sparkling waves, a blur as she chased the taunting seagulls, her shrill bark carrying on the breeze. The pup's sheer joy made Kelsey chuckle. She waved the hand holding her shoes, keeping a firm grip on the long, heavy skirt of her dress.

"Kelsey!" Aunt E exclaimed again. Hustling forward, caftan flowing, she engulfed Kelsey in her yellow, floral-printed chiffon arms. "Aren't you just a sight for sore eyes?"

"It's good to see you too." A lump lodged in Kelsey's throat, and she hugged as good as she got. Though her aunt and her pals added to her trepidation because of their meddlesome matchmaking ways, her spirits lifted.

Everyone talked at once, getting their greetings and their hugging out of the way.

Millie raced between her feet, and Kelsey picked up the curly-haired mass of wriggling pooch, giving her a hug. The pup licked Kelsey's jaw, then strained to run free, the cawing birds just too tempting.

Aunt E's scarlet hair whipped about her face like flames in the wind as she studied Kelsey from head to toe. "My, don't you look radiant tonight! Norma Sue, Adela, isn't my niece the most beautiful sight in gold?"

"Lovely, Kelsey. Just lovely." Admiration warmed Adela's blue eyes, making them even more vivid than usual in contrast with her soft cap of snow-white hair.

"Yup." A ranch woman with a large personality and a smile as wide as her ample hips, Norma Sue had shed her Stetson for the occasion, and her short, steel wool–curls ruffled freely in the breeze. "Honey, you're gonna blow the socks off of every single male at this shindig tonight."

And there it was. Two minutes in and they'd already started matchmaking. No wonder these three innocent-looking ladies were known far and wide as the Matchmakin' Posse of Mule Hollow, their tiny Texas hometown.

"Now, y'all, I'm telling you right up front," Kelsey said. "I'm not looking for love or even a relationship, and y'all aren't pushing me into anything either."

Aunt E harrumphed. "That low-down, lying Lance Carson did you a favor walking out of that church. If you'd married that scoundrel, look what you'd have been tied to for the rest of your life."

"That's right, young lady," Norma Sue huffed. "You were raised on a ranch. You know you've got to get back in the saddle after you're bucked off. It's been two years. That's more'n time to saddle up."

Her mouth dried up. True, Kelsey's life on her family ranch on the outskirts of Boerne, Texas, had taught her that, but she didn't want to get back on the horse, and that was the difference. And she had good reason. She looked to Adela for help.

"I agree, dear. You don't want to let what he did define your life. You have to move forward."

Her heart fought the steel band tightening around it. "I agree. Lance did me a favor, really. If we had married, I never would have found my calling here in Corpus Christi. I love my life." It was true. She'd traded in her boots for flip-flops and a bistro by the beach two years ago. She was doing fine. *Fine.* Enjoying herself and running a business that allowed her a laid-back way of life

with good friends and lots of happy customers.

Of course, after what Lance had done,
she'd been hurt, embarrassed, and madder
than — well, let's just say she'd been one
hot Texas cowgirl. But that was then. She
was no longer a cowgirl. She was a surfer
girl — okay, so she didn't surf, but she did
have an array of flip-flops fit for every occasion. She made the best coffee in the city,
the best pastries and sandwiches too. And
her soups were to die for — customers'
words, not her own — but exactly what she
was aiming for with everything she created.
Making her customers happy made her
happy.

Her life was fantastic.

*It was.* Sure, she'd love to drum up a little
more business, maybe get some catering
jobs so her employees could pull in some
extra income for themselves, but that would
come. It would.

Looking at the three expectant faces of
the matchmakers, her pulse stuttered and
her stomach knotted. They were going to be
on her like syrup on a hot pancake tonight.
To them, a single woman needed a man.
End of story.

Kelsey was having none of it, though. And
she was about to say so when Millie zipped

past them heading toward the water and dove for a low flying sea gull. Was she a pup or a bird?

Millie landed on the receding wave, her fur splayed out like a mop as she floated. Yipping and barking, she began paddling wildly, but instead of returning with the waves, she was pulled farther out. She had to have traveled more than twenty feet in the time Kelsey had watched.

"My baby!" Aunt E exclaimed, running for the water with Norma Sue and Adela on her heels.

Millie was about to be lost at sea.

Kelsey dropped her shoes, hiked up the narrow skirt of her sequined dress, and took off running. "I'll get her, Aunt E," she shouted. She plunged into the water, maneuvering a shallow dive in the direction of the black mass of yelping fur.

She came up where the puppy had been, only to find Millie had been swept farther away, still treading and yelping frantically. As Kelsey pushed forward, the heavy sequined dress caught water like a sponge. She floundered, scrambled, and fought to no avail — the dress tangled around her legs and dragged her beneath the waves.

She clawed for the surface and gasped for air, only to be sucked under once more.

Thrashing and twisting, she fought her way back up and kicked her gold-encased legs up and out of the water, but the dress clung to them.

Her lungs burned. Flipping and flopping, she tried to reach around for the zipper but couldn't — the ridiculous fabric weighed her legs down like actual gold. She managed to reach the surface and gasp for air before the ocean claimed her again.

This, she thought, was not how she'd envisioned herself going out.

And what about the poor puppy?

Brent Corbin yanked at the collar of his starched white dress shirt and strode out of the Castle and onto the hotel's back patio. Heading toward the outer corner, he breathed in the scent of ocean air. Soon he'd have to go back inside to join the wedding celebration. But not for a few moments yet.

Brent was happy for his college rodeo pal Steven, and a little envious that Steven had found what he hadn't been able to find himself. Love seemed elusive for Brent.

He'd just reached the railing when screams erupted down by the beach. Three older women in bright colors were waving and jumping and getting all kinds of crazy in the sand.

What could they be so excited about? Brent looked out over the water for signs of trouble. The evening sun glinted off the blue water, flaring suddenly off of what appeared to be the golden tail of a — of a *mermaid.*

The tail flipped and rolled, and suddenly the body of the mermaid appeared, arms flailing, before she sank back beneath the water. An instant later she burst again from the waves, her form glowing gold in the sunlight, long blond hair flowing over her like flaxen seaweed . . . and then she was gone.

The mermaid was in trouble.

Brent vaulted over the hotel rail, landing boots first in the sand, and plowed forward, fighting the sand as it sank beneath each step. He kept his eyes on the spot the mermaid had disappeared, yanking off his jacket as he ran. He dropped it to the wet sand, passed the three hysterical women standing ankle-deep in the waves, and kept on going. He plunged into the surf just as he saw the blonde emerge yards away. Her eyes were wide with terror that pierced his heart and drove him forward.

Swimming hard, Brent made it to her before she sank again. He reached for her and grasped a flailing arm. She latched onto him, throwing her free arm around his neck, and nearly took him under too, trying to scramble on top of him. Her thick blond mass of hair covered his face and filled his hands as he struggled to gain control of the situation.

"Whoa, darlin'. It's all right," he soothed, holding her at bay while some of her desperation eased. "You have to give me room or we'll both drown. I gotcha."

"M-my dress, it's too heavy! I can't move." Huge eyes, blue as the water, locked on him. His heart skipped a beat as a wave crashed over them.

"Millie," she gasped, and he realized only then the puppy that was floating beside them, looking almost finished.

Snapping to, he dragged the mermaid close, fully aware that every nerve ending in his body hummed with new energy when she clung to him. Twisting to his back, he scooped up the bobbing puppy, then, holding tight to both, he kicked hard toward shore doing a one-armed backstroke.

When his boots touched ground in shallow water, he'd never been so happy. Standing, he folded his arms beneath his mermaid's knees and carried her and her puppy out of the water.

"Kelsey, honey, I thought we'd lost you,"

285

the redhead exclaimed as he trudged to the shallow surf. She reached out a hand. "Here, let me get Millie, you sweet, amazing man, you."

The pooch leaped from him to the redhead, wiggling and whining with happiness.

The mermaid's arms wound tighter around his neck as her heart thundered against his. He tightened his hold in response, not at all ready to give her up.

The other two women were talking too, but he didn't hear what they were saying. He was too focused on the treasure he'd plucked from the sea.

The glitzy gold number weighed the mermaid down in his arms and fabric dangled well past her feet. It was no wonder she'd almost drowned.

"I don't think this thing was meant to be a swimsuit," he drawled, hoping to calm the erratic beating of her heart. "You're trembling."

"You saved me," she said between gulps of air.

She was staring at him as if he could jump tall buildings in a single bound. With her looking at him like that, he thought he probably could. "Well, yes, ma'am, that's what we Texans do when we see damsels in distress."

She smiled at that and her hand on his shoulder squeezed. "Thank you. You can put me down now."

"Whoa, not so fast. I've got you, so stay put as long as you need to."

"You are one strong swimmer," the robust woman with bushy gray hair declared. Planting her hands on her floral-print hips, she grinned at him. "I don't think my horse could have moved as fast as you did getting out there to these two. We can't thank you enough. I'm Norma Sue."

"And I'm Adela. You were a true blessing to us today," said the third woman, a delicate wisp of a woman with wise blue eyes that shone against her short, snowy white hair. "The Lord sent you along at the perfect moment."

"Yes, he did," the redhead gushed. "I'm Esther Mae, and this is my niece, Kelsey Wilcox. She would have drowned if not for you. And she was looking so stunning in that gold evening dress too. You should have seen her racing out there to save my Millie."

"I'm fine now. Got my breath back," the mermaid insisted, her voice watery but stronger. "You really can put me down now. I'll be fine."

"Are you sure?" he asked. She looked pale,

and the silky skin of her arms still felt cold. "That was quite a scare you just had."

Esther Mae scooted close. "Yes, it was, Kelsey. Why, he might need to do mouth-to-mouth resuscitation on you."

"Hush, Esther Mae Wilcox," Norma Sue snapped, booting her out of the way with a well-aimed hip. "You only do that with victims who aren't responding."

Brent laughed and so did Kelsey, although with a tremor. His arms tightened about her before he finally complied and set her on her feet. "There you go. Easy does it," he urged when she wobbled. He kept his hands on her, steadying her.

A brief, uncertain smile fluttered over her lips, and he felt it wing its way through him like a butterfly caught on the breeze. She was captivating — no matter that her hair clung to her in dripping sheets. Her blue gaze called to every protective instinct he had.

"Thank you." Her soft words pulled him from thoughts of kisses in the moonlight.

"That was . . . scary." She looked down at her ruined gown, tugging at the shimmery cloth. "No, on second thought, *this* is scary." The dress stretched out like a sweater on her slim figure and puddled in the sand. She half gasped, half laughed, then her head shot up, alarm on her face. "My cousin's wedding rehearsal party. Aunt E, I'm going to be late. I have to go change. Can you explain things to Tiffany before I get there? But *don't* alarm her," she warned.

Esther Mae's mouth dropped open. "I wouldn't dare," she said.

Her last name finally clicked with him and Brent's pulse kicked into high gear. "Your cousin is Tiffany? Steven's Tiffany?"

Esther Mae brightened — if that was possible. "Yes, do you know my other niece, Tiffany, and her fiancé, Steven? Are you here for the wedding?"

This day couldn't get any better. Brent went to tip his hat, then realized it was floating out to sea. "We rodeoed together in college. I'm one of his groomsmen, Brent Corbin. I missed rehearsal earlier."

"You *are,*" Esther Mae said with emphasis. "Did y'all hear that? Brent, here, is in the wedding party!"

He still had one hand on Kelsey's left arm and felt her stiffen.

"Rodeo?" She took a step back. Her gaze swept down him, only now taking in his dripping shirt, dress jeans, and finally his ruined ostrich skin boots. "You're a . . . a *cowboy,*" she gasped. "With *boots.*"

His heart tightened at the way her kiss-

289

able pink bottom lip dropped and her expression filled with hurt and anger snarled together like thorns and blossoms in berry vines.

It cut to his core as if she'd just accused him of using his boots to kick Millie. *What has a cowboy done to her?* Because Brent knew without a doubt that she'd been hurt and hurt deeply. Nothing else explained that pain in her incredible eyes.

Distinct groans echoed from the threesome beside him.

"Yeah, I am. I own the Sandbar Ranch, right down the road from Corpus."

"Sandbar. I do love the name of your ranch." Adela's interjection smoothed the tension. She picked up his discarded suit jacket and began brushing it off, then offered it to him with a smile.

"Yes," Esther Mae jumped in, glancing at Kelsey. "It's a perfect name, since it's close to the ocean, right, Kelsey?"

He could feel Kelsey withdrawing. She rubbed her hands on her arms, and he noticed goose bumps.

"The ranch has a long strip of secluded beach. That's how my dad and mom came up with the name." He leaned forward and dropped his jacket over her shoulders, wanting to hug her, but instead drew away and gave her space.

Norma Sue slapped him between the shoulders. "There you go, Brent. Ain't he a gentleman, Kelsey?"

"Yes, thanks," Kelsey said, swaying toward him, then drawing back she clutched the jacket around her. "I . . . I have to go." She turned and started down the beach, dress dragging in the sand.

Brent was speechless.

Esther Mae shot him an apologetic glance, then hustled after his mermaid, her yellow tent of a dress shaking.

Norma Sue slapped him on the back again. "Well, that didn't go over so well. One no-count cowboy breaks her heart and she locks it away."

So that explained it. Brent couldn't take his gaze off of Kelsey as she hurried along the edge of the water where it licked the sand. His interest had been caught from the first moment he'd touched her.

And she didn't like cowboys.

Just his luck.

Esther Mae came tromping back in the last of the fading light, looking flustered.

"Ladies, if you'll excuse me, I need to go change into something dry . . ."

"We have to do something," Esther Mae told her friends.

They were all studying him. "Is something wrong?"

"Are you seeing anyone?" Esther Mae asked.

"No, ma'am. Not at the moment."

"Perfect." She clapped her hands together and her face lit up. "You might be just the cowboy to help my Kelsey jump back in the saddle."

Norma Sue started nodding. "I do believe she's right."

Not at all sure what to make of the sudden turn of events, and still reeling from his reaction to Kelsey — and her reaction to him — he smiled with caution.

"Ladies, I'm thinkin' that's somethin' Kelsey's gonna have to decide," he drawled, only to watch all three of them wilt before him. "Look, I get that y'all care for Kelsey. And she's a lucky woman to have y'all on her side. Especially after the bad hand I gather she's been dealt. But she looks strong. She'll find her way." Promising to see them at the party, he headed toward the hotel to change.

His boots sloshed with water and his sandy clothes scratched as they clung to him, but his heart felt lighter than it had in a very long time. The weekend he'd been dreading for months had just taken an unexpected turn for the better.

Kelsey Wilcox — the most beautiful mermaid he'd never dreamed of — had splashed into his life, and she would be at the wedding.

And that changed everything.

He smiled as he climbed the stairs to the Castle. What other unexpected treasures would the night bring?

# TWO

"No, no, no," Kelsey mumbled, while her mind cheered, "Yes, yes, *yes!*"

Brent Corbin was gorgeous.

*Gorgeous.*

But he was a cowboy. Just like the boot-wearing, slow-drawling sweet-talker sporting a cowboy hat who had broken her heart into itsy-bitsy pieces. Did she need to remind herself that she no longer trusted cowboys?

But he was so gorgeous.

And he'd just dived in there and rescued her and poor Millie. She knew ostrich boots like the ones he'd ruined were very expensive. And he hadn't given them a thought before plunging in.

He had to be a nice guy.

But *still* a cowboy. Her heart needed to stop with the pitter-patter it was doing, because there was only one thing she mistrusted more than a cowboy.

And that would be her heart.

She was so glad when she reached her tiny bungalow. It was the perfect little spot just behind the boardwalk, close to her bistro and only about three football-field-lengths away from the hotel. Tonight it seemed even more perfect because it gave her a place to duck out of sight to try to reclaim some semblance of calm.

Her skin still tingled from Brent's touch. Her heart still raced from the way he'd looked at her — no. *No.* That was from the adrenaline lingering in her bloodstream after nearly drowning.

Because of this horrible dress. She pulled the blinds shut and peeled the offensive disaster from her body right there in the kitchen. Then she kicked it into the corner for good measure.

Hurrying to her bedroom, she took a quick shower, then got busy drying her long, thick hair and finding a replacement outfit from her closet. This was Tiffany's night. She had to ignore the persistent buzz inside her head. She told herself it was from all the salt water she'd ingested in the bay an hour earlier, not from anticipation.

Anticipating seeing a certain cowboy again was not what Kelsey wanted for herself.

But was "herself" listening? Nope.

■ ■ ■ ■

Brent stood beside Tiffany, Steven, and several other members of the wedding party on the lower level of the ballroom discussing honeymoon plans. He was trying hard to concentrate on the conversation, but thoughts of Kelsey kept interrupting.

Now that he knew Tiffany and Kelsey were cousins, he could see the resemblance. They were both willowy blondes with similar fine-boned beauty, Carrie Underwood smiles, and gigantic Pacific-blue eyes — not that he knew what Carrie's eye color was, but there was a resemblance. However, Tiffany's eyes, or Carrie's smile, didn't slam him in the chest and knock all thoughts from his brain like one look from Kelsey had done.

An hour and a half later and he was still reeling from his reaction to her. He thought maybe it had something to do with the high stakes way they met — after all, it wasn't as if he saved someone's life every day.

He scanned the upper level where the entrance was to the room, hoping to spot Kelsey as she arrived. When he didn't see her, he took in the room in case he'd missed her entrance and caught Norma Sue and

Esther Mae watching him — again. He shot them another smile. They were making him a little nervous. He tugged at his collar and turned so that Steven blocked his view of them.

Tiffany nudged his arm and leaned his way. "I guess I should have already warned you that the posse has its eyes on you."

"The posse?" he asked.

Steven laughed and squeezed Tiffany's waist. "He has no clue what you are talking about, Tiff."

She chuckled. "My sweet redheaded aunt and her friends, or I should say her cohorts, are the notorious Matchmakin' Posse of Mule Hollow. They had a part in getting us together." She looked at Steven with adoration and kissed his cheek. "And we couldn't be happier now. I can tell you, though, we had our moments."

Brent had heard that there had been some older ladies meddling in their courtship. "They call them that?"

"Oh yeah." Steven nodded toward their table where they were having what looked to be a deep discussion. "Those three ladies are something else, and you, buddy, had better watch out. Speaking of which, when are you going to start dating again? It's been way too long."

"Haven't been in any rush." Up until this afternoon, he hadn't even been thinking about women — not after the last couple of dating disasters. Now he couldn't get one particular mermaid out of his mind.

"Oh, there's Kelsey, finally," Tiffany said, waving up toward the entrance.

Tension coiled in Brent's gut. Kelsey stood at the top of the steps that led down to the ballroom floor. She was looking their way, a vision in the ice-blue dress that reached just above her knees and swirled as she began walking down to them. Where the gold dress had hugged her every delicate curve, this dress skimmed her body and flirted about her legs. He couldn't have looked away from her if he'd been hit by a cattle hauler.

"Just so you know, you've done good for being a cowboy," Steven said. "Saving Kelsey's life like you did might get you past barriers one through five with her."

"Barriers?" Brent asked. His attention remained on Kelsey as she wove through the crowd, stopping to say a word here and there. Each time her soft lips lifted into a smile, tension coiled tighter inside him, tugging deep on emotions that were new to him. Emotions that told him there was something different about how she made him feel. Maybe it was because nothing seemed fake about her. He liked that. Liked it a lot because he was so tired of fake women it hurt.

Steven gave a blunt laugh. "It's simple with Kelsey. Her five Rules of Dating and Life are: no cowboys, no cowboys, no cowboys, no cowboys, and —"

"No cowboys," Brent finished for him. He'd heard what Norma Sue had said about a cowboy breaking her heart and locking it away. But — his heart sank — the look he'd seen in her eyes when she'd spotted his boots made sense now. It wasn't that she'd been hurt by a cowboy and stopped dating in general — no, she'd just stopped dating cowboys.

He looked at Tiffany, feeling that question in his gaze.

She winked at him. "The best cowboys don't give up that easy, though, do they, Brent?"

He laughed with relief. "No, ma'am." What had that cowboy done to make her turn against all of them?

Whatever it was, seeing those amazing eyes across the crowd, Brent knew it wouldn't matter. If there was one thing Brent understood about himself, it was that he liked a challenge.

Steven nudged him and hiked a questioning brow. "Like I said, bud, when you gonna start dating again?"

"After the last two fiascos, I guess I've been dragging my boots a bit."

"With good reason." Tiffany frowned. "I'm sure it's hard finding out someone is only after what you can give them financially," she continued, then her voice dipped into teasing. "You know, given your bad luck with women, a posse of matchmakers picking someone for you is probably a good thing. They can spot gold diggers a mile away."

Kelsey made it to them through the maze of ribbon-tied chairs and ruffled tables topped with vases overflowing with an array of beautiful flowers. The room practically glowed with beauty, but all of it dimmed next to Kelsey. Brent's knees grew weak when her gaze met his, and he was thankful Tiffany dragged her into a big hug that gave him a minute to find his footing again. Or so he thought until she looked at him over Tiffany's shoulder and the ground shifted again beneath his feet.

"I am so glad you are okay," Tiffany said, releasing Kelsey after a moment. "We've been thanking Brent. He's a real hero."

Kelsey looked uncomfortable. "Thanks

300

again." Even her brief smile knocked the breath out of him once again.

Brent had met a lot of women in his twenty-eight years, and he'd never been affected like this before. "You look beautiful," he blurted, suddenly feeling clumsy.

She glanced down at the dress, then gave a tiny shoulder shrug. "It's not as formal as Tiff wanted for this party, but at least this dress isn't trying to drown me."

"You were in a bad way with that gold mermaid dress. I never thought about a dress being dangerous."

Tiffany linked one arm around Kelsey's waist and squeezed her. "That was my fault! We were shopping and I talked her into it. Kelsey is much more laid back than that. Glamorous, just not flashy. And you're right, Brent, I bet she did look like a mermaid."

He grinned at that. "I thought I was seeing things at first, and then she burst out of the water with all that blond hair — I'm glad I finally kicked myself in gear and came and got you." She just looked at him with those big eyes — probably trying to figure him out.

His fingers itched to run through that mane of hers, bury his face in it, and breathe deeply the sweet floral scent. Unable to resist, he picked up a lock of her hair and gently rubbed it between his fingers. It was pure silk, just as he'd thought. "You're real, all right."

Steven cleared his throat and Brent dropped Kelsey's hair like it was hot coal. What had come over him?

Thoughts of how her thick hair had filled his hands when he'd reached for her in the water rolled through him. He wanted to draw her slowly into his arms again. His gaze dropped to her lips. He yanked his thoughts out of the dangerous territory it had gone and focused. "So, what do you do, Kelsey?"

She inhaled sharply, as if she knew the direction of his thoughts. "I run Sunflower Bistro on the beach."

"A bistro, huh? Are cowboys welcome for lunch sometime?" he asked. When she hesitated, he raised his brows just enough to prod.

"We get a few cowboys on the beach. But we don't serve much steak."

"Not all cowboys like steak for lunch."

"Most do. I'm afraid I know a thing or two about cowboys." Her defensiveness proved Steven was right.

Brent didn't like being stereotyped. "Not all cowboys are the same, you know. Some of us even have brains," he challenged, more irritated than he had been in a very long time. If he could have found the cowboy that put that look in Kelsey's eyes, he'd have tied him to a runaway bronc.

Kelsey's heart thundered as she became lost in Brent's gaze. She swallowed hard. What was wrong with her? She'd made him mad. She felt like a fool.

Good, because she was mad too — mad that the man drew her like a moth to a flame. The moth *always* came out on the bad end of the deal.

Forcing her nerves down, she smiled at Brent. He'd saved her, after all. He deserved for her to be nice to him — despite being a cowboy. "Sorry, I didn't mean to imply . . ."

"It's okay." His grin hitched to one side, but the tension tugged between them. "Are you feeling all right? You didn't take on too much salt water?"

Oh, that smile did funny things to her insides. "I'm fine, thanks to you. It's really embarrassing. I *can* swim . . ."

"I'm not complaining." He chuckled. "Though I'd rather you hadn't been in trouble, that dress let me meet you sooner."

"Glad I could make your day," she quipped. What else could she say? *I love your chuckle and your eyes are amazing.*

Argh! Everything else faded into the background when he laughed. The sound, as deep as his eyes were brown. *Oh my* — Kelsey suddenly felt a headache forming.

The lights in the overhead chandeliers suddenly dimmed as the band began playing a new song.

"Hey, that's our cue. Let's liven up this party." Steven nudged Brent, then took Tiffany by the hand. "I'm taking my soon-to-be-bride for a spin. You two join us."

With that, Steven swept Tiffany onto the dance floor into a lively two-step as the band began a rendition of an Alan Jackson favorite. Brent looked at her. "Join me?"

"No. I think I'll pass. I've had enough excitement for one day."

"Chicken?" Brent prodded her.

"You are impossible." She was only half-teasing.

His eyes warmed. "Dance with me, Kelsey." He held out his hand.

She started to refuse, but instead she placed her hand in his. Tingles of awareness shot through her like a Roman candle bouncing around.

"That's my girl," he soothed like he had out in the water. It made her insides go soft.

Still, she opened her mouth to inform him

that she was not his girl. That she hadn't meant to accept the dance. But then she was in his arms and all coherent thought fled as her feet followed his lead across the floor . . .

# THREE

Being enfolded by Brent's muscular arms again, dancing beneath the softly glowing lights, had not been in Kelsey's plans when she'd come to the rehearsal celebration. She knew the room was beautifully decorated for the wedding party. That it was filled with gorgeous floral arrangements, cream roses and an array of pale flowers that mixed elegance and country so as to give the room an extremely romantic feeling — but all of it had faded to the background the moment she'd spotted Brent in the crowded room. Her knees had wobbled as she'd walked down the stairs, and it had taken every ounce of self-control to not turn and run. What was wrong with her? She was not interested in anything that had to do with a romantic relationship. She wasn't.

But here she was, one hand warm in his, the other resting on his powerful shoulder, her nose very nearly brushing his chin as they stepped together to the beat of the country music.

"You're good. We're going to give Steven and Tiffany a little competition." His breath against her ear sent delicious shivers racing over her skin.

She wanted to ignore the sensation, but . . . there were moments in life. Being rescued by Brent and this intimate dance were among those moments. She knew the rescue saved her life, she wasn't sure what the dance signified. She only knew it meant something.

Something special and dangerous at the same time.

Alarms rang and clanged as he set the rhythm and she went along with it. Turmoil rolled through her like waves.

"You've done this before." He looked down at her.

He was holding her at a respectable distance. Could he feel her heart beating with the band?

"Misspent youth. I was always at one dance or the other," she admitted.

"I did a little of that myself."

Her nerves were really trying to beat her up inside. "So, Brent Corbin, how do you know Steven?"

He spun her in a slow twirl and her insides

dipped. He pulled her back to him, and she bumped into him as they resumed two-stepping together. She laughed to cover her confusion.

"We were both on the college rodeo team out in Lubbock," Brent answered her question. "After graduation, Steven set his sights on making it to the National Finals Rodeo."

"So you didn't want to go for the NFR?" Lance had lived and breathed the rodeo; the NFR was always foremost in his thoughts. And in the end, that's what had left her standing there alone at that altar. He said getting married would tie him down and prevent him from hitting all the rodeos needed to gain the qualifying points for the finals.

"Not me. I came home and took over running the Sandbar Ranch. Not all cowboys fall in love with the rodeo."

Brent stared into her eyes, and she lost a beat and stepped on his foot. "Sorry." She couldn't think when he was looking at her like that.

"No problem." His eyes twinkled.

"So, you love your ranch?" She tried not to think about how his hand slid from her waist to the center of her back, making it seem all the more like he was embracing her.

"Yeah, and my dad had a heart attack during my third year of college. He needed me. And even if he hadn't needed me, I was anxious to put my education back into the ranch. See if I could build on what my dad had started."

"Oh," she said, thinking of her dad and the ranch she'd left behind — the ranch she hadn't put anything back into. She'd left him just like Lance had left her. She pushed that thought out of her head. She'd had her own life to worry about. "So where is the . . . Sandbar Ranch?"

"Aransas Pass. About twenty miles away."

"That close?" She'd forgotten that he'd said it was close when they'd talked on the beach. He'd even said his ranch *had* a beach. With all the excitement of the moment, it was a wonder she had remembered him saying anything.

"Very close. You'll have to come out and ride with me."

She stepped on his foot again. "Sorry."

His eyes crinkled at the edges. "It's all right. I don't mind. So, what about coming out and riding? If you don't ride, I'm a pretty good teacher."

"No, I mean, yes — I ride. I used to ride. I don't anymore." *Get a grip, Kelsey.*

He paused their steps and studied her

309

with sincerity in his eyes. "What happened? Why don't you ride anymore?"

Her stomach seemed to do a neat three-sixty. "My —" She caught herself before she spilled anything more personal about herself. She didn't want to get friendlier with Brent. "Do you do this to all the women you meet?" The question escaped before she could stop it.

"What do you mean?"

"Charm your way past their defenses."

He tugged her a little closer. "Is that what I'm doing? I thought I was just being interested. I want to know what makes you tick, Kelsey Wilcox."

She swallowed and tried to form a coherent thought. But he'd stumped her.

He chose that moment to spin them three times in a circle that had her clutching him and feeling exhilarated at the same time.

Her heart was trading places with her good sense.

The dance ended, and Kelsey had never been happier about something in all of her life. "Thanks, I . . . I need to go see my —" Her mind went blank. "My aunt."

Tugging her hand from his, Kelsey hurried off the dance floor.

She'd suspected it and now it was confirmed . . . Brent was dangerous. Her cheeks burned, and she was sure her skin was flushed a humiliating fuchsia.

She needed to stay away from him.

If her aunt and her comrades glimpsed even a hint of her attraction, she would be toast.

*Perfect, buttery, topped with strawberry jam toast.*


Brent watched Kelsey flee. What had he said?

That amazing dance had given him time to learn new things about her, and he was intrigued all the more.

What had a cowboy done to her to make her run like that?

The party was a success as far as Brent could tell. All around him people were laughing, talking, and dancing. He watched his friend Tru Monahan, who was one of the other groomsmen, doing the Jitterbug with one of the four bridesmaids. The crowd had formed a circle around them as they spun and wove to the fast music. Tru was from Wishing Springs, a little Texas town on the other side of San Antonio, and he was also leading the world in the Quarter Horse Championship. He knew how to kick up his boots.

"Boy, Tru's having a good time," Steven

observed, coming to stand beside Brent.

Brent struggled to focus on his friend. Thoughts of Kelsey made it difficult. "With all the pressure he's under with the championships coming up, I'm sure he's glad to have a weekend to let off a little steam." Tru's success had come with extra stress — he had major sponsors he answered to and who demanded he maintain his status every year.

"Tru seems to handle it well," Steven said. "But he's seemed a little tense to me. Did you notice?"

"I noticed. That's why this is good for him." Brent didn't envy any of his rodeo buddies their success. But sensing the pressure Tru was under was one more reminder to Brent that he was comfortable with the life he'd chosen on his ranch. Steven laid a hand on Brent's shoulder. "I'm just glad you both could be here to share in my celebration."

"It was a whole lot easier for me than for Tru, but I wouldn't have missed it, buddy." Brent had chosen a different path than Steven and Tru — a quieter, more laid-back path. He'd never regretted it. He answered only to himself. Both Steven and Tru had sponsor obligations and unbelievable competition schedules. "You know I'm no party animal, but I have to say I'm having a great time."

Steven laughed and nodded toward Kelsey. She was visiting with Esther Mae, Norma Sue, and Adela. "If that's so, then why are you standing here alone? You should get over there. Ask her to dance again."

"And you should go find your fiancée and show Tru how it's really done."

"Soon as she gets back from taking a breather, we will. Speaking of, there she is. Catch you later."

Brent smiled, glad for Steven and Tiffany. He glanced back at Kelsey and found her looking at him. He nodded and touched the brim of his hat. She looked away instantly. But his gaze caught Esther Mae's. She winked at him with a broad smile. He'd found some allies, that was for certain.

Esther Mae waved him over. When he took her up on her invite, he noted Kelsey's tight expression.

"Sit down right here and visit with us," Esther Mae urged, patting the seat beside her. "So, tell us what kind of ranch you have. Kelsey tells us it's a family ranch and you've been running it since right out of college."

"Yes, ma'am." Now he understood why Kelsey had looked uptight — they'd been grilling her about him. "My family's been ranching over forty years. We run cattle, breed quarter horses, and offer boarding and a place for people to come out and ride. We also have a pavilion for events that can be rented — weddings, reunions, all sorts of events."

"Oh, that sounds lovely," Adela said. "You'll have to tell us more. Do you cater the events?"

He glanced at Kelsey and noticed she'd now given him her full attention.

"Funny you should ask. We've been thinking about it as something to offer, though that's undecided. Until then, we just provide the location and the folks can bring in caterers on their own, if they like."

"Isn't that interesting, Kelsey?" Norma Sue looked from him to Kelsey.

"Our Kelsey is a ranch girl," Esther Mae added.

"Was, actually. I've chosen another path with my life." Kelsey gave her aunt a pointed look.

Esther Mae looked at him and back at the ladies, and there was a little frown between her eyes. "Y'all remember when she was a girl? You couldn't get her off of a horse to save your life!"

"She did love it," Adela prompted. "Still,

314

people change, Esther Mae. Our Kelsey does seem to flourish here on the beach — look at that tan. Besides, her bistro is wonderful. You'll have to stop in and try it, Brent. It's just down the beach. Everything she creates is delicious."

Kelsey's eyes warmed at the praise. "Thank you, Adela."

It was easy to tell she loved what she was doing. "I'd love to check it out. I come to Corpus a lot, you know. I love to fish."

"You fish?" she asked, looking as if he'd just told her he was from outer space.

"Sure. I like to drop a hook in the surf."

She seemed skeptical. "What do you like to fish for?"

"Tarpon is my favorite."

"What is a tarpon fish?" Norma Sue asked. "I like the sand here, but I know beef, not fish."

"It's a sport fish. They're hard to hook and a fight to reel in. And they are as silver in the light as Kelsey was gold in that dress." He looked at Kelsey, "I do love a challenge."

She ignored his implication. "I'm sure with the demands your ranch makes on you, you don't have much time for anything else."

He thought of his dad's health problems and sobered.

"I make time, Kelsey. I work hard, but a well-rounded life is important."

She looked as if she really couldn't figure him out. "When I was growing up, my dad worked sunrise to sunset on our ranch."

"Mine too. Till he had that heart attack. Guess it helped us have some perspective on what's important in life. Your dad still work those hours?"

"He lost his ranch several years ago. All that hard work was for nothing."

Her words sounded bitter.

Esther Mae patted her hand. "But he loved it while he was doing it."

Kelsey stood. "Yes, he did." Her expression shadowed. The conversation seemed to have hit a sore spot. "I'm going to go see if I can help Tiffany with anything." She nodded at him and then glided off.

"She's beautiful," Norma Sue said from across the table.

"Yes, ma'am. She is that."

He tore his gaze from Kelsey's retreating form to find the three women grinning at him. "So, how long are you ladies in town?" he asked, deciding to change the subject.

"Till Sunday evening," Esther Mae said. "We wanted some time to visit with Kelsey."

Norma Sue began drumming the beat of the Randy Rogers band on the table. "We love Mule Hollow, but this fantastic place is a real treat. Tell me more about your ranch. What breed of cattle do you run?"

He spent the next little while telling them about his ranch in Aransas Pass and found himself having fun visiting with them. His own aunts would have loved these three, and he felt almost as if he'd known them for years. They told him funny stories about their tiny town, and he found himself determined to visit the outer edge of the Hill Country. Clint Matlock's large spread there was known all over Texas. It rivaled Tru Monahan's in Wishing Springs, on the outskirts of Austin. He supplied quarter horse colts to both ranches, which were within four hours of his ranch.

"You need to get back out there and dance," Adela said after a few minutes. "You're a young man. You should be having a good time."

"I am having a good time, ladies," he said, telling the truth. Then he caught sight of Kelsey. "But I think I will go see if Kelsey will dance with me again."

"Oh, that would be wonderful," Esther Mae gushed.

He said good-bye, then wove through the crowd. He tapped Kelsey on the shoulder.

"I've come to test my luck and ask you to

dance with me again."

She spun around and her eyes clouded. "Look, Brent, thank you again for saving me today. I owe you, okay? But this" — she waved a hand between them — "isn't going to work. Besides, I could have saved myself."

"If you say so," he said, startled by her outburst.

She lifted her chin. "I . . . I could have. I don't need some cowboy rushing to my rescue or teaching me to ride or dance, or anything. I'm not interested in this" — she looked genuinely perplexed — "becoming anything more than what it is."

Without waiting for his reply, she scooted through the crowd and disappeared through a service door.

He watched her go. He'd just come off the end of two back-to-back bad relationships that had him skittish. And obviously Kelsey Wilcox was running scared too. He could feel it. And after what she'd been through, he could understand it . . . to a point.

But she had turned his world upside down when he'd spotted her in the water this afternoon. After he'd rescued her, held her in his arms, and looked deep into those eyes . . . and felt the connection that he'd felt . . .

A man didn't walk away from something like that, no matter what.

A cowboy didn't either . . . at least not a real cowboy, and maybe that was what Kelsey needed to learn.

# FOUR

The morning after the party Kelsey walked to the bistro at sunrise as usual to begin preparing her pastries, soups, and specialties for the day. Julie, who helped in the kitchen prepping and baking, showed up soon after, along with Candy, Kelsey's waitress. Together, they had everything ready by seven when the Sunflower Bistro officially opened.

Aunt E, Norma Sue, and Adela showed up at eight, all smiles and excitement over the party and what would come — a brunch cruise at ten for immediate family and the wedding party and then the wedding that evening on the beach beneath the stars. Millie, the now-dry tiny ball of fluff, bounced on the thin leash Aunt E had snapped to her collar. Of course they were as animated as Millie when it came to the party the night before. Much to Kelsey's dismay, they had absolutely fallen in love with Brent Corbin.

They settled around a table on the outside patio, and immediately Kelsey had to start dodging inquiries about Brent. Since he'd fished her out of the bay last night, her life had . . . well, it had turned upside down — the man had been constantly on her mind. Millie sat on her foot and looked up at her with tiny black you-and-me-both-sister eyes.

No, this morning Kelsey had a whole set of emotions and thoughts duking it out inside. Talking to the posse about Brent was not on her to-do list.

"Kelsey, I do love your bistro," Adela said, looking through the bistro's open patio doors. Kelsey could have kissed the wisp of a woman for steering the conversation away from what she thought of Brent.

"Sunflower Bistro is a perfect name for it," Aunt E added, taking the bait. "It makes me want to smile every time I come here and see this sunny, happy place you've created."

"You did good," Norma Sue agreed.

"I tried." Kelsey smiled. It was true. She'd painted the walls a rich ocean blue, then added touches of sparkling jewel tones with vibrant ocean photos and an array of amazing sunset and sunrise photos in hues of mandarin orange, lemon, and sunflower yellow.

Looking at it through the open doors, her insides felt light and her heart smiled. She'd put so much of herself in her business. She'd taken the photographs, and the tables were great little works of art she'd found at a thrift sale. They had driftwood pedestals and ceramic tops that she'd tiled herself using a vast array of swirling colors. She loved this place. She was proud that she'd created it with her own two hands.

"It gives me peace each time I walk inside," she admitted.

"As I'm sure it does everyone else who comes here. How did you come to find this spot?" Adela asked.

Candy and Roxie, the part-time waitress, had the customers handled and Julie had the kitchen under control, so Kelsey took a moment. She sat down, hoping she could get the posse to understand what this place and the life she'd built meant to her. Hoping she could remind them of what had brought her here and that she wasn't interested in complicating her life with another man right now. She was doing great without a man in her life.

"Y'all know how I came to be here," she said, shooting them a frown. "Yes, I'm better off without Lance, but I was so upset when my wedding fell apart. I think God led me to find this spot on the shore," she answered. And she really did. "Remember, I just got in my car and drove. I was so angry and hurt and walking on the beach is soothing to me. I think it's the vastness of it. So I ended up in Corpus for the night."

Sympathy filled their expressions.

She gave them a tiny shrug. "Looking at the vastness of the ocean helps put life into perspective. And believe me, I needed perspective. I was a blubbering, brokenhearted wreck." It was true. Embarrassing — but true. "I was trying to figure out my life that next morning — there was a lot of walking and tears. I came across this closed-up building. And this place captured my imagination when I looked through these doors. It gave me something to hope for."

"God is good, Kelsey," Adela said.

Kelsey nodded, remembering how much cleaning and painting it needed. But that was okay, because it gave her something to focus on other than the failure she'd felt like after what she'd just been through. But maybe reminding them of her broken heart would help them to stop pushing her. "Working on the bistro helped me through.

It helped me find strength again. And a new purpose. You know, like working with the homeless shelter providing meals. I can't express how fulfilled that makes me feel." It was so true. "Knowing that my bistro has helped give a boost to Julie, Candy, and now Roxie, warms my heart just thinking about it." All three of her employees had been hired while they had been at the shelter.

"Honey," Aunt E said. "You're doin' good."

Norma Sue picked up a pastry. "Yep, you sure are, sweet-pea. Cleaning and scrubbing are good ways to get over the past. Baking is too. These are fantastic." She took a bite, her expression blissful.

"I always loved to bake. Mom taught me that." She thought of the ranch and her heart ached a little. The bistro had also helped her family when she had to watch her father lose his ranch because of drought conditions and low cattle prices. Her dad wouldn't accept any help from her, said it would cost too much to start over. It had broken her heart for him and her mom, and made her all the more thankful that she'd chosen a new path. For her, there was no looking back now. And they seemed to enjoy the travel that came with his new job — they were on a sales trip right now. It couldn't be helped, and so they were missing Tiffany's wedding because of it . . . It bothered her some, but Tiffany understood.

"Anyway." She stood as a fresh wave of customers entered the bistro. "I better help. I'll be back in a minute."

She got busy helping fill orders, but found her thoughts wandering to the feel of Brent Corbin's arms holding her as they'd danced.

She fought the memory off just like she'd been doing all night and morning.

If she didn't want that life again, then she certainly didn't want to date a cowboy and chance the past repeating itself.

She had once loved everything there was to love about being born a cowgirl. A person changed, though, and this was Kelsey now. After Lance had pulled out on her and then seeing her father struggle, she wanted no part of ranching anymore. The sound of wind and surf, these were the things that filled her with excitement now. No more hot dusty days fixing fences and wrestling with cattle or worrying about the lack of rain or the fluctuating cattle prices that held a rancher hostage when things were going bad. That was her past. And that was where it would remain. It didn't matter that her skin tingled thinking about the touch of his hand and the warmth of his breath near her ear as they'd talked . . . His scent, musk and sandalwood, so masculine . . . *Forget that! All of it.*

Lance's sweet-talking, lying ways had forever tainted her view of men in Stetsons — even one who smelled better than fresh cinnamon rolls baking. Even if getting Brent out of her head was proving to be harder than she'd expected.

She sighed and placed several of her freshly made croissants on a plate. She had enjoyed dancing with him, though. And when he'd asked for a second dance, she'd said no because she'd enjoyed the first one far too much.

Like Aunt E always said with one of her malapropisms, Kelsey hadn't fallen off that cabbage truck yesterday — she knew when to walk away from temptation. She hadn't fallen off the turnip wagon either.

And she recognized that any thought of involvement with Brent Corbin might threaten her orderly, manageable, happy new life.

And she was about to be forced to spend three hours on a brunch cruise with him while the posse pushed her hard. Her little talk moments ago had to have opened their eyes to the reasons why Brent was not the man for her. It had to have.

Hopefully they would ease up.

"You okay, boss?" Candy asked as she passed by with a plate of breakfast muffins.

"Sure, Candy, why?"

The waitress paused before moving on. "You've been distracted all morning, and your cheeks keep flushing. Got a man on your mind?"

"No! Why would you say such a thing?"

Candy laughed so hard her dangling hoop earrings danced. "Your aunt just told me you got rescued from the bay by some hunky cowboy last night."

"Do not encourage them," Kelsey said.

"So it is true! You'll have to give me all the details."

"Don't you have an order to deliver?"

"Yes, I do. But don't think I'm forgetting about this." Candy gave her a grin, then went to deliver her order. Kelsey watched her go, reminded of the other little problem she had been facing. Candy really could use some extra hours. There was a lot going on in her life, and Kelsey really wanted to help her. The small catering jobs that the Sunflower Bistro had recently begun to do were picking up, but were sporadic at best. She knew if she started catering weddings, things might improve. Competition was fierce, but if she got in with a wedding venue, it could really prove helpful to Candy, and her other employees too. With everything that had gone on, Kelsey hadn't wanted to participate in weddings. She just couldn't face them. But maybe it was time for her to get over herself.

And that brought her right back to the idea that had been hanging around in the back of her mind ever since Brent had mentioned the pavilion at his ranch. Could that be a possible venue for her bistro to get involved in?

*No.* She squelched that thought again. Like she'd been doing every time it whispered to her.

She well knew it was not a good idea.

Especially with the attraction she was fighting toward Brent.

Work. She shoved hard at all the crazy, tangled-up thoughts whirling around in her head and went back outside to serve the pastries to the couple who were now sitting at the table beside the posse. She sucked in the tangy salt air and fought to let the serenity calm her suddenly riled-up spirit.

"Mmm-hmm." Norma Sue paused to smell her cinnamon-apple muffin before taking a bite. "These are delicious, Kelsey."

"They're a new recipe . . ." Kelsey's voice trailed off as she spotted a tall, lean man in cargo shorts and a bright orange T-shirt jogging down the beach. The breeze whipped his dark wavy hair across his forehead. He jogged with long strides, in a graceful, smooth gait. Her mouth went dry. Brent.

Now, *that* was a man.

As he drew near, he smiled and gave an open-hand wave before altering course, jogging from the wet sand toward the boardwalk.

A small sigh eased from Kelsey. If she hadn't seen his boots and Stetson the night before, she never would have pegged him for a rancher today.

Why, oh why, did he have to be so . . . hunky?

"That is one good-looking man."

She didn't even register who said what everyone was thinking. For the past two years, since her fiasco of a wedding, Kelsey had met a lot of men — a lot of good-looking men. A lot of interesting men, but none of them had made her heart skip or her skin heat with a blush like Brent.

She wanted to say it was just a normal reaction to the man who'd saved her life. What woman wouldn't feel some inkling of excitement toward the man who'd rescued her? Especially if he was tall, dark, and had a smile that struck like lightning.

"Mornin' ladies," he drawled. "I thought I'd take y'all up on your offer of breakfast before our little ocean getaway." He scanned the posse and then his chocolate gaze met hers.

"Oh? Well, welcome," she blurted, forcing her voice to be light and unruffled — an Oscar-worthy accomplishment.

"Hey, I've heard only good things. *And* I've been seeing those little yellow bags you put your pastries in with your Sunflower Bistro logo on them. They are everywhere this morning. That's got to mean only good things."

Her cheeks heated at his praise.

"Good-looking and smart too. Sit here." Norma Sue patted the empty chair beside her. "Kelsey redid this place all by herself. You'll have to go inside and see all her creative table designs."

"Yes, but her food is the real treat," Adela added.

Okay, so this was crazy. "Would you like coffee?" Kelsey asked, needing out of there.

"Sure, Kelsey. I take it black if you don't mind. You've got a great place." At the sound of his voice, Millie woke from where she'd curled up under the table. With a joyous yap, she jumped to greet Brent.

"Hey there, is this the little seaweed pile I

pulled from the surf yesterday? Little girl, you clean up good." He picked Millie up and snuggled.

"Coffee, black, coming right up," Kelsey squeaked, spinning round and hurrying away. *Breathe,* she told herself. *Just breathe. Men snuggle puppies every day. It doesn't mean any of them are your type. Put one foot in front of the other and keep your mind on the end result . . . This is only temporary.* By Sunday evening things would be back to normal. He would be back at his ranch. The posse would head home to Mule Hollow, and she would have her life back just as it was.

She only had to keep her head on straight between now and then.

# FIVE

Brent's spirits soared as high as the seagulls overhead in the cloudless sky. The midmorning August sun blazed hot, but the breeze as the cruiser cut slowly through the bay minimized the heat. The yacht, a beautiful split-level outfit built to entertain large groups, had awnings to offer shade for those who wanted it and easily held the entire wedding party of ten plus friends and family. But it was also intimate enough that he could keep Kelsey within view at all times.

Brent mingled with Steven and Tru and a few other college buddies on the lower level of the yacht.

"Seven hours. Are you ready?" he asked Steven. Like Brent, Steven hadn't been paying much attention to the water. While Brent's gaze kept straying to Kelsey as she talked with Tiffany and the bridesmaids on the upper level, Steven had hardly taken his eyes off of his soon-to-be bride.

"I'm ready. More than I can express."

The love and emotion rang clearly in his friend's voice, and Brent felt a pang of envy. What would it feel like to love like Steven and Tiffany?

The instant the thought was out there, his gaze locked back on Kelsey. He'd enjoyed breakfast at her bistro. Bubbly and engaging, she hurried about making sure the eight tables outside and the ones inside were well taken care of. He tried hard to imagine her in ranch wear, even though it would be a shame to cover up those tanned legs with jeans and boots. Or that thick golden mane of hair with a hat. She looked perfect in her sundress and flip flops.

"Where did you disappear to last night and this morning?" Steven asked.

"Sorry, I had some ranch business to take care of last night. This morning I went for a run — and ended up at Kelsey's bistro having breakfast with Esther Mae, Norma Sue, and Adela."

Steven laughed. "You better watch out for those three. It's safe to say they have you in their sights. You good with that?"

"I think I can handle three little old ladies. Besides, Kelsey's great."

"As badly as she's been hurt, I'm startled she's even giving you the time of day, buddy.

It took awhile for her to warm up to the idea of Tiffany falling for a cowboy."

"So, I'm curious about this original cowboy — what did he do? I know he broke her heart, but how?"

"He dumped her at the altar for dreams of the NFR and ran off with a barrel racer while he was at it. It did a number on her. Then toss in the fact that her dad lost his ranch to foreclosure a few months later, and you, my ranch-owning friend, are about to fight an uphill battle where that little gal is concerned."

"So, you're telling me she associates every bad moment in her life over the past few years with ranch life and cowboys."

"That'd be a fair assumption."

He let that info sink in. He'd had his fair share of bad luck with women; that didn't mean he'd sworn them off completely, just temporarily. He hadn't lumped all women into the same category.

He hadn't been left at the altar, though. What would something like that do to a person? He could only imagine how that had to have ripped away every bit of trust from Kelsey.

He knew how to rebuild trust in a broken, mistreated horse. Could he do the same with a woman? They were completely different. Still, patience, kindness, and building up a personal relationship had to be the winning elements.

Steven nodded toward the upper deck where Tiffany stood. "I can tell you finding the love of your life is well worth any trial and tribulation you have to endure."

Brent watched Kelsey tuck her blond hair behind her ear and laugh at something Tiffany was saying. His gut tightened. He couldn't have looked away from her if he'd wanted to. He'd never felt like his heart was driving him toward a woman before, but that was exactly how he felt about Kelsey.

She was laughing again, having a good time with Tiffany. He smiled. She might have had her heart broken, but she'd pulled herself together. She'd gone on with her life. Almost . . .

He realized that maybe he could help Kelsey move forward and realize all cowboys weren't the enemy.

Or at least that he wasn't.

Kelsey sipped her iced tea and studied the horizon in the distance. The ocean softly lapped at the boat.

"You fit in here."

Brent's words softly spoken in her ear made her jump as a tingle raced across her skin where his breath had touched, instantly reminding her of the night before.

Looking like a man comfortable at sea, he sat on the edge of the boat. The wind whipped his dark hair across his forehead and the sunlight warmed his skin. He fit here too, and the thought needled at her.

She'd managed to avoid him most of the morning. "I love it. But what's surprising me is you seem to love it too."

He looked baffled. "Why is that so surprising to you?"

She laughed, embarrassed. "I mean . . . you don't even look like you own a ranch, sitting there in your shorts and deck shoes."

His brows knitted. "You know, you really need to lay off judging people by their occupations."

"I just mean a cowboy is rarely out of his jeans —"

"Not true," he challenged. "Though I'll say that if I lived deeper in the heart of Texas, I might be less likely to be sporting cargoes and deck shoes."

"Okay." She laughed. "I don't mean to herd you into a group. But —"

"This jerk really did a number on you, didn't he?"

She blinked and stepped back from him. "How?"

"It's not hard to figure out. But the posse filled me in on some of the details of your bad experience. And I can't say that I blame you. I just hope you give me a chance since we were brought together in the most unorthodox way. That should count for something, don't you think? I mean, I'm just wanting you to look at me and not my occupation." He gave a crooked grin, then hitched a brow in a question.

Her stomach dipped and she leaned toward him, so drawn to him . . . She wished — She yanked herself upright. "It's more than that. Being a cowboy and a rancher is a lifestyle."

Before he could answer, Steven called for everyone to gather on the top deck. He lifted his glass and hugged Tiffany close. "I just wanted to lift up a toast and a prayer, out here on this beautiful body of endless blue, for my soon-to-be wife, Tiffany."

Brent stood up behind her as she turned to give her attention to the wedding couple. She had to admit that it had taken awhile for her to warm to Steven. She'd feared for the longest time that her cousin would suffer the same fate that she had.

Was she wrong to put Brent into the same category with Lance? When it came to her future, she was taking no chances, she reminded herself. She'd meant what she'd said. Being a cowboy was also a lifestyle.

She thought of her dad. Of the ranch.

"They are a great match, don't you think?" Brent said, taking a drink from his bottle of water.

"Yes, they are." It was so true. Kelsey was riveted to Tiffany, her expression glowing with love. What would it be like to be loved like that? To be so cherished? So adored? Kelsey's heart ached thinking about it.

*Steven's a cowboy!*

She gave herself a mental shake. *Focus, Kelsey.*

"So, besides serving mouthwatering bagels and croissants and wearing gold dresses into the ocean that make a poor cowboy think he's seeing mermaids, what else do you like to do?"

That pulled a laugh from her. "You really thought I was a mermaid?"

"Hey, the sun was reflecting off of the dress and that long part at the bottom flopped around."

His smile was sheepish and adorable. Drat!

She laughed again, unable to help it. She was suddenly feeling a little reckless; after all, she was on a yacht, the sun was gleaming off the cerulean water, the breeze was skimming her skin like a kiss . . .

"So, would you have dived in after an ordinary woman, or is it just mermaids that you dive in to rescue?"

"I'd have come in for you, no matter what."

The way he said it sent a dangerous thrill racing through her. "You didn't know me," she challenged.

"I'd like to get to know you, Kelsey. Diving in after you, mermaid or not, turned out to be a startling blessing."

Her skin heated with a blush. She didn't know if anyone had ever said she was a blessing. What a word choice.

"That's a very nice thing to say —"

"It's the truth." He crossed his arms and studied her for a beat. "So, tell me how you're really doing."

She stared at him, her thoughts turning. She knew instinctively what he was asking. "Why are you asking me this? Why do you want to know?"

"Because I can't imagine a man walking out on you. I hate that you went through that."

Was he for real? "When my fiancé left me at the altar, it was embarrassing. And it hurt. I cried like a baby. And now, thinking back, it makes me so mad that I was such a fool. And just to let you know, I haven't admitted that to anyone."

"You had every right to feel upset and mad. But ashamed, embarrassed — no, I think you should let that go. Some people are good at lying. I'm not one of them — just so you know."

She took a deep breath. Her hand shook thinking about it. And why had she told Brent something so personal?

Feeling reckless could get her into trouble. Then again, at least he'd tried to make her feel better.

The yacht made a wide arc as it turned back toward Corpus. "It doesn't matter. I'm happy. I've found my calling here with my bistro, serving coffee and good food. No one has a better job than I do. I love being able to cater to people."

*Cater.* Kelsey wondered again about the facility he'd mentioned on his ranch. She would love to be able to help Julie and Candy have more opportunities. And Roxie was part-time, but could really use more hours.

"You are really good at what you do. I agree —"

"Dolphins!" The high-pitched yell from Esther Mae broke into his reply. Aunt E was leaning out over the rail, pointing with one hand and holding her big floppy hat with the other. Two gleaming bottle-nosed dolphins popped out of the water, and everyone moved to the edge of the yacht to watch them.

"I hope Aunt E doesn't fall in. You might have two rescues in one weekend." She wasn't completely joking.

"I hope she doesn't either, but I would. She is a very" — he hesitated — "enthusiastic lady."

"Tell me about it." She smiled and watched as the beautiful dolphins ran with the yacht, diving and jumping from the water as if choreographed. "I really do love this place," she confessed, leaning out to let the breeze sift through her hair.

She looked over to find him watching her with intense eyes. Her pulse leaped when he wrapped a hand around the railing on one side of her, then the other, and she found herself boxed in. Breathless, she angled toward him. She couldn't stop herself.

"So," he asked. "I've heard you out. And I'm still here. Do you ever think you could consider going out with a cowboy? This cowboy?"

# Six

Kelsey's eyes widened in what looked like disbelief — and why not? She must think Brent had lost his mind asking her if she'd go out with a cowboy after what the last one had put her through.

"That's not a good idea, Brent."

"Okay, so I love a challenge," he teased, coaxing a reluctant smile from her. "That smile tells me there's still a chance here for a lonely cowboy to change a Texas mermaid's mind."

She laughed. He loved her laugh, a lilting sound that danced through him.

"I don't believe you're lonely. If you are, it's because you choose to be."

"The truth is I don't date much. I haven't even felt inclined to think about it for months."

"Like I said, you chose."

"I'm choosing to try to convince you to go out with me." He was being relentless and he knew it, but she was fun to spar with.

"I can't, Brent."

She studied him and nibbled on her lip, drawing his gaze.

He still had his hands on either side of her, and all he had to do was lean in and steal a kiss. That would not be the smartest move on his part, but it didn't stop him from thinking about it.

"Do you really have a pavilion on your property? For events?"

His mind filled with different things she could have said in this situation. A question about his pavilion wasn't one of them. "Yup. I do. Why?" An idea hit him like a brick between the eyes. Kelsey loved her restaurant, loved working with people. It was obvious when he'd watched her interacting with her customers. "You wouldn't by chance be interested in catering our events, would you?" That exact interest flared in her expression even before he finished asking the question. It was perfect.

She pulled away from the landing. "I know that I just turned down your date, but yesterday you mentioned that you were thinking of offering catering as an option to anyone who wanted to rent the pavilion. I was thinking the Sunflower Bistro might be just what you were looking for."

*Thank you, Lord.* He smiled, unable not to. "Your Sunflowers at my Sandbar. Hmm, I like the sound of that. Kinda like us. Those two words don't seem to go together at first, but when you think about it, they're perfect. Who doesn't need sun on a sandbar?" Brent hoped he hadn't gone too far, but it really did make sense. At least to his way of thinking. And it gave him more time.

"This would be purely business, Brent," she warned.

"It will be whatever you want it to be." He meant that. But it still gave him the opportunity to make his case.

They were approaching the dock. The wedding wasn't until later that evening, and he wasn't ready for the cruise to be over.

"You would need to come out and see the ranch — the pavilion. See what we have to offer."

"Yes. You're right." Her forehead crinkled slightly at the thought.

"How about tomorrow?" Brent was rushing things, but he didn't want to give her time to talk herself out of her brilliant idea. "You could come out, bring your aunt and Norma Sue and Adela. I could give you all the tour."

"Yoo-hoo, you two," Esther Mae called,

hurrying over. "Y'all look like you've been having fun. I hate to see the cruise end, but then, if we are to have a wedding this evening, we need to get off the boat. It *was* romantic, don't you think?" She looked from Kelsey to Brent. The palm tree on her hat swayed with the movement.

Adela joined them and Norma Sue followed. They launched into the plans for the wedding that evening.

"Ladies," Brent said, not wanting to miss his shot. "Would y'all like to come out to the ranch tomorrow for lunch and let me give you a tour of the Sandbar? It's just twenty minutes away."

"Does a rooster crow?" Norma Sue asked, grinning.

Esther Mae clapped her hands together. "Oh yes. That would be the perfect ending to our trip."

Brent wanted to pick up the smiling redheaded aunt and give her a hug. "I'll treat you ladies to lunch and a ride over some of the most beautiful ranch land in these parts. We'll even ride on the beach."

"The *beach*! Oh, how romantic. Isn't it, Kelsey?" Esther Mae elbowed Kelsey, who glared at her. "We'll be there right after church."

"This is perfect," Adela said. "Just perfect.

You, young man, have made our day."

"I'll furnish lunch," Kelsey said. "You know, since you're showing me what you have to offer, I'll show you what I have to offer."

Brent laughed. "I like the sound of that — I mean, sure. Great. Show me what you've got."

# SEVEN

The sunset wedding was extremely romantic. So romantic that as Kelsey took her place beside the other bridesmaids, the most rebellious feelings took hold of her. Capital D-dreamy feelings that went against every bowed-up, hard-knuckled thought she possessed about weddings.

Tiffany had chosen a quiet stretch of beach where the land merged into the sand, leaving a beautiful grassy area for the reception under the stars. They'd sparkled it up more by stringing twinkling lights overhead and splendid, fifteen-foot palm trees in huge pots had been brought in by the wedding planners. The trunks were wrapped with lights all the way from the top to the base. Though it was sunset now, the lights still glowed happily in promise of what would come as the sun went down and the reception began.

Her gaze flickered to Brent standing with

the other groomsmen beside Steven. He was watching her; his lips quirked when their eyes met. Kelsey's fingers tightened around the flowers. Her breath caught in a knot of longing.

*You hate weddings,* she reminded herself. But that was the problem — did she?

She looked back at Tiff and Steven and her heart lifted with a light spirit, not an angry one. Her fingers relaxed on the flower stems. She'd gotten over Lance a long time ago. It had been the lingering effects of the wedding that had been the hard part to overcome. Which actually said something for what she'd realized she'd felt for Lance. She took a cleansing breath. He'd done her a favor and she knew it. She'd been more in love with the idea of him than with him. What a disaster their marriage would have been.

But she'd trusted her heart and it had led her wrong.

As the preacher pronounced Tiffany and Steven husband and wife, a surge of true joy ran through Kelsey in a rush. Instantly, her traitorous eyes slid to Brent — he was smiling with happiness for them too. Longing she didn't dare soften to swelled in her chest . . .

Then those heart-stopping, smoldering

348

eyes shifted to her.

Drat! Double drat!

She snapped her gaze back to Tiffany. She and her Prince Charming practically floated together down the aisle.

Kelsey's gaze flicked to Brent again, and she wanted to make like a crab and disappear into a sand hole. Because the moonlit beach reception was about to happen, and she wasn't certain suddenly that she could trust her actions.

Of course first, she had to take his arm and walk back down the aisle with him.

"They made it," he said, smiling as he held his arm out to her not nearly enough seconds later. She slipped her hand through his arm, and they started off behind Carrie, the maid of honor, Tiffany's best friend, and Tru, the best man.

"Like a fairy tale," Kelsey said, keeping her gaze locked firmly ahead of them. As soon as they made it to the last row, Kelsey slipped her hand out of the crook of Brent's arm.

"Tiffany," she said, hugging her cousin. "It was such a sweet wedding. Congratulations."

Tiffany sniffed. "It was, wasn't it. I'm so happy."

Kelsey laughed. "Then stop crying."

"I know it's crazy, isn't it?" Tiffany smiled. "Happy tears are wonderful, though."

Brent stepped in and hugged her too. "Happy tears are always good. Not that I tear up that much, but that's what my mom always says."

"Thank you, Brent."

Steven grinned, pulled Tiffany into his arms, and brushed the tears from the corners of her eyes. "As long as they're happy tears," he said, then kissed her and winked at them. "I'm one happy cowboy."

As Steven and Tiffany were engulfed in a wave of other congratulations, Kelsey felt Brent watching her, but she refused to look at him. She didn't trust her heart. Couldn't trust her heart. And right now, in this moony, oh-so-romantic setting, the last thing she needed to do was put herself within touching distance of the handsome cowboy who'd plucked her out of the sea.

Later, after the cake was cut and the wedding party had danced — she'd been all too aware of being in Brent's arms again — she stood alone lost in thought. The gorgeous moon shimmered on the water and the lights from the wedding reception cast pinpoints of brightness across the sand and out over the ocean, and all she could think about was that Brent was heading home as soon as Tiffany and Steven left for their honeymoon. It was a good thing.

It was.

Brent stood on the outer edge of the light, his thoughts ebbing and flowing with the tide. The reception was in full swing, and Brent had felt restless all evening. What was going on with him anyway?

*Kelsey.*

He hadn't been able to forget her expression as she'd watched Tiffany and Steven recite their vows. His heart had ached thinking about how Kelsey said she'd been hurt and embarrassed when she'd been stood up at the altar. And that she'd been mad.

He could understand why weddings would be hard for her. But she'd seemed mesmerized by the ceremony, and when she'd looked at him, he'd felt it all the way to his soul.

What was he doing?

He'd wanted to march across that sandy aisle and sweep her off her feet and into his arms. He'd wanted to right the wrong done to her on her wedding day.

But he'd only known her for twenty-four hours. And he'd never been known for being impulsive. He couldn't start winging it now, not with something this important.

Especially not with Kelsey.

He hadn't been looking for someone like her at all. Hadn't expected the effect that meeting her had had on him.

But all he could think about was her from the moment he dove into the ocean.

Deciding he better join the party or Steven might think something was wrong, Brent headed straight for the cake. He grabbed two pieces of the creamy white confection and crossed to where Kelsey stood beside the dance floor watching the guests.

"Hey, you don't line dance?" he asked, stopping beside her. He offered her the cake and she took it with a smile.

"Not really. I'm not one to jump out there."

"I'm with you. Though I don't mind watching everyone else mess up their steps, I don't want to be the one who turns left when the rest of the line turns right."

She laughed. "Oh, the nightmare of it."

"Yeah, that's what I'm talking about." He took a bite of his cake. She did the same. He'd never had a better time eating cake.

"So." He cleared the lump out of his throat. "You doin' all right?"

In the glow of the tea lights, her eyes clouded. After a beat she nodded. "Tha-thanks for asking. Actually, I am. I couldn't always say that. But I truly could see Tiffany and Steven's love shining through during the ceremony."

"It was clear to everyone."

"As it should be," she said, looking up at him with amusement.

She was having a good time. The expression on her face then had been both tender and sad. Normal emotions at a wedding.

"Hey, would you like to go for a walk on the beach? It's a beautiful night. Of course, if you'd rather dance —" Silence radiated between them despite the music blasting from the loud speakers.

Kelsey cut another forkful of cake, and he was certain she was going to turn him down. Instead, she gave him an uncertain smile. "I would like that."

*Yes.*

They put their plates on a tray and walked toward the water. The surf swept in with a hush and swept out, bringing with it the damp, briny scent of a beach evening. The music from the wedding and the laughter lingered in the background as they walked on the firm, damp sand just at the edge of the water.

"You know, Aunt E and the girls are thrilled about coming to your place tomorrow. They couldn't stop talking about it all the way back to the hotel today." She laughed, a husky, completely feminine sound.

Brent's pulse hummed faster — it had been in an uproar from the moment his and Kelsey's gazes locked during the ceremony.

Kelsey paused to pick up a shell and then held it out to him. The moon caught on the pale swirls of pinks and gold melded in the creamy white pearl tone. "Beautiful, don't you think?" She smiled, then looked out to the ocean.

Brent swallowed hard and willed himself to say something. Words were hard to come by, though, when all he wanted to do was pull her into his arms and kiss her breathless.

Coming for a walk had been a bad idea. He didn't want to run her off before she came out to his ranch and they got something worked out with the catering. That was his way in with Kelsey — his way of keeping in touch and hopefully getting past her "cowboy" barriers.

"There's nothing like the vastness of the ocean to put things into perspective."

Kelsey looked at him. "Yes, I always say that too."

He could breathe again at least now that he got a few words out. "I spend a lot of time at my beach on the ranch. It's a good place for me to think."

"I can't imagine having your own beach. That's amazing. I mean, I can walk out of my bistro or my bungalow and see the beach anytime, but to own a piece . . . it's just too cool."

He laughed. "Well, I look at it as the Lord owns it. I just get to enjoy it while I'm here. It's also something else the ranch has to offer as a venue, not that I'm using the pavilion and beach to their main potential at the moment. I have a ranch to run."

"It really sounds like the perfect setup. I have to admit that the more I've thought about it, the more excited I am to see it."

"Good, I think it's a perfect match."

"Just like us," he wanted to say, but didn't.

When she'd turned to look up at him, she was suddenly almost too close, kissing close. The sweet scent of her had him wanting to be even closer. Her beautiful hair was pulled up in a soft bunch of twists and curls with tendrils that escaped about her face. He couldn't help himself and gently tucked one behind her ear.

Her gaze searched his, suddenly wary. She swallowed, and as he watched her throat move, he wanted to place a kiss there.

He had it bad.

Suddenly, from the band platform, the microphone crackled to life. "It's time to throw the bouquet," someone announced.

He shook himself. He'd been seconds away from kissing Kelsey and more than likely running her off.

He shifted to look toward the sound, and Kelsey did too. Tiffany was waving her rose bouquet in the air. She laughed as several of the single women raced each other to the sandy area in front of her.

"Kelsey Wilcox, get yourself over here," Tiffany demanded with a smile, looking toward them. Obviously they were still well visible despite the shadows.

Norma Sue marched from the crowd and across the sand. "Kelsey, come on and get on up there."

"I don't think so." Kelsey held her hands out as if warding off the bouquet. "I'm fine right here." Her cheeks flamed red.

Esther Mae came hustling over from the punch bowl.

"Kelsey, Tiffany wants you in the group. You might catch it." The redhead beamed.

Kelsey crossed her arms. "No. I don't want to catch it."

"Nonsense." Norma Sue planted her hands on her ample hips. "Have a little fun. Get in there or be a party pooper."

"Okay, fine," Kelsey huffed, shooting a stern look at Norma Sue. "But I'm not going to catch it. I'm not kidding that I'm not ready to think about marriage. Even if it's just through a bouquet toss."

That said, she let them hustle her to the group. She stood on the edge of the growing flock of women.

Everyone was joking and pushing playfully at each other. When Tiffany turned her back on the group and prepared to toss the flowers, Kelsey looked wary instead of ready and took a step back. Brent wondered if she really wouldn't reach for the flowers.

"Reach for the flowers. Really reach," Esther Mae called, holding her own arms up in the air to show Kelsey how to do it. The redhead looked like she was playing outfield for the Texas Rangers, with her knees bent and hands extended. Kelsey turned to stare in disbelief at her aunt. Tiffany threw the bouquet over her shoulder. It sailed hard through the air and hit Kelsey smack in the face — then fell like a rock at her feet.

# EIGHT

Kelsey stumbled back when the flowers hit her — what were they wrapped with? Someone dove for the flowers and knocked her farther off balance, and she braced herself to land in the sand.

"Gotcha," Brent said, catching her in his strong arms and holding her steady. "Are you all right?" He turned her so he could look at her and moved her hand away from where she'd covered her throbbing forehead.

She squinted at him, wondering if she was going to have a black eye. "I think so. What was that? A bouquet or a rock?"

"Oh, Kelsey, I'm sorry," Tiffany gushed as everyone else gathered close. "The stems were wrapped with that handcrafted silver wire and jewel decoration. I didn't dream it would hit anyone." She gasped. "You have a lump."

"Let's sit you down," Brent said, taking charge and leading her out of the crowd and over to a chair. "You need some ice."

"Here's some," another guest said, and handed him a cloth napkin filled with ice that he placed on the tender spot just above her right eye.

"Thank you," she said at last, feeling really ridiculous.

"Hold that there and let's see if we can keep you from getting a black eye," he said gently.

*Who got a black eye from wedding flowers?*
Obviously she did.

*Or at least a lump,* she thought, the next morning after church as she drove over the Bay Bridge. As soon as Sunday services ended, Aunt E had herded them all out the door and to the parking lot like cattle. Kelsey forced her eyes back to the road, and thoughts buzzed in her mind like bees preparing for winter as she drove.

Today was about catering. Every catering option she could imagine shuffled through her mind one right after the other. As they arrived at the Sandbar Ranch, she prepared to be completely professional. It didn't take much imagination to see that Brent was hoping for more than a working relationship with her. And last night she'd been tempted to go along with the hope she saw in his eyes.

But she couldn't.

That did not stop her heart from teeter-tottering on the edge of some serious — no, she wouldn't let herself imagine more between them.

Couldn't.

The growth of her business was at stake here. The posse had decided they would be heading home to Mule Hollow after their tour of Brent's ranch and so Kelsey followed them in her vehicle.

It was a setup.

Praying for patience and peace in the midst of turmoil, she tried to think positively. If something she didn't like happened now, she could hightail it out of there. But she didn't plan on letting anything get out of hand. She was going to keep this strictly about catering.

Norma Sue and Adala rode together, and Aunt E and Millie squeezed in with Kelsey. The high-strung ball of black fur had barked at everything they passed. Her shrill, little bark set Kelsey's nerves on end today — which didn't take much since Kelsey was feeling extremely high-strung herself. And like a ditz, sporting that lump on her forehead. It was mortifying!

"This is a beautiful place," Adela said as

they all got out of their vehicles in front of the barn. "Don't you think so, Kelsey?"

"Very nice." And it was. The moment they'd driven through the gate, it was evident from the beautiful upkeep that the Sandbar Ranch was doing well for itself. Colts frolicked in the front pastures beneath the huge oak trees. And in the distant pastures black Brangus cattle grazed as far as she could see. The same kind her daddy raised.

This wasn't her father's ranch.

Brent came striding from the barn — tall, lean, and rugged in his work boots and faded jeans. He looked like the cowboy he was. The sun-bleached chambray shirt stretched across his broad shoulders looked invitingly soft with age. When he whipped his straw hat from his head and grinned at her, it was enough to throw Kelsey into cowboy relapse.

Still, her pulse skittered crazily. Went berserk, was more apt.

"I'm glad you like it," he said, not stopping until he was close enough to dance with her again. Looking down at her, he gently touched the lump above her right eye. "It's looking better. And not bruised like I thought it would be." The suntanned skin around his eyes crinkled. "I guess you

361

showed that bridal bouquet."

Goodness, Brent smelled of man and leather. She leaned into his touch even as she was trying to keep herself upright. She smiled, she couldn't help it — the man sorely tested her willpower. "I guess I did."

Norma Sue snorted. "If her aunt hadn't distracted her, she might not be sporting a goose egg today."

"It wasn't Aunt E's fault. I wasn't going to catch the bouquet."

"You could have at least deflected it," Norma Sue pointed out.

"A-hem," Kelsey said dramatically. "Did we or did we not come out here to look at Brent's ranch?" She stepped away from Brent, away from his gentle touch and the warmth of his laughing eyes. Away from the nearly overpowering need to touch him back.

She was grateful that he'd come to her rescue immediately last night — that he'd caught her and kept her from falling — but she did not need to keep thinking about being in his arms.

"I'm glad y'all are here," he said. "I've got everything ready."

Norma Sue's smile burst across her face beneath the shadow of her white Stetson. She slapped him on the back. "This here is going to be a great day."

"Oh, it is," Esther Mae gushed. Her red hair matched the bright red blouse that she'd worn with her jeans and boots — they were red too. "I can't wait to see everything. Especially the beach area where you told us you like to ride your horses. In Mule Hollow we have plenty of lakes and rivers to ride beside, but no beach. A beach is so romantic, don't you think, Brent?"

Brent chuckled. "You and I think alike."

Kelsey had to admit that the thought of riding on the beach was nice. With Brent, romantic, even. She wasn't thinking about romance! *Yeah, right.* No, she was thinking about how much a group renting the venue would enjoy the experience. This was all about the venue. The catering. And what the Sandbar Ranch and Sunflower Bistro could do together.

The fact that her gaze kept lingering on Brent was a little aggravating and distracting. She could ignore it, though. She could.

As it turned out, Brent had two magnificent palomino horses hitched to a fancy white carriage that would carry them around the ranch. More points for chivalry on his part.

He did know how to make a woman light up. The carriage had two wide-cushioned benches that faced each other and then a narrow seat up top for the driver.

Of course, Aunt E immediately spoke up, "You young people ride up there in the driver's seat. That way you can talk business ideas. I think the two of you putting your heads together on this catering and ranch setting for parties and weddings is a fantastic idea."

"I do too," Norma Sue added. "Just brilliant." "Absolutely," Adela encouraged, then followed Norma Sue and Esther Mae into the carriage, leaving Kelsey with no graceful way of getting out of sitting beside Brent. And really, it would give them more time to talk business.

Though Brent looked too pleased with the seating arrangements, which made her worry that she was encouraging him when she really wasn't meaning to. She wanted to believe he was just thinking about how much more they could talk about business, but she knew better. She could see it in the sparkle of his smoky eyes.

She was being ambushed, no doubt about it.

He climbed up to the driver's box and offered her his hand. She hesitated, wanting to say she could get in by herself, but then that would just be rude.

His muscled shoulders bunched beneath his shirt as he leaned farther down, arm outstretched, eyes inviting. Her pulse rushed like the Brazos on a flood day, pounding in her head as she looked at up at him.

She was not interested in a cowboy.

She was *not* interested in a cowboy.

*She was not.*

Dragging in a ragged breath, she slipped her hand into his. "Thank you," she said, climbing up beside him.

*Business.* Strictly business, she reminded herself again as their hips nearly touched on the narrow bench. Other than hanging off the edge, she had no room to move farther away from him. Each time he moved, his shoulder bumped hers and friction sparked — if it had been night she was certain the sparks would have been visible to the naked eye.

"I'm glad you came." His smile grew.

"Thanks," she growled as an unwanted urge to add "me too" hit her.

He chuckled and leaned in close. "I know you got rooked into riding up here, but it's okay. Relax."

Kelsey fought the temptation to lean into him.

Behind them, Aunt E sighed. "This reminds me of the way they used to court

365

in the old days."

Kelsey shot a warning glare over her shoulder. Her aunt just winked. Norma Sue gave her a thumbs-up. And Adela wore her serene, angelic smile that she hid behind a wispy hand.

*They're out of control.*

Those poor people in Mule Hollow. Surely women didn't *move* there to get their lives meddled in like this?

"Hey, boss, where do you want these?" asked a cowboy leading two striking saddled horses from the corral.

"Just tie them to the back, Toby. Thanks." Brent turned to the ladies. "I thought I'd bring two horses, and if any of y'all want to ride on the beach after we eat, then you can do so."

Aunt E's joyful squeal said it all.

"Way to grab those brownie points," Kelsey muttered. She cleared her throat. "I mean, that's really a great idea to advertise for the venue."

He chuckled. "Yes, it is."

She wasn't sure if he meant that for the brownie points or the business. "Brent, remember this is about business today," she said, then looked straight ahead as he started the carriage moving toward a stable that sat down the road a little way.

366

"Sure it is. But you can't fault a guy for trying to impress a beautiful woman." The carriage rocked along to the rhythm of the horses, and her insides dipped at the thought of him trying to find ways to impress her. She was such a sap.

# NINE

"Is that your stable?" Kelsey asked. "I'd love to stop and see what you have to offer in the way of horse rides for events that might want them."

"I thought you might. I'm raising a quality horse here on the ranch. I'd like y'all to see the new crop." He also wanted to let Kelsey reexperience ranch life in hopes something would rekindle good memories.

Her reaction looked promising so far. As soon as he pulled to a halt, she scrambled down from the seat to the ground before he could assist her and hurried inside the large stable. The soft nickers of the horses greeted them as they entered the building.

"Hi, pretty lady," Kelsey was saying as he entered. She had chosen one of the soon-to-be mothers, so large she could drop her foal any moment.

While the posse spread out looking the place over, he stepped up beside Kelsey as she rubbed the mare's silky white star between her velvety brown eyes.

"Delta likes you," he said.

"Horses always did love her," Esther Mae offered. "Isn't that right, Kelsey?"

"Yes, it's just because I used to enjoy them and they could tell."

"Horses have a keen sense of people," Norma Sue added from where she and Adela were checking out a couple of twin foals a few stalls down from Delta. "They know if you care or if you're indifferent."

Brent watched emotions play over Kelsey's expression.

"Oh, there're more out back," Adela said, walking gracefully out the back of the stable with Norma Sue and Esther Mae hurrying behind her.

Suddenly he and Kelsey were alone.

"Did your dad raise horses? Or did you just have a few for the ranch?" he asked, spying a wishful expression in her eyes as she looked at Delta.

"We raised a few."

Yes, wishfulness was definitely in her tone. "That was a part you really enjoyed." It wasn't a question. He could see it in her face.

Her hand stilled. "I . . . I loved it." She lifted bright eyes to his. "Birthing foals was just a joy to me. It was like Christmas each time a new one was born. I was always involved. I can't tell you how much time I spent cleaning stalls and brushing down horses after a ride." She smiled. "I am actually startled at how welcome the memories are to me."

Brent could barely breathe looking at her. How badly had it hurt when her dad had lost his ranch?

"I'll never forget the night before my wedding . . ." She paused, and he wasn't sure she'd keep on, but she gave a quiet huff of a laugh, then looked back at Delta. "Anyway, my favorite mare, Morning Star, was due, and Daddy and I worked all night to save the baby. I ended up not making it to my own bachelorette party." She smiled at that and it warmed Brent's heart to see it.

"Wow, you were dedicated."

"I wouldn't have missed it. Tulip made it into the world healthy and beautiful, and . . . and Daddy and I shared a wonderful experience together."

She turned from Delta, then, wrapping her arms together, blinked hard. Tears glistened in her eyes.

"You okay?"

She waved a hand and gave a quick grin that was far from joyful. "Yes, I just haven't thought of that in a while. It's a hard memory."

He draped his arm over her shoulders and pulled her in for a sideways hug. "I'm sorry your dad lost his ranch."

She cleared her throat and moved away. "Me too. He loved it. It nearly broke my heart to watch him lose it." Before he could say anything, she pinned him with a pointed stare.

"I've left that part of my life behind. I could never go through that again. You know, becoming a part of that life." She took a deep breath and her eyes brightened. "To cater the experience of others for a few hours I can definitely do, though."

"But you love it."

"I love my life now. I don't want to look back. I'm sorry, Brent. I don't." She headed toward the entrance and he followed.

That hadn't gone as he'd hoped.

He followed her out, and they found the posse waiting beside the carriage. Once they were all loaded up, he drove the carriage down a dirt road that crossed the ranch and led toward the beach. It was a nice stretch of beach, a lonesome, undeveloped spot.

Kelsey was quiet most of the ride, clearly lost in thought. She had been completely up front about why she was here from the very beginning. Was he hoping for too much? Was he wanting something out of his reach? Something that wasn't right for Kelsey?

Or could he help her be brave enough to reclaim a part of her life that she'd loved? Because she might say she didn't want to go back, but the emotion in her voice had said something different.

He was grateful for the opportunity to get her to his ranch. Today was about more than business, and he didn't care what Kelsey called it. And he didn't plan to waste a single moment.

The instant he pulled to a halt beside where the grass and the sand met, the ladies were climbing out.

Norma Sue pushed her Stetson off her forehead, causing her bushy gray hair to spring out at her temples. "We're going to see your beach, Brent."

Esther Mae was grinning. "That's right. Y'all stay here, take your time."

Adela shielded her gaze with her hand, looking so dainty he was afraid the wind might blow her over. "We'll be back. I just have to see your beach close up. The windswept beauty of this area is God's perfect handiwork." And then she left them with a twinkle in her iridescent blue eyes.

"Sure, take your time." Brent chuckled and watched them wander over the sand dunes, through the beach grass, talking as they went.

He turned to Kelsey.

She smelled of sugar and cinnamon, and he leaned in close — again. Though it defied logic, he was unable to get enough of her. "You baked some delicious pastries for lunch, didn't you?" he asked, moving the conversation away from the ranch. "You smell good enough to eat."

Her eyes flared. They were close enough that if he leaned in a little more, he could kiss her.

And probably get himself slapped in the process.

She sat straighter. "I wanted to show you what I have to offer. I start out about five thirty every morning to have them fresh each day. I did the same this morning in order to make it to church too."

He grinned. "We keep the same hours. I start exercising my horses about that time. They work better for me in the cool of the morning. Especially in August with all these scorching days we have. Suits me fine, though."

She frowned. "Not me. I drag myself out of bed for work because I have to."

"Yeah, right. You know that's not true. You wouldn't have opened the bistro if that were the case. Wanna help me set up lunch? I was thinking lunch on the beach would be good." He moved out of the wagon, needing to move away from her before he hauled off and got himself into hot water.

"I'd love to," she said, taking his hand when he held it up to her. He grabbed the blanket and the big hamper she'd packed and started toward the beach. Kelsey followed. "You like sunrises too," he called over his shoulder, unable to stop teasing her. "Standing on the beach watching that sunrise peek over the horizon makes you smile."

"You —" She caught up to him as he hit the rise of the dune. "How do you know that?" she snapped, making him chuckle again.

"I feel it about you. Almost everyone watches the sun set. But seeing a sunrise — that takes effort. Sure, some see it because they have to get to work that early. You, on the other hand, chose the bistro for a reason, and enjoying sunrises must have been part of that."

Her brows knit together. "That's almost too perceptive. Did my aunt tell you that? I'm going to —"

"Hold on, don't go wringing your aunt's neck or anything. I'm really just shooting in the dark here, but I saw all those sunrise and sunset photos on the walls of your bistro and had a hunch." He led the way down the dune, then set the basket down about twenty yards away from the water's edge.

"Oh, this is . . ." Her voice trailed off as she stepped past him to gaze out at the water. "Just spellbinding."

The posse waved from farther down the beach. She waved at them, then turned back to him and took one side of the blanket. "Is that why you ride so early?" she asked.

She was so beautiful. *Focus, Corbin.* "There is nothing like the quietness of a morning just before the sun comes up and my horse and I are stirring up dust. It's as if it's just the two of us alone in the world. And then the sun starts to rise, and I stop to watch it and say a prayer for the day." He didn't normally share this detail with anyone. Kelsey was different.

"I . . . I do that too. I'm usually on the deck before I unlock the bistro and I say a prayer for the day." She looked at him as if she was really seeing him for the first time and not the cowboy that she was constantly trying to deny.

He couldn't help feeling a triumphant jolt — a hopeful jolt like the adrenaline burst of a runner when the finish line comes into view. "I knew it."

She looked away, breaking the thread of contact. Backing away, she shook out her end of the blanket and he did the same. It fanned out, then settled over the sand. "I think we're going to work well together, Brent. I see all kinds of possibilities." She had neatly changed the subject.

He grabbed the basket and set it in the center of the blanket, and she dropped to her knees beside it, looking up at him. "You've shown me what you have, now settle in and I'll show you what I have."

He knelt beside her, his heart thudding. Kelsey could believe what she wanted, but she was wrong.

This was much more than working well together.

She could run scared and deny all she wanted, but he knew he didn't want to watch sunrises by himself anymore.

He wanted to watch them with Kelsey.

# TEN

"What do you mean, you're leaving?"

Why was she surprised? This had been coming all weekend.

Still, for them to tromp back over the sand dune and inform her they suddenly needed to get back to Mule Hollow, pronto, was a little overboard even for them.

"Yes, we need to get back. Millie nearly took another dive into the ocean, and the last thing we want is a repeat," Norma Sue said. She surveyed the food Kelsey had spread out on the blanket. "That looks great, Kelsey. You two will really enjoy that."

"That's right," Aunt E said, trying to control a soaked and squirming Millie. "Norma Sue had to run in and grab Millie before she got swept out to sea again." She looked genuinely upset. "I'm never bringing her to the beach again. It's just too dangerous for everyone. But that looks so delicious. Y'all stay here, have lunch, then ride the horses back to the barn."

"Nope, you'll need me to drive y'all back," Brent said.

Norma Sue yanked her chin up indignantly. "Son, I've been driving wagons since before you were a twinkle in your daddy's eye. *I'll* drive that carriage back to the barn."

"She can do it too," Adela assured him.

"She surely can." Esther Mae might have been upset about Millie, but she had quickly gotten back on board with the matchmaking.

Kelsey really had wanted to talk to Brent about the catering, but her emotions were not behaving. She was struggling not to get personal. The trip into the stable had awakened some long-ago feelings she'd shut away deep in her heart. And then, he was just so stinkin' charming. He was a hard man to ignore.

"No, we'll all go," she said, deciding the safest thing to do was go. "We can talk about this another day." Staying out here alone with Brent was just too dangerous.

"You will do no such thing." Holding Millie tight, her aunt came over and gave her a one-armed hug. Millie licked her cheek. "You've prepared all of this, and Brent's mouth has got to be watering. It looks and smells so delicious. It would be cruel for you to leave."

"I can leave him the basket."

"No," Adela said, coming over for her hug. "We have a long drive ahead of us, so we need you to stand in the gap for us with this wonderful man. And eat that cheesecake."

As frustrated as she was, Kelsey laughed. Who could say no to Miss Adela? "All right. I'll stay." Her stomach fluttered when she glanced at Brent.

"You sure you've got this?" Brent asked Norma Sue.

"Does a chicken lay eggs? Yes, I have got this."

That said, the posse climbed into the carriage with Norma Sue in the driver's seat.

"You know, my great-grandmother was a stagecoach driver," she called from her perch, tugging her Stetson down low on her eyes and grinning so big her plump cheeks were shiny. "I've always felt the hankerin' to live a month or two back then. But today, this will do just fine. Girls, hang on to your hair."

She flicked the reins, and the horses started moving so abruptly that Esther Mae and Adela had to grab the sides of the carriage.

"Norma Sue!" Aunt E shrieked. "Don't you *dare* drive like a crazy woman. We are not Wells Fargo or the Pony Express!"

Norma Sue hooted with laughter and maneuvered the team and the carriage in a perfect semicircle to turn them around and then off they went. Shouts of laughter rang out behind them as they charged toward the horizon.

And Kelsey was on her own, with a man who was breaking down her defenses one smile at a time.

She knew without doubt she should have gotten in that carriage. But that was just it.

She hadn't . . .


Silence enveloped Kelsey and Brent.

"Well, they couldn't have gotten any more obvious," Kelsey said finally, watching them go.

Brent laughed, feeling a lightness sweep over him. He liked the ladies, he really, really did. But lunch on the beach — just him and Kelsey — won hands-down. "I don't think they try to be secretive. I think they've grown quite comfortable with their role as the matchmaking posse. *And*" — he paused as the ocean breeze lifted strands of her hair across her face — "I think they're really good at what they do." He reached for the strands, his fingers brushing her forehead as he pushed them from her face.

She swallowed hard. "What do you mean?"

The need to kiss her overwhelmed him. "You know what I mean."

"I . . . I don't," she stammered. Her gaze dropped to his lips.

He breathed in the sweet scent of her. "They know how to spot people who match up well. They recognized exactly that when I carried you out of the ocean."

She shook her head. "We don't match. I'm not interested in a cowboy. Or a ranch."

"Your eyes say differently."

"What is that supposed to mean?" she asked, her gaze flaring with indignation.

He chuckled, letting his finger trace the curve of her jaw. And then, lifting her chin up just a little, he kissed her.

He hadn't planned on it. Not since Kelsey was in denial about the amazing chemistry between them. Not since she wouldn't recognize that what was happening between them went much deeper than just chemistry and attraction.

She gasped as he claimed her soft lips with his, and all thought went up in smoke. For the briefest moment she melted into him — met the kiss with equal emotion. Their hearts thundered together as he tightened his embrace. This was all he ever wanted; his breath grew ragged. *Whoa!* Alerts clanged inside of him. *Whoa!* Immediately, but not without regret, he pulled back.

He was playing for keeps and that required self-control.

God had sent Kelsey his way, and he was not going to be the one to mess this up. Not when his world had just clicked into place.

Kelsey looked stunned. She planted a hand to his chest as if to push him away and glared at him with confusion. "What?" was all she said.

"Yup, there is definitely something going on here."

He would be lucky if she didn't hop on her horse and leave him in her dust after that line. Needing something to do, he bent and grabbed a couple of cans of cold sodas from the hamper. His fingers shook slightly as he popped the tops. He held one out to Kelsey.

She cocked her head to the side and studied him. He smiled and wiggled the soda. She huffed and snatched the can, sloshing the caramel-colored liquid out of the lid as she took it.

"You might be right," she snapped. "The problem is, it doesn't matter. I'm not going to do something I don't want to do. And dating a cowboy — even one I'm attracted to — is not an option."

He'd gone too far. He knew it, and also knew he'd better fix it now. "Fine. Let's have lunch and then enjoy a ride back to the barn." She stared at him like he'd lost his mind. He believed he had.

"Relax," he urged. "I promise. I'm not going to kiss you again today. Even if you decide you want me to." He winked, still humming inside from the kiss.

She grunted and sank to the blanket. "You are incorrigible."

"Thanks. I'm trying."

"That's not a compliment, you know," she said dryly. She plucked a plump strawberry from the dish.

"I don't know." He hiked a brow that had her pausing with the strawberry halfway to her lips. "From what I know about that word, it means persistence, and my middle name is Persistence. When it comes to getting something I really want."

Her azure eyes narrowed. "Oh," she said, then plopped the strawberry into her mouth and yanked her gaze from his to study the ocean intently.

A slow smile spread through Brent. She had been more affected than she was letting on, and he was thankful for that. He knew she could easily continue to push him away and maintain she didn't want anything to do with him or the life he led. But he could tell she was wavering and that gave him hope.

Score one for the cowboy.

# ELEVEN

Kelsey sank to the blanket right after the kiss. She wanted to run away — on legs as flimsy as wet noodles — but that was not happening.

So, she'd been stuck eating a picnic lunch with Brent and pretending there was nothing growing between them.

In truth, she was scared out of her mind.

She was falling for Brent Corbin.

He had really done a number on her. And she'd completely forgotten about the reason she'd come to his ranch in the first place. Catering. What catering? She wasn't sure she could do this. Not after that kiss. Not after the way being here on the ranch with him was affecting her.

"Brent, let's ride." She jumped to her feet, the instant her legs felt steady, and went to check the saddle of the horse she'd picked to ride earlier. His name was Ransom, and he looked sleek and fast. Just what she needed.

"How long has it been since you rode?" Brent asked, coming up beside her, dangerously close and yet not touching.

"About two years." She stepped away from him. She planned to have a little conversation with the Lord when she got home. God had gotten her through the breakup with Lance, and he was the only one who knew exactly what she'd felt afterward — how low and worthless she'd felt. So what was he doing now by putting Brent in her path?

Yes, they were going to have words.

"You'll do fine," he encouraged.

She'd realized over the weekend as she'd gotten to know him that he was good at encouragement. Now it made her chuckle.

"Yes, I'm sure I will," she managed. Reaching for the saddle horn, she stepped expertly into the saddle and swung a leg over. He had to back up to get out of the way.

Her tennis shoes felt alien in the stirrup when she'd always ridden in her broken-in boots that she'd had for years. She'd thrown those boots into the sea that morning after Lance left her. And she'd never planned to put any back on.

She still didn't.

Settling into the saddle, she looked down at him, feeling more in control now from the higher position. "I may not have ridden in a while, but it's not something you forget."

"Not when you can ride well. You can, can't you?" The warmth of his touch sent a jolt rocketing through her. She jumped and Ransom jumped too, dancing sideways; his ears flattened and he threw his head back. She tightened her hold on the reins, feeling Ransom's flight instinct even more than the horse did.

She glanced down at Brent, who had started to reach for the horse's bridle when it had started acting up. At his touch, her pulse had instantly taken flight again. "Let's find out. Race you." She saw the glint of surprise in Brent's eyes, and she imagined a little fist pump of triumph that she might have put him a little off balance, like he'd done to her.

With just the slight squeeze of her knees, she set the gelding moving. Brent's husky laughter followed her as Ransom charged down the smooth dirt road. The wind in her hair, brushing across her skin, and the thrill of the run had Kelsey smiling wide. Leaning slightly forward, she laughed with exhilaration . . . She'd missed this.

The thundering of hooves behind her signaled that Brent was in pursuit. A glance over her shoulder had her heart racing at the challenge of the chase. Brent rode hard, holding the picnic basket balanced on one knee, reins in the other hand. He had a disadvantage, but he'd also had more saddle time than she'd had over the past two years.

Ransom was fast. She'd thought he would be by the look of him and had appreciated his beauty, as well as Duke's, Brent's horse.

Concentrating on what was ahead, she could tell by the pounding of Duke's hooves growing louder that they were gaining ground.

Leaning down low, Kelsey felt Ransom's mane tickling her nose. She rubbed his neck. "Come on, boy," she urged and let him have his freedom. Instantly she felt his muscles bunch and another gear kicked in as if he knew she'd given him control.

Laughing with joy, Kelsey glanced over her shoulder again and saw that Brent and Duke were barely two horse lengths away. Brent should be proud at Duke's speed. She let Ransom enjoy the moment of pure abandonment before pulling back.

Conceding, though it wasn't her favorite thing to do, she reined Ransom in and slowed him to a trot so he could cool down before they reached the barn. Brent did the same with Duke, pulling up beside her.

"That was amazing," she said, breathless with elation.

His smile was dazzling, his gaze dangerous. "I knew you were a cowgirl."

"I'd forgotten how fantastic it feels to ride. To just let go and fly," she said, high on the ride as she smiled at him.

"It is pretty amazing. And so are you, Kelsey. You belong here, no doubt in my mind."

It was the perfect dash of ice-cold reality for her and doused the flame of excitement as it hit.

Kelsey was out of the saddle in one fluid movement and had Ransom tied to the rail before Brent and his picnic basket were dismounted.

Seething inside, she rushed toward her car. What had she been thinking?

"Hey, wait up," Brent called.

She kept on going, making him jog to catch up with her.

"So, you're just going to leave? Are you upset?"

Was she upset? She spun and glared at him. "Yes, Brent, I am. You are relentless. *Relentless.* I had a great time, all right, I admit it. I did. I find you —" She almost lost herself in his expressive eyes before she snapped out of it. "I find you *amazing.* You rescued me, ruined a suit and probably those expensive boots with all that salt water. So, yep, I like you. And yes, I also like your ranch. And again, I like you. There, it's admitted. Out in the open. Done. Does that make you happy?"

His jaw had dropped, his brows scrunched as if she'd just slapped him with a fish or something. "Yes, it does," he said, snapping out of his momentary stupor, the confusion in his gaze clearing, his expression turning serious.

She poked a finger in his chest, backing him up a step. "The problem you don't seem to understand is that it doesn't make me happy."

"You've had a blast. You said it. I saw it."

"For a moment I almost felt like . . . like I was back home. But I don't want to go back home. Don't you understand? I have a new life that I *love.*" She slapped her hand on her hip. "I've only known you for a weekend. But you should know this about me — I'm not changing for any man. I can't give up who I am. Not again." Yanking her gaze from him, she turned back to her car and pulled the door open.

Brent grabbed the door and crowded

close. She could feel him at her back, even though he wasn't touching her. The sudden urge to lean back into him overcame her and she started to get inside instead.

"Kelsey, wait." His voice was soft. "Just wait."

She closed her eyes, one hand rested on the roof of her car and the other on the door. He placed his hand over hers on the door. "Don't leave upset. I shouldn't have pushed. It's just . . . you were amazing the way you were riding after being out of the saddle. You ride with such grace . . . Stay. Would you? Just stay."

Turning, she found herself almost encircled by him with the car at her back. "Maybe I overreacted," she admitted, confusion clouding her judgment.

"I'm going to do everything I can to change your mind so you'll give us a shot. I really think we have a lot of things going for us."

She couldn't think straight with him standing so close. The man muddled her mind. She forced herself to harden her heart. "Good-bye, Brent."

Sliding into the seat, she was relieved when he stepped out of her way, allowing her to pull her door closed.

She had to get out of there.

She did not belong here.

Why, then, did she feel so rotten? It wasn't until she was far down the road toward Corpus that she realized she'd forgotten all about looking at the pavilion and talking about catering.

The fact that she was failing her staff — whom she loved — made her heart ache. But she would just have to figure something else out. She had to. Because she couldn't work with Brent.

She knew that now. Understood that she had to keep as far away from him as possible.

He was a blamed fool. Brent jabbed the posthole digger into the hard earth and rocked it back and forth and hauled out the last of the dirt. Tossing the two-headed shovel to the side, he stared into the scalding August sun and berated himself one more time. He'd been doing it ever since watching Kelsey's taillights disappear over the hill yesterday.

The scene played again and again through his mind relentlessly. He'd blown it.

Moving to the tailgate of his truck, he hefted the new gate post to his shoulder and carried it to the hole, letting it drop into place with a dull thud.

He wiped his shirtsleeve across his forehead and closed his eyes for a moment. Kelsey had been right. He'd plowed right through everything she wanted and pushed for what he wanted.

Now what?

He wanted to go after her and try to make sense of everything. But he couldn't make sense of it himself. And he couldn't do what she asked — which was to leave her alone. He wanted Kelsey.

Pure and simple, he wanted her in his life. He'd never met a woman who captured his every thought and dug into his heart like Kelsey did. He knew they could have something special . . . something lasting. Forever, if she'd give them a chance.

But he lived on a ranch and she didn't want to.

So what was he supposed to do about that?

He kicked the dirt back into the hole with the side of his boot. When it was done, he hung his head and prayed.

He didn't have the answers. He couldn't very well throw her over his shoulder and make her marry him just because that was what he wanted. They'd known each other three days. She'd think he was crazy.

Time and space. That was what she needed. She needed time.

And he would give it to her. If it took every ounce of willpower he had, he'd give it to her.

# TWELVE

"*Kelsey!* You have found your calling," Lillian Sebastian raved as she swept through the bistro door two weeks after Kelsey had run from Brent's ranch. A dull and stagnant cloud had been hanging over her ever since. Lillian's excited declaration was just what she needed to put a little oomph in her otherwise oomph-less day.

"I take it your family enjoyed the platters we fixed up for you?" she asked, forcing herself to sound excited. That was what she needed to do. Fake it till it happened. Lillian was the wife of a well-respected lawyer in town and they all attended the same church. They'd ordered several large platters of specialty Danish and pastries along with sandwiches and soups for a family party. Kelsey had decided to go ahead with the Sunflower Bistro catering program and it was starting to pick up.

"Are you kidding?" she asked in her thick

Texas drawl. "They *fought* over the last Danish — I kid you not — practically licked the bowls of that to-die-for potato soup, and there were not even crumbs left of those Monte Cristo sandwiches. Seriously, Kelsey, I've never tasted food like yours. Your twist on recipes is unique. Simply amazing. You should speak to my husband, Bill, about the process of franchising this place. Tell her, Julie," she called to Julie in the kitchen. "You've told me that Kelsey taught you everything you know. And you are doing an excellent job."

Kelsey stared at Lillian in astonishment. Bedecked in a pristine white suit, Texas-sized jewels, a mixture of lamb chop — sized turquoise and diamonds the size of a pecan pie, Lillian and her praise were overwhelming, to say the least.

Julie stuck her head through the kitchen pass-through. "Absolutely, you are doing a great job, Kelsey," she agreed. "I could barely butter toast when we met at the shelter. Mrs. Sebastian, you probably don't know that Kelsey gave me this job when I was helpless and homeless."

From where she was clearing a table in the corner, Candy cocked a skinny hip and grinned. "I think it's a great idea too. I was in the same situation and Kelsey helped me too. Think of how many others you can help if you have more restaurants."

"See there," Lillian continued. "I doubt you'd have any problem getting investors if you needed capital. I'd back you in a heartbeat. As would some of your other clients."

Franchise. Kelsey rolled the idea over in her mind. "I've never really thought about franchising the Sunflower. I'm not sure it's something that interests me." Right now nothing did, but what Candy had just pointed out about helping more people appealed to her very much. She had to pull herself out of this funk hanging over her. Still, it was a large commitment. "I enjoy working hands on and the freedom I have just the way it is."

The classy blonde smiled. "Well, young lady, you've got a gold mine here if you are aggressive and make a plan. Bill is an expert. I'd urge you to consider this. You've got a future to think about. And you're so young and single — no husband or kids. You have nothing to hold you back. Think about it. I'll tell Bill you might be calling. Oh, and I almost forgot to tell you that my niece's wedding plans have changed. There was a fire and the venue burned to the ground over the weekend. So, as you can imagine, we are frantic to find a place. We have a few on our list, but they're mostly places we'd already decided against before, so none of them seem promising. If you hear of something you think might be perfect, could you let us know? Got to rush. Call Bill."

"Sure," Kelsey said, her mind churning. She'd agreed to cater Lillian's niece's wedding reception, though at the time she'd almost turned the opportunity down. Thankfully, Lillian was very good at getting what she wanted out of people, which had helped Kelsey see the light and was what had gotten her to think about more catering opportunities. Still, feeling a little like she'd just been rolled over by a very classy steamroller, Kelsey watched Lillian leave. *No husband or kids* — right now not having them did not feel like an advantage. Not when her mind was so full of Brent and the idea that if she just gave in she could very well have a future with him.

Was it real, though? And was it the future she wanted?

Candy stared at her. "I can tell you aren't feeling it. Though you haven't been feeling much of anything since that weekend you went to your hunky cowboy's ranch."

"He is not my hunky cowboy," Kelsey

snapped. "Honestly, Candy, I barely know the man." *Liar, liar, pants on fire.*

Candy threw up her hands. "Hey, I'm just making an observation. Lillian's right, you know. You've got the goods going on here with all the wonderful food and desserts. However, if you're not feeling it, then you need to do what your heart tells you."

Her heart? Ha! She'd leave that out of it for now. The fickle, thumping lump was causing her all kinds of problems.

Scowling, she went back to the kitchen where she'd been finishing up a large batch of vegetable soup to go with the sandwiches that she and Julie had made earlier.

"It's true, Kelsey," Julie said from where she was working on an order for a group out on the deck. "You are an amazing baker and cook. And you have the best heart. I'm amazed every time I turn a lump of dough into something people will eat. And it's because of your generosity."

"Ditto!" Candy agreed, following Kelsey into the kitchen and setting two dirty plates in the sink. "Y'all are making me want to learn to cook." She grinned. "Not really. I'm good right where I am. Kelsey, I've got a little apartment all to myself and a cat I can feed, and it's all because you brought that amazing soup to the shelter and gave a gal like me a shot. You deserve the best. Lillian isn't telling us anything we didn't already know."

"Y'all, stop." Kelsey stirred the soup. "I love you gals. Y'all deserve credit. You're the ones who did all the work. You showed up every day and made it happen."

Candy gave her a yeah-right look. "Whatever. You know what you did and we know what you did, giving us a shot. You're doing the same for Roxie now, giving her a hand up. This little bistro is a powerful place because of your heart. Only, the way I see it right now, you haven't been yourself lately. And I got a feeling it has to do with that delicious hero who pulled you out of the ocean."

Kelsey stared at Candy in dismay.

"Hey, don't look at me like that. I'm just stating the facts."

Julie gave her a tiny smile. "That's right. This place is fantastic without a franchise. I have to agree with Candy, though. You haven't been yourself. It's easy to tell something is wrong. Do you need to talk?"

Tears filled Kelsey's eyes. These two were so important to her. They'd come through far more than she'd had to and they inspired her.

"Group hug," she said, walking over to

Julie and waving Candy over to join the hug.

"I can't talk about it," she said, her voice thick with emotion. "But thank y'all for caring." She released them, sniffed, and went back to her soup. "Y'all just gave me exactly what I needed — a reminder of why I love this bistro and the life I've made for myself here. It is a blessing to me and has been from the day I saw my dreams inside those empty windows."

It *was* true. And as she took a deep breath, she felt so much better. "Okay, back to work." She laughed. "It's going to be a great day. And I have to get this soup over to the shelter by four."

She tasted the soup, the flavor as good as its tantalizing aroma. She *loved* soup — comfort food number one. She added a couple of dashes of salt, then stirred. For the first time in days she felt some semblance of calm. This was where she belonged.

*But you miss him.*

It was so true. How that could be, after only knowing him for such a short time, was unbelievable.

Especially when she didn't want to.

Everything she'd told him that afternoon had been true. She wasn't interested in cowboys or ranching. And yet she kept thinking about how much she'd enjoyed being on the ranch, seeing the foals, and riding Ransom, racing Brent.

In her heart of hearts, she knew he wasn't like Lance. She knew that she'd judged cowboys unfairly and that it was what was in a man's, any man's, heart that counted. Then again, it had been two weeks and she hadn't heard from him or seen him the entire time.

If he'd really cared, would he have given up so easily?

*Okay, this is ridiculous.*

She glanced at the clock. It was time to load up the food. She grabbed the large cake box full of assorted sandwiches on fragrant bread, then headed out the back door.

"You need help?" Julie asked.

"Nope, I've got it." The afternoon warmed her with its startling beauty. The clouds gleamed so white against the baby blue sky that she looked up to admire them — and missed the step down.

"Gotcha," a familiar voice said, and Brent stepped into her path. Grabbing her around the waist, he plucked her out of the air and steadied the box with the other. Somehow both she and her sandwiches made it through as he set her upright.

"We have to stop meeting like this," he drawled, looking at her from beneath his Stetson, that devastating smile quirking into a lopsided grin.

Kelsey stared at him. He was here. After all the torture she'd put herself through for two weeks and then the little heart to heart she'd just had with herself, she wasn't sure if she was supposed to be happy or mad that he had finally showed up.

Mad. Definitely mad. *And elated.*

"What are you doing here?" she asked, her heart making such a racket she could barely hear herself asking stupid questions.

"Saving you — again," he teased.

He looked better than . . . well, better than everything. "Right." She couldn't keep herself from smiling. She took the box from his hands and placed it in the rear of her car.

"Where you going?" he asked.

"On a delivery." She scooted past him and headed back into the bistro, her stomach tied up in knots.

"Well, hello, *cowboy,*" Julie crooned. "You must be the handsome hunk who rescued our Kelsey from the bay. Candy wasn't lying."

Kelsey glared at her friend.

"Hi, I'm Brent."

"And I'm Julie," she answered as she shot a grin at Kelsey. "So, now I know where your mind has been for the past couple of weeks, boss."

Brent looked pleased with himself. "Oh really?"

Kelsey's mouth dropped open and she slammed it shut again. Spinning, she reached for the soup.

"Whoa, I'll do that," Brent said, moving in beside her, his hands grabbing the handles. With reluctance, she forced herself to let him have the pot. "Where do you want this?"

She knew when she was beat, and on this she was. "In the trunk beside the sandwiches."

She trailed him as he led the way to the door. His muscles flexed as he placed the heavy pot in her trunk and her mouth went dry, remembering how they felt around her. He looked up and caught her looking. Drat.

He quirked a brow. "You were going to carry that pot? All by yourself?"

Relieved that this was his question instead of one about her ogling his muscles, she relaxed. "Not exactly. I was going to try. I'm realizing that I could never have done it alone. I made more soup than usual this time. Thanks for taking over for me."

He smiled, charm oozing from him. "You're welcome. I was wondering how you could carry that heavy pot. My muscles were groaning. That had me thinking I was getting soft."

"Hardly." The word was out before she could stop it.

He chuckled that husky chuckle that she liked. *Loved.*

"Training horses and wrestling cattle do that."

"Better than a gym any day." She surprised herself with her sudden laugh. He winked and her insides tightened. She stepped back. "I, um, I need to go. This is supposed to be there in fifteen minutes," she said, pausing to check her watch. Time had sped by.

"Can a cowboy catch a ride?"

He wanted to go with her. "Sure, I guess. It may take awhile. I never know."

"I've got all evening."

"Why did you come by?" she asked, shutting the trunk.

"I just wanted to see how you were doing." He stared at her over the hood of her car. "Is that okay?"

Her mouth went dry. She nodded. "Sure," she said, then got in the car and fumbled with her seat belt as he got in beside her and buckled up. He'd come to see how she was doing. She had to hold back a smile as she pulled out of the drive and headed down the road.

All the air had been sucked out of her small car — she was going to suffocate. She glanced at Brent. He seemed to be breathing fine.

He turned those deep expressive eyes on her and her heart jumped in her chest like a sailfish on a hook. Oh dear.

"So, where are we going?"

She'd just told him two weeks ago that they weren't going anywhere.

"Is it a catering job?"

"Oh! The soup. No, not a catering job. We're taking this over to the shelter for displaced families. A few other restaurants in the area supply the evening meals. I only serve fresh food at my bistro and advertise it that way." Okay, so now she was rambling. Of course she sold fresh food at her restaurant.

He turned and studied her. She kept her eyes on the road. "So, instead of wasting the leftover food, you put it to good use."

"Yes, that's what I meant. Though it's not technically leftovers. I plan for the meals, coordinating my menus so that I can combine what I don't end up using into a hearty soup and sandwiches the same day, like this one. This is one of the favorite parts about being my own boss."

She pulled into the parking lot of the church-supported shelter. Together they carried in the food and set it among the other food that had been delivered by other restaurants. Although there were plenty of volunteers, she and Brent stuck around and helped serve.

It was all she could do to keep her mind on what she was doing over the next two hours. She'd been so distracted watching Brent make himself useful. He'd stepped right in and helped serve food. Then he'd grabbed a tea pitcher and a coffee pot and began walking through the dining area offering refills. That he would be willing to serve like that touched her. She wondered about his ranch duties. Her dad would have never taken time to do something like this. She didn't understand Brent in many ways. But, unlike her father and all of his nonstop work, Brent seemed successful at his ranch despite taking time to enjoy his life.

When they finished and Brent had taken out the trash, which he'd insisted on doing, Kelsey drove them back to the parking lot behind the bistro. Julie had closed it up for the evening, so Kelsey left the washed pot in her trunk. Brent's truck was parked several spaces down the less-packed parking lot now.

"Thanks for helping me," she said, confused by the emotions she was feeling. He'd jumped right in there and joined in like he'd been ladling soup all his life. He'd been kind and concerned and helpful. Brent Corbin was one of the good guys.

He was a great guy.

He was still a cowboy.

"You're welcome. I enjoyed it. You're doing a good thing, Kelsey. See you later."

That said, Brent strode toward his truck. Kelsey watched him go, feeling sad and a little shocked that he was leaving so abruptly. He'd never said why he'd come by. She had the sudden urge to call out to him and ask him if he wanted to grab a bite to eat somewhere . . . or take a walk on the beach. She caught herself just in time and instead watched him climb into his double-cab black truck. He backed out of the space, tipped his hat at her, then drove off into the sunset.

# THIRTEEN

It had taken every ounce of willpower Brent had to stay away from Kelsey for two weeks. He'd done it on purpose, giving her time and hoping that if he took his time, started dropping into her life every so often and built a friendship with her, maybe she would give him a chance.

But it still took his willpower and trust in the Lord for him to walk away now.

*Patience.* When he'd started praying, that was the word that kept coming to him continually. Patience.

He wasn't a patient man.

But he'd forced himself to be. Not that he'd been in the best of moods during that time. He was lucky that he still had ranch hands at the ranch. His foreman had finally come to him and told him he had to do something to alleviate the bad mood or there was going to be a revolt.

That had been all the excuse he'd needed

to make the trip to the beach.

Now he was walking away.

Kelsey had been right when she'd told him two weeks earlier that they had only known each other for less than three days. It wasn't normal for a man to fall in love with a woman in that short a period of time. That he had wasn't what mattered. What mattered was that she'd told him time and time again that she wasn't going to date or fall for a cowboy. And she'd made it clear that she had no intention of living on a ranch ever again. She made it clear that she'd come to the ranch that day purely for business purposes.

He hadn't listened. He'd had his mind made up and plowed ahead as if she'd said nothing.

She'd had every right to walk away from him.

So, he aimed to fix that. He'd laid low, giving her some time, and then he'd come by to say hello and test the waters. Nothing planned, just a check to see how she was doing and if just maybe she'd missed him in the two weeks like he'd missed her.

She'd seemed glad to see him. That was promising. And he'd enjoyed seeing a whole new side to her. Kelsey had a good heart. That she'd put up with the posse's schemes had already shown him that.

He liked seeing this part of her. Brent drove back home over the Corpus Christi Harbor Bridge with the wind billowing in through the open window and Kenny Chesney singing "El Cerrito Place," a low, lonesome love song, on the radio. Brent understood a little more about Kelsey than he did before. She had a good life. What she did made others' lives better, and she was good at it. She had found purpose.

A good thing. It just made getting her to fall in love with him that much harder.

He was up for the challenge. Because today, he'd known even more than before that Kelsey was worth whatever it took to win her heart.

# FOURTEEN

Kelsey didn't see Brent for another week, and she finally gave in and called him. He picked up after several rings.

"Hello, Sandbar Ranch."

Butterflies fluttered in her stomach at the sound of his voice. She'd missed him. "Brent, it's Kelsey."

"Hey, how are you?" There was no mistaking the way his voice warmed when he realized it was her. The idea sent a shot of sunshine through her.

"I'm great. I, um — I was calling to ask if the pavilion was open for the second week of September."

"Really? Hold on a sec and let me look at my calendar."

She realized she was on pins and needles as she waited for him to get back to her.

"It's all yours," he said within seconds. "If you need it, that is."

She smiled into the phone. "Yes, I just

might. I have a client looking for place for a wedding reception. I'd need to bring them out and see it."

"Anytime. I'll be out of town for the next two days delivering horses, but you can come out whenever you need to. If it's when I'm not here, my foreman will show you around if you need him to."

Kelsey's hand tightened on the phone, and she could almost see him smiling even though he wasn't standing beside her. "I'll find out when it is convenient for them and let you know something."

"That's great." There was a pause. "Kelsey, I'm glad you called."

"I think this will work well," she said. "And I'm glad I called too," she added. "I'll call my clients and set this up."

"Sounds like a plan to me." His drawl sent a little shiver through her even across the air waves.

As she hung up, her pulse was skating at the thought of what this meant: she was going to be seeing more of Brent Corbin.

Things had happened quickly after that. She'd suggested it to Lillian and then she'd taken her and her daughter, Sabrina, out to see Brent's place. They'd loved it.

They'd said it was the perfect venue.

And so she found herself driving through

the front entrance of the ranch on Tuesday afternoon after closing up the bistro. Rain was in the forecast, thankfully only a slight chance. As she headed up the drive, there wasn't a cloud in the sky.

However, there was a very dark one hanging inside the car. Her palms felt damp on the steering wheel as she pulled to a halt once more on Brent's turf.

The ranch was beautiful, but nothing looked as good as Brent when he came out of the barn carrying a roll of barbed wire to the bed of his truck. He was dressed simply, scuffed boots, form-fitting jeans with fringed chaps, a T-shirt stretched tight across his muscled chest. The look was finished off with buckskin-colored work gloves and his ever-present Stetson. He took her breath away and made her knees weak — even though she was sitting in her car.

Two other cowboys were loading supplies into the truck too, but her gaze stuck to Brent. She'd been praying for the Lord to help her through this. He strode toward her, tugging his gloves off as he came, and before she shut the engine off, he was pulling open her door.

"Hey, welcome back," he said, holding a hand out. His eyes drank her in. She smiled in spite of herself.

"Thanks. I hope I'm not here too early. There was less traffic than I anticipated."

"It's not a bad drive. Only takes me twenty minutes from the downtown marina. Not much farther from your bistro." He closed her car door for her as he continued. "It's really good to see you. I need to finish up over here and then we'll go check out the pavilion. You should go say hello to the new baby in the stable."

"Did Delta have her baby?" A jolt of excitement sprang through her.

"Last week. They're both doing great. She's the spitting image of her mom."

Thrilled, Kelsey hurried toward the stable and found mother and filly inside. She was all gangly legs and sleek amber, as sweet as caramel candy when she came trotting over to investigate Kelsey.

"You are a beauty, little darling," Kelsey said when the filly nuzzled her hand. "And look at you, so friendly." Kelsey smiled at the mother. As gentle as a lamb, she was watching Kelsey. Obviously she'd decided that Kelsey wasn't a threat and was more than happy to let her baby sop up the attention — as long as she got some too. Delta carefully maneuvered next to her baby and nuzzled Kelsey over the top rail. While Kelsey tickled the baby with one hand and

Delta with the other, mamma horse nibbled at Kelsey's hair as if she did that every day. Memories flooded back of happy times she'd shared with her dad birthing foals. A lump of emotion clogged her throat just as Brent came through the entrance of the stable.

"The filly is adorable."

Outlined by the sun behind him, Brent made quite a statement striding toward her, from his hat to his spurs and fringed chaps. It was that rugged square jaw and penetrating eyes trained on her that stilled her heart. She was so glad to see him. She'd missed him.

"I knew you'd think so."

Kelsey tried to calm the raging storm of emotions suddenly sweeping through her. She'd missed him so much.

"Amazing," she managed, and she wasn't looking at the horses. Kelsey's stomach felt as if it were free-falling. And her heart clutched as Brent walked right up to her and, in one smooth movement, cupped her jaw with his work-roughened hands.

He held her gaze with his own. "You take my breath away, Kelsey. It's good to have you back out here," he said, his voice gravelly with emotion. His gaze touched every part of her face, lingering on her lips.

She could barely breathe, and though she told herself to break away, her feet ignored her.

He was going to kiss her.

But he didn't. Instead, his eyes clouded and then, in an instant, he moved past her to the back of the stable. Kelsey had never been so disappointed in all of her life. Not even the day Lance had walked out of the church on her.

She grabbed the stall rail and steadied her weak knees.

Silence filled the stable as Brent filled a bucket with feed, then came back to let himself into the stall. "Come on in and meet little Tulip."

Kelsey went still. "Tulip?"

He winked. "I couldn't resist after the story you told me. I hope you don't mind."

"Mind? Brent, I love it."

She eased into the stall and held her hand out to Tulip. She was touched deeply at Brent's attempt to ease the pain she'd felt at losing her Tulip. Years of hurt and pain rushed her suddenly and it was all she could do not to cry. But she'd stopped crying a long time ago.

Still —

"I knew you'd lost Tulip before, and I wanted you to be able to come here and watch this beauty grow and flourish here on the ranch."

She wasn't sure what to say, how to react to something like that. Her every instinct, every cell, every emotion demanded she throw herself into his arms. Why had he done this?

"It's a very sweet gesture. But —"

He poured the feed into the trough and shot her a knowing look. "Didn't mean to give you something to have to veto. You ready to go see the pavilion?"

She should have been relieved that he recognized he'd just put her in an uncomfortable situation. But she didn't. "Whenever you are," she said, too brightly.

"Then let's go. I had Toby saddle the horses, thought you might want a quick ride while you were here. It's not a big deal, though. I know you don't really want to have anything to do with ranching. I just thought if you wanted to enjoy a horse ride, I'd have them saddled already."

This was not the action of a man who just wanted to have a business relationship with her. Part of her wanted to run again, but part of her undeniably wanted to stay. And there was no denying the delight that ambushed her at the thought of riding again.

His disclaimer eased her mind. She could

ride a horse without the pressure of reclaiming a love of ranching. "I would love it."

They rode down the gravel lane to the pavilion. Its rustic wood and stone façade stood out in the windswept pasture and, if not for the trees, it might not have been such a romantic venue. The wide-branched oaks along with the western landscaping just fit. Abundant blooming yellow lantana and red roses in perfectly maintained beds softened the view — like rawhide and lace, the building and the landscape complimented each other.

"You've done an excellent job with this place, Brent."

He halted Duke and stared at the pavilion, which was still a good five hundred feet up ahead of them. The storm clouds had begun to gather in the distance behind the pavilion. "I just built something I liked. I saw a picture of a similar place in a magazine and I kept it for years, until I decided to go for it."

She relaxed in the saddle and reached forward to pat Ransom's shoulder. "Why did you choose to do this? It was after you took over running the ranch, right?"

He took a heavy breath and flicked the reins through his fingers. As if he were thinking deeply. "My dad had worked most of his life out here on this ranch. Like your dad, he'd put a lot of blood, sweat, and maybe even some tears into this place. If *he* didn't put in the tears, I know for a fact that my mom did."

Kelsey looked away, remembering the tears her mother had cried. Many of which she tried to hide from Kelsey. "My mom too," she said, looking back at Brent with regret. "I hated watching them struggle."

"I understand. My dad had done a good job and I'm sure your dad did too. But there are so many things in ranching that are out of the cowboy's hands. My dad struggled to keep up with the times, and then the drought set in for three years and it was hard. Then, in the middle of the drought, my dad had his heart attack. I knew when I took over there were some things I wanted to implement in how we grazed our cattle, and so many other things that had to do with the cattle operations. That included the horses. The pavilion was an extra. A rainy day extra."

She smiled at that, unable to take her eyes off of him.

"I knew I was going to meet a fantastic baker one day and she would need a place to cater a wedding. And so I built this building in preparation. How did I do?"

His answer was so unexpected that her laughter bubbled out of her.

"Cute, cowboy. Real cute. And you almost had me."

He grinned. "I try. I first dreamed it up when I was at school. One of my classmates got married and it was at a ranch over in Wharton, and they had something similar. The manager said it stayed booked most of the time, so it provided a steady source of income for the ranch. That's all I needed to know. You coming out here to cater is just icing on the cake."

He gave her a grin as the first big raindrops plopped thick and heavy down on them.

"We better take shelter." He rode the rest of the way with her beside him, and by the time they'd dismounted, the heavens had really opened up. He jumped from Duke and turned to her. Grabbing her around the waist, he lifted her from the saddle before she had a chance to dismount.

Breathless and damp, she laughed as he carried her beneath the open pavilion. She'd missed the feel of his arms and the beat of his heart next to hers. And she missed his kiss. His gaze fell to her lips, and then in a quick motion he set her on her feet and stepped away.

That was twice now.

Of course she knew it was the right thing for him to do. She'd told him point-blank before that she had no desire to have anything to do with a cowboy.

Still, it was frustrating.

"We better check out the kitchen." Taking both horses' reins, he moved them into the shelter of the pavilion and tied them to a beam. "This way," he said, and led the way to the back of the building. "Feel free to look around. The kitchen is well-equipped, but you can bring in whatever you want. And as far as setup goes, you tell me how you want to serve and I'll have my guys put the tables just like you ask."

The storm was coming down — a regular Texas thunderstorm, with lightning and a massive downpour. Inside the kitchen, though, it sounded more like a pleasant rushing of water over the metal roof. Kelsey moved about the room, trying not to think about how separated from the world it felt inside the kitchen under that deluge of water with Brent. *And if you decide this is a partnership you want us to continue . . .*

Her thoughts kept going to what he'd said about the ranch. She looked through the cabinets and catalogued what she'd need.

She had a really hard time concentrating.

At last, she led the way out of the kitchen and walked to the edge of the pavilion watching the rain.

"I think we're stuck." Brent came to stand beside her. She glanced at him.

"Looks that way." She felt as if time were standing still. And she loved it . . . She cut off her thought and moved away from him. It was entirely too dangerous to be near him. To be stuck with him and knowing she could be stuck with him for the rest of her life — and be happy. This was not what she needed to be thinking.

They should have brought the truck.

He tilted his head and studied her. "Are you afraid of me?"

She wrapped her arms around herself. "What makes you say that?"

"For one, you won't stand near me, and for two, you seem nervous." He stepped toward her, stopping to hang his head and stare at his boots. When he looked at her, there was storm in his eyes. "Kelsey, I've been praying, and I've been trying to stay away from you and give you space and time to get to know me. But I am not a patient man, and this has been the hardest thing I've ever done. I know it's crazy. It's not logical, but since when has love ever been logical? I am in love with you. I am."

Kelsey's mouth went dry and her knees wobbled, but her heart leaped for joy. It *was* completely irrational. Illogical.

Brent yanked his hat from his head and pushed his fingers through his hair, looking so torn. His deep, expressive eyes captured hers as he took another step toward her. He was so close, and yet he wasn't touching her with anything except his beautiful gaze.

"I've thought about nothing other than this ever since kissing you. I'm a cowboy. My heart is deep in this Texas soil — soil ranched by my grandfather and my father, and I want with all my heart for my kids to ranch here too. But, Kelsey, I love you. And I knew that after I'd only known you for three days. My heart connected with yours. And I know you may need more time. I'm willing to wait. But know that my heart is true. It can love you wider than the Grand Canyon and deeper than the ocean if you could trust me."

She started to speak.

"Wait," he said, taking her hand, finally touching her. "I have one more thing to say before you tell me to hit the road. I can live in town with you. I can watch the sun come up over the bay as long as I'm doing it with you. And I can come home to you and watch the sunset with you in the evening wherever you want me to. As long as I'm doing it with you, I can live anywhere. There is nothing that says you would be the one who would have to commute or even think about giving up your bistro."

Kelsey felt them come. The tears swelled in her eyes and spilled over. He would do all of that for her?

She shook her head. "No," she gasped through the tears clogging her throat.

He pulled her into his arms. "It can work, Kelsey. I know you feel something for me. I felt it in your kiss. You can't kiss with your heart like that and not have it mean something."

She smiled and sniffed and giggled because it was so unromantic. "No," she managed.

He dropped his hands and, looking so hurt she could barely stand it, he backed a step away. "You can't mean that. I'm good with my finances, Kelsey. I know you have a fear of loving a place and losing it. That's not going to happen here. I've got backup plans."

Oh, how she loved him. She knew it. She'd known it.

She'd just denied it.

She moved to him and placed her hand over his mouth. "Shhh, please." She held his startled gaze with her smiling one. "I need to talk. I do trust you, Brent. And I love you. I was trying to say no, I couldn't let you move into town. I love it here. And this is where I want our babies to grow up."

She removed her hand and watched as his expression lifted, and then in one swift motion, he pulled her into his arms and his lips captured hers. At last.

When he finally pulled away, he was smiling. "But you'll keep the bistro?"

She chuckled. "Yes. And there is only one term that has to be met."

He was grinning now, cocky and full of fun and love, just like the cowboy she loved. "Anything you want."

"We have to have a beach wedding, here on our beach."

He squeezed her close. "It's the only way. You going to wear that gold dress?"

She laughed. "God might work in mysterious ways, but I have a feeling he's done with that mermaid dress."

He spun them and then took her into a slow dip. "Darlin', you can wear overalls for all I care, as long as you say 'I do.' "

Looking up at him, she wrapped her arms around his neck. "I do. I do in good times and in bad, with or without a ranch, as long as I have you."

He brought them out of the dip and tenderly kissed the tip of her nose. "That sounds like the perfect plan to me."

And then he kissed her with all the promise of tomorrow . . .

# ACKNOWLEDGMENTS

I had a long and lovely acknowledgment written, and then I realized it would have taken up several pages of the e-book! So, I've condensed it but hope everyone knows how much I love and appreciate you so very much. Thanks always to God for loving me and giving me the gift of writing. To my editors on this novella, Ami McConnell and Becky Philpott: you ladies rock. I loved bringing my love of cowboys and the beach together in this story — and thank-you for letting me have the "Mule Hollow Matchmakin' Posse" visit Corpus Christi for this story. I do believe readers are going to love it! And for letting me be a part of *A Year of Weddings* — I've loved it. Thanks to associate editor Karli Cajka for all you do, especially not letting me overlook things! And thanks to my fantastic agent Natasha Kern for your unwavering efforts on my behalf. And with all my love to my husband

Chuck whose love of Tarpon fishing inspired me to bring cowboys, sun and surf to this fun story. And finally, thank-you to you, my dear readers. I couldn't do this without you.

# DISCUSSION QUESTIONS

1. Why did Kelsey not like weddings?
   Did Kelsey feel like a failure after
   she was left standing at the altar?
2. Working with the shelter, providing
   meals, and providing a few women
   with jobs gave Kelsey something
   very rewarding to focus on other
   than her own problems. When you
   are hurting, have you ever thought
   of volunteering? How can being of
   service to others give you new
   perspective?
3. Kelsey judged Brent the moment
   she saw his boots. And as the story
   developed she continued to try to
   put Brent in a neat little mold that
   her mind had of what a cowboy
   was. What were some of the things
   Brent did that were not typical of
   what she thought he would enjoy?
4. When they were on the yacht, Brent

called Kelsey a blessing. No one had ever called her a blessing before. He also altered the conversation and asked her how she was really doing after being left at the altar. He was interested in her feelings, her emotions. He was digging deeper to get to know her. To get past the superficial exterior and really find out about the woman he'd saved in the surf the day before. How did this affect Kelsey?

5. At Tiffany and Steven's wedding Kelsey faces the fact that she'd been over Lance, her ex-fiancé, for a long time, but it was the lingering effects of his betrayal that had caused her so much pain. How does she react to this epiphany? What held her back from moving forward at that moment of realization?

6. After the matchmaking attempts from the posse, and after Kelsey leaves the ranch, Brent realized he was pushing too hard for what he wanted. He wanted a relationship with Kelsey — but he hadn't listened to what she wanted. Have you ever gone after what you wanted without considering the

other person's wishes?

7. How about this — have you ever gone after what you wanted without asking the Lord what it was that He wanted for you?

8. In the end Kelsey learned to trust and move forward with her life, and in doing so she was able to fully embrace the emotions and love she felt for Brent. What did you think about how things worked out with their situation? What did you enjoy most about this book?

# ABOUT THE AUTHOR

**Debra Clopton** is a multi-award-winning novelist who was first published in 2005 and has more than twenty-two novels to her credit. Along with her writing, Debra helps her husband teach the youth at their local Cowboy Church. Debra is the author of the acclaimed Mule Hollow Matchmaker series, the place readers tell her they wish were real. Her goal is to shine a light toward God while she entertains readers with her words.

The employees of Thorndike Press hope you have enjoyed this Large Print book. All our Thorndike, Wheeler, and Kennebec Large Print titles are designed for easy reading, and all our books are made to last. Other Thorndike Press Large Print books are available at your library, through selected bookstores, or directly from us.

For information about titles, please call:
  (800) 223-1244

or visit our Web site at:
  http://gale.cengage.com/thorndike

To share your comments, please write:
Publisher
Thorndike Press
10 Water St., Suite 310
Waterville, ME 04901